SAY GOODBYE

FIRST CHAPTER WINNER
2011
UP
Awards

by
Robert Capko

A John Paxton Novel

A Class VI Publishing Book

SAY GOODBYE

Published by
Class VI Publishing
Philadelphia, Pennsylvania

ISBN 978-0-615-44664-6

Acknowledgements

There are so many people to thank, it is impossible to know where to start. First I am eternally grateful to my late parents, Mike and Lillian Capko. I also thank my agent and confidant, Melba J. Griffith, LLM Esquire, Philadelphia lawyer extraordinaire. Also I thank my editor, Michele Bardsley, and my copy editors Davilynn and Bill Furlow. Any mistakes remaining are my own, not theirs. I also thank the following, in no particular order, for their numerous and invaluable contributions to this project: Jennifer MacDonald, Andy Warren, Michael Perry, Lisa Capko, RNC, Jean Jacobs, Pat Goodwine, Cathy Jo Williams, Kristen LaRiccia, Tammy Lukander, Kristin Merrifield Smith, Lante Craft, Karen Rydlewski Rizzolo, Maggie Benko, Kathy Ellis, Dr. Paula Cain Vickers, Meri Beck, Matthew Bracken, CMSgt. William D'Avanzo, USAF (Ret), Caylen C. Perry, USAF (Ret), Explosive Ordnance Disposal, Thomas Murray and K.C. Cali. All the things you like about this book are directly attributable to them; I am solely responsible for everything else. Last but not least I would like to thank the United States Military for their tireless sacrifices without which we wouldn't have the freedom or security to engage in whimsical pastimes such as creating or reading this novel.
— *Robert Capko*

In loving memory of Michael and Lillian Capko

"These things I do, that others may live."
— Pararescue Motto

Part I

CHAPTER 1

**Pararescue / Combat Control
Indoctrination School
("Superman School")**

**Lackland Air Force Base
San Antonio, Texas**

March 27, 1999

"Crazy!"

In the office too small for the three men, Senior Master Sergeant Paxton saw Colonel Ward cringe at his outburst. It was, after all, no way to address a two-star general.

"Crazy or not, it's the only hope we have," Major General Reed explained, showing no reaction to the remark.

Paxton studied Reed in the bright light that shone through

the single window. The general seemed overdressed for the occasion. He wore his full Class A uniform: dark blue suit jacket, matching pants, light blue dress shirt, solid dark blue tie and lots of ribbons. Was he trying to impress someone? Other than special occasions, most of the officers in Paxton's immediate chain of command wore their camouflage Battle Dress Uniforms (BDUs), or at most, their light blue long-sleeve shirts with ties. Then again, General Reed was not in Paxton's chain of command.

"Why me?" Paxton stood behind the towering clutter on his battleship-gray desk. Paxton wore starched standard woodland-green BDUs and mirror-polished black leather jump boots.

"You're qualified."

Paxton knew immediately that wasn't the reason. "So are lots of men. To me, this sounds like a mission for the SEALS or Force Recon, not Air Force Pararescue. I'm not the man you want."

General Reed looked around Paxton's cramped office and stepped toward a framed citation on the wall. The Air Force Cross had been awarded to John Paxton for service to his nation above and beyond the call of duty in the Persian Gulf Theater. The medal was one of the Air Force's highest awards. Of course, Reed had seen other Air Force Crosses awarded in Desert Storm, but he had never seen one quite like Paxton's. The narrative portion of Paxton's citation certificate, which ordinarily would describe the actions taken to earn the medal, had been blotted out by a black marker.

"You're the right man. When does this get de-classified?"

General Reed tapped the thin glass covering the redacted citation.

"I have no idea," Paxton replied.

"Look, Pax." Urgency edged Colonel Ward's voice. "Budget cuts have left us strapped for qualified personnel. We need you on this one."

Paxton looked at his commander, irritated at the lack of support. Colonel Ward opened his hands in a gesture of helplessness. Paxton rolled his eyes. This silent exchange took place behind the general's back. The look Colonel Ward gave him sunk Paxton's heart. *Damn it.* No point in fighting. He was going to Yugoslavia.

"When do I leave?"

"Now," the general said.

"Now?"

"A car is waiting downstairs to take you to the flight line," Ward said.

"But I'm not packed." An active Pararescue Jumper (PJ) was always packed and ready to deploy. They each had special mobile lockers in which they stowed all of the equipment that they might need on a mission. Ordinarily, an active PJ would be itching to get into the action. Paxton was, however, no longer an active PJ.

"You'll be given everything you need on the flight over," the general assured him.

"What about my PJ trainees?" Paxton asked.

"Colonel Ward will see to it that the Pararescue training program stays afloat. Now let's go."

"What the hell's the rush? I want to see my family before I leave."

General Reed shook his head. "No time for goodbyes, Sergeant. We have a Stealth fighter down in Yugoslavia, and we need you there pronto."

Paxton picked up the phone and started dialing. Reed turned, reached across the desk, and struck the cradle of the phone with the side of his hand, cutting off the connection. "No calls, Sergeant."

"Colonel!"

Ward nodded and put his hands out, palms down. "I'll call her, Pax. I'll make sure everything is taken care of. Believe me, nobody here likes Operation Allied Force. But the eggheads in Washington think it's a good idea to bomb Yugoslavia. So now *we* have to deal with the fact that the Serbs shot down a Stealth. That's why we need you … and I shouldn't have to explain why we need secrecy."

Paxton looked at Ward and then at Reed who still held the cradle of the phone. Paxton slowly lowered the handset until it hovered over the general's hand; both men stared at each other.

"It's getting late, gentlemen," Ward said.

Reed pulled his hand off the phone and Paxton dropped the handset onto the base. As Reed and Ward turned and headed out the door, Paxton opened his desk drawer and grabbed three items. The first was a nylon pouch containing a medical kit. The second was his definitely-not-standard-issue customized .45-caliber Kimber semiautomatic pistol. It was in a nylon holster attached to a web belt containing four eight-round magazines. He buckled the belt around his waist and adjusted the location of the holster. The last item was his cell phone, which he discreetly slipped into his pocket.

Paxton slammed the drawer shut, walked around to the front of his desk and grabbed his sunglasses. He lingered to look at the photograph of his wife, son, and daughter. He was amazed at how much his life had changed since he had gotten married. And now he was being sucked back into the old life. A feeling washed over him that he hadn't felt in years. Fear.

He didn't like the way the hair on the back of his neck tingled, not one bit.

"Lives are at stake. Let's move it, Sergeant," the general insisted from the doorway. Paxton broke free of his thoughts and grabbed his maroon beret from the desk. Then he followed the other two men down the hallway.

The men hurried down the stairwell, through the front doors, and out into the sunlight. As promised, a blue sedan was parked in front of the building with its engine running, an airman sitting patiently behind the wheel. Paxton fitted his beret onto his closely cropped head and followed Reed and Ward to the sedan. The general and the colonel stopped near the back door and turned toward Paxton.

"Good luck, Pax." Ward extended his hand.

Paxton returned the Colonel's firm handshake. "Thank you, sir. Please take care of my trainees." He let go and smartly saluted his commander.

"I will." Ward returned the salute. Then, he turned and saluted the general, "Take good care of Sergeant Paxton, sir.

We need him back."

"From what I understand, he is quite capable of taking care of himself." General Reed touched his hand to his brow.

Both men climbed into the back of the sedan. Paxton had to bend way down to slide his muscular 6'2" frame into the backseat.

"Oh, and Pax…"

"Yes, sir?"

"Give me the cell phone."

Paxton's eyes iced over as he reached into his pocket and handed the phone out the still-open car door. Ward took the phone and Paxton slammed the door shut.

• • •

Ward watched as the car sped off and wondered if he would ever see Paxton again.

Probably not.

CHAPTER 2

"WE ARE GOING TO HURLBURT FIELD IN FLORIDA TO PICK up the rest of your team," General Reed explained as he and Paxton walked from the sedan toward a parked T-1A Jayhawk, the Air Force's version of the Beech 400A corporate jet. The drive from Paxton's office had taken only a few minutes. The driver had dropped the two men off on the flight line about fifty yards from the plane.

Paxton squinted behind sunglasses. The Jayhawk was a small plane, slightly longer than 48 feet with a wingspan of just over 43 feet. Its short three-point retractable landing gear made it look like it was squatting on the tarmac. The plane's hatch was open and its small stairway was down.

From the plane's markings, Paxton recognized it as one of the 99th Flying Training Squadron's Jayhawks used to train instructor pilots at Randolph AFB on the Northeast side of town. San Antonio was the consummate military town. It had an Army installation, Fort Sam Houston, and no less than four Air Force installations, Randolph, Brooks, Lackland, where Paxton was stationed, and Kelly, the base on which he currently found himself. Since Lackland had no runways, Paxton surmised that Reed had called one Jayhawk over to pick them up at Kelly, which was separated from Lackland by a fence.

The general jammed a stapled packet of orders into Paxton's hand as they reached the plane's stairs. Paxton glanced down at the documents. They ordered him to Ramstein Airbase, Germany, with "variations authorized" annotated in the itinerary block to keep the ultimate destination classified. Paxton knew from experience that he wouldn't be going anywhere near Ramstein.

"At Hurlburt you will change planes and fly directly to Serbia," the general explained referring to the province of Yugoslavia.

Paxton followed Reed up the three steps into the plane. The general stepped all the way into the cabin, making room for Paxton to clear the doorway. A female senior airman inside the plane pulled up the stairs and the door thudded shut behind them. She then ducked into the flight deck where there were two extra seats used for training purposes, and closed that door behind her.

Paxton took off his sunglasses and blinked until his eyes adjusted to the relative darkness of the cabin. The interior was too small for Paxton to fully stand up. On each side of the cabin were two cloth-covered seats and behind them, a cloth-covered bench stretching across the entire rear of the tiny plane.

The Jayhawk already had a passenger onboard. He lounged in the seat on the starboard side of the aircraft. The man unfolded from the seat as the general approached, but Reed waved him down and took the chair to the man's left. The lanky stranger was dressed in green camouflage BDUs bereft of any insignia, rank or markings whatsoever. The pattern and cut of the BDUs were unfamiliar. He had salt and pepper hair, cut in the style of a Marine, and piercing blue eyes.

Reed indicated the passenger across the narrow aisle. "Senior Master Sergeant Paxton, I'd like you to meet McMurphy. He'll be joining you for this mission."

Paxton, partially crouched because of the low ceiling, shook the man's hand. "Glad to meet you. Would that be Sergeant McMurphy, Colonel McMurphy, or perhaps, Mr. McMurphy?"

"It's McMurphy," the stranger replied.

"I see," Paxton said, seeing all too well.

Paxton turned to the general. "You didn't mention anything about him." Paxton spoke as if McMurphy wasn't sitting there.

"McMurphy has his own special mission. He'll join you for your team's airdrop. He's highly trained. I think you'll find him very useful."

The plane shuddered and the lights flickered as the engines groaned to life. Paxton met McMurphy's enigmatic gaze. "What's your special mission?"

"Sorry." His tone was not apologetic.

He would get nowhere questioning McMurphy. Paxton turned again to the general, his agitation mounting, "Who does McMurphy answer to? I'm not going to lead a mission with free agents."

"He'll listen to your orders."

"Listening isn't good enough. Every member of my team must *obey* my orders, or people might get killed."

Reed's face reddened. "Obey this order, then, Sergeant. You will take McMurphy as a member of your team with you into Yugoslavia. I assure you, he'll follow your orders to the extent they're consistent with his mission."

Paxton couldn't believe his ears. "Who the hell decides if my orders are 'consistent with his mission'?"

Reed looked at Paxton and his lips stretched into a thin, wry smile. "He does."

• • •

High over the Serbian terrain, somewhere between the Bosnia-Herzegovina border and Belgrade, a NATO F-16 Falcon jet fighter, called a Viper by its pilots, flew close-air support for the Combat Search And Rescue (CSAR) mission near the last known location of the downed F-117 Nighthawk Stealth Fighter plane. The Viper pilot's headphones crackled and then picked up a distress signal. He keyed his mike. "Identify."

"This is Cue Ball."

To confirm the identity, the pilot said, "Authenticate:

Band saw."

"Royal Flush," came the correct reply.

He had located the missing F-117 pilot. The downed pilot was safe and not under duress. Had he been captured and forced to communicate, he would have used a different code word. "Good to hear from you, Cue Ball. This is Screwdriver. Are you injured?"

"Negative, Screwdriver. But the bad guys are on my ass. Get me the hell out of here."

"Roger that," the Viper driver replied to his stranded comrade. He keyed his mike again. "Help is on the way."

• • •

Paxton sat on the left side of the bench seat in the rear of the plane. He looked out of the port side window at the blue-green Gulf of Mexico far below as the plane sped toward the panhandle of Florida. Before takeoff, Paxton had squeezed between Reed and McMurphy and sat down on the bench, which was the only open seat. The Jayhawk's takeoff and climb to cruising altitude had been uneventful. Paxton had spent the first part of the flight trying to get comfortable in the cramped cabin. His knees pressed on the back of the general's seat, which was directly in front of him, and his legs extended into the aisle. To his right, on the bench seat next to him, was a large black nylon bag.

General Reed turned around in his seat and over the drone of the engines said, "Sergeant Paxton, it's time to get changed."

"Changed?"

"Everything you need's in there." Reed pointed to the over-stuffed nylon bag sharing the bench with Paxton.

Paxton unzipped the bag and peered in. On top was a pair of jump boots. Under the boots was a set of green BDUs. Paxton took the boots and uniform out of the bag. Like McMurphy's uniform, this one lacked any indication of rank, unit or nationality. They also had the same unusual pattern and cut as McMurphy's. "You don't expect me to wear these, do you sir?"

"As a matter of fact, I do."

Paxton held the uniform out toward the general, "This isn't the uniform of the United States military."

"I know that."

"You want me to parachute into Yugoslavia, a combat zone, behind enemy lines, wearing whatever the hell these are?"

"Mercenaries fighting for Serbia wear that uniform," Mc-Murphy explained, speaking for the first time since the plane had taken off.

"I don't give a damn. I'm not going to wear it." Paxton tucked the uniform into the bag. "Do you know what'd happen to me if I'm captured and I'm not wearing a U.S. military uniform?"

"You'll be considered a spy," Reed answered without feeling.

"Damn right I will, sir." Paxton shoved the boots into the bag on top of the uniform. "No Geneva Convention protection. After I'm tortured, and interrogated, I'll be shot."

"I wouldn't be surprised."

"If that happens, will the government admit I was on an official mission?"

SAY GOODBYE | ROBERT CAPKO

"Probably not," Reed replied. "Particularly since this mission doesn't officially exist."

"General, this is not what I do. I'm a PJ. I rescue downed pilots from behind enemy lines. In fact, I don't even do *that* anymore. The Air Force pays me to take younger airmen and turn them into PJs."

"There's a downed F-117 Stealth fighter pilot behind enemy lines involved in this mission," Reed said.

Paxton looked at the general. "But we're not going to rescue him."

General Reed matched Paxton's cool stare. "True. But we're sure going to make it look like you are."

• • •

Colonel Ward hung up the phone, a sick feeling in his stomach. He sat in his office, down the hall from Paxton's. He hated making that phone call, but he knew its importance. Besides, he had promised Paxton that he would call Jill. Paxton's wife sounded okay on the phone after he explained Paxton's whereabouts. As the wife of a PJ, or, more accurately a PJ instructor, Jill was used to her husband's crazy travel schedule.

Ward put his head in his hands and agonized about what he had just done. He knew John Paxton's wife well. Their families had spent time together on the weekends.

He hoped she would someday forgive him—for the lies he'd just told her.

CHAPTER 3

Field Headquarters
6ᵗʰ Serbian Army
Federal Republic of Yugoslavia

March 28, 1999

"Sir, good news!"

General Dragisa Rugova looked up as Lieutenant Colonel Vojislav Nikolic walked into his office.

"We have located the main portion of the American Stealth plane and have secured the crash site. It's about forty kilometers from here, sir. I can take you there if you wish." Nikolic's heavy topcoat hung below his knees. His uniform pant legs were neatly tucked into the tops of his shiny black leather boots. He had a full dark mustache that matched his hair and penetrating Mediterranean eyes.

"Excellent. What condition is it in?" Rugova had a booming voice. He was a large man, but not fat. He was very tall, with broad shoulders. His hair had turned gray, but his body was still solid. Seated behind his desk, he looked up from the map he had been examining when Nikolic interrupted. A cup of steaming coffee sat on one corner of the map, a brown stain growing around the base.

"It's in bad shape, sir. But the fuselage is in one piece, more or less."

"What about the *special* part?"

"Intact, sir. We should have it for you soon."

"I hope for your sake that you're right." Rugova returned his attention to the map.

"Sir, we need reinforcements to secure the site."

"Why do you need more men to secure the site?"

"Townsfolk want to see the famous American Stealth plane. They saw coverage about it going down on their satellite feeds from the American cable networks," Nikolic explained. "They are climbing on the wreckage, taking pieces as souvenirs. Women, children, old men, they all came out. They are snapping pictures of it and even posting them on the Internet."

"Pull your men back. Let the villagers satisfy their curiosity."

"But sir—"

Rugova waved away Nikolic's protests. "Let our people revel in our great victory. We brought down the great American Stealth plane. That's something the Muslims in Iraq were never able to do. It serves the Americans right for attacking us when all we are doing is protecting ourselves from terrorists." Rugova turned toward Nikolic. "What do you think the Americans are going to do now that their secret plane is lying in pieces outside Belgrade?"

"Rescue the pilot?"

"Yes, they will try. What else?"

Nikolic stared at Rugova. "Bomb the anti-aircraft artillery that shot it down."

Rugova shook his head in disappointment. "You must learn to put yourself in your enemy's shoes. Think how they think."

Nikolic stood in silence.

"The Americans want to destroy the plane so we can't get the technology."

"We have skilled engineers, but even so, will we be able to use this technology?"

Rugova laughed. "Its value to us is monetary. Our allies will pay us handsomely for the Stealth technology. In exchange, they'll be very helpful to our efforts against the Americans. And you and I, Nikolic, will be heroes to our country." He tapped the map, smiling. "The Americans won't bomb the Stealth if little children sit in the cockpit, smiling as their pictures are taken. They have no stomach for killing innocents. That's why they're weak. It will be their downfall."

"Yes, sir."

"Call the press. Allow television cameras to film the crash site." Rugova looked at Nikolic. "No more *souvenirs*. Make sure our prize remains intact."

Nikolic nodded sharply.

"Take me to the wreckage." Rugova stood up and put on his overcoat. The two men walked out of the room. "Any luck locating the pilot?"

"We picked up a recent transmission between someone we believe to be the pilot and one of the American planes looking for him. We're triangulating the position of that transmission and should be able to locate him very soon."

"I want him alive."

"Even if we capture him alive, sir, I don't believe he'll tell us anything."

Rugova stopped walking and looked at Nikolic with dead eyes. "He *will* talk—of that, I am certain."

• • •

The lone F-16 flew over the general area of the downed Nighthawk pilot. But the F-16 pilot was careful not to linger where he had located Cue Ball. He knew that his presence in the air would attract the Serbians on the ground. The Viper driver keyed his mike. "Cue Ball, this is Screwdriver, do not, I repeat, do *not* reply. I'm still here. We haven't forgotten about you, buddy. We're going to get you out of there, but have patience. Help is coming. Keep your head down and maintain radio silence."

He then banked the jet into a sharp left turn as he looked down at the scene far below that had caught his attention a moment ago. In the morning sun, he could make out what looked like ants swarming over a tiny black arrowhead. There was no question in his mind that he was looking at the wreckage of the Stealth fighter.

He could also see intermittent flashes of unmistakable small arms fire aimed at him. *I'm too high up to worry about them, but whatever brought down the Nighthawk is probably dialing me in right now.*

He reached down and switched encrypted frequencies on his radio and keyed his mike again. "Aviano, this is Screwdriver, over."

He continued his left turn making a complete circle around the activity below. The radio crackled the reply from the base in Italy. "Screwdriver, this is Aviano. Go ahead."

"Aviano, I've located the package. I'm over it right now."

"Good work, Screwdriver."

"Standby for the GPS coordinates."

"Negative, Screwdriver. Not over the air. We don't know who's listening."

Screwdriver looked down again at the activity below. "Um, from the looks of things, it ain't going to be a surprise to anybody. I'm sure they already know its exact location."

After a pause came the reply. "Okay, Screwdriver, go ahead with the coordinates."

Screwdriver read the numbers from the computer screen in front of him and then he repeated them. The NATO controller in Italy read the coordinates back for confirmation. "You've got it, Aviano."

The Viper completed another orbit around the downed Stealth fighter. "Aviano, I've a clear visual and a full complement of ordnance. Permission to engage with a GBU?" The Viper was carrying two 500-pound guided bomb units (GBUs).

"Negative, Screwdriver. Do not engage package."

Screwdriver shook his head. "I really think I should engage, Aviano. This is a good opportunity, and I have a clear shot."

"No, Screwdriver. Do not drop your bombs!"

"Why not?"

"Not my call, sir. The boss says no. So the answer is no."

Stupid HQ pricks. "I've hung around here long enough. Somebody's gotta be drawing a bead on me. Permission to come home?"

"Permission granted."

"Over and out."

Screwdriver leveled off as "WNW" scrolled to the center of the compass on his heads-up display. He felt the kick in his kidneys as he engaged his afterburner and headed for home.

Far below, Cue Ball looked up as he heard the Viper scream overhead, headed in the direction of Italy. He shook his head as he drew deeper into the brush, trying desperately to conceal himself from the brightening morning.

He felt more alone than he had ever felt in his life.

CHAPTER 4

"WHERE ARE YOU GOING?"

"The flight deck." Paxton had gotten up and squeezed between McMurphy and Reed and was moving up the Jayhawk's narrow aisle. Paxton still wore his Air Force uniform. He refused to wear the mercenary clothing. The plane was still high above the Gulf of Mexico on its way to Florida. The three men were alone in the small cabin as the pilots and the female airman remained unseen behind the flight deck door.

"Don't bother trying to use the radio to make a call."

"Why not, sir?"

"It would compromise mission security."

Seeing that the conversation did not involve him, McMurphy, who was still seated, pulled out a tiny portable compact disk player with a pair of headphones. Paxton watched McMurphy as he put them on, pushed play and closed his eyes.

Gritting his teeth, Paxton turned back to the general and said, "I've no intention of revealing where I'm going or why. I want to say goodbye to my wife and children."

"*No,* Sergeant."

Bastard. Paxton looked away, emotions welling up inside him, and then returned his gaze to the general. "My wife's expecting me home for dinner tonight."

"Colonel Ward has already contacted your wife and let her know you'll be missing dinner."

"What the hell did he tell her about my whereabouts?"

"He's told her that you've gone TDY at the request of the Air Force."

Paxton stared at the general. "He told her that I've accepted a Temporary Duty assignment?"

"Which is accurate, of course."

"You've got to be kidding me. You make it sound like I've gone off to some training course. She knows I wouldn't go TDY without telling her. She'll be worried sick."

"Do you think she would worry less if she knew the truth?"

Paxton glared at the general. "This whole mission is nuts." He had a bad feeling about it. He didn't want to be on the plane. He wanted to be at home, digging into Jill's meatloaf and telling her about his day. He wanted to kiss his children and read them a bedtime story.

"Put on the uniform, Sergeant." General Reed's stare was cold. "That's an order."

•   •   •

Jill Paxton pushed her blonde hair back and adjusted the portable phone with her right hand so she could hear more clearly. She stood in the kitchen of her modest home that afternoon, dressed in tan slacks and a brown pullover sweater. Buying the house had been a dream come true for her and John.

They had lived on base since they had gotten married. The housing on base was nice, but it wasn't theirs. But, after much scrimping and saving, they had enough for a down payment. They found a house in a nice safe neighborhood just outside the city limits of San Antonio and bought it. 324 Casa Verde Way, San Antonio, Texas. That address belonged to them. The drive was reasonable to Lackland Air Force Base, and John started work so early in the morning, that traffic was never a problem. The school district was solid and the neighbors were friendly. It was the perfect home for a growing family.

The door to the large pantry was open revealing neatly organized groceries. Candles, pictures and knickknacks were smartly arranged throughout the kitchen. Jill always added those extra touches that made the house into a home. Looking around at the spotless dwelling, it would be difficult to detect that she was the mother of two small children. One would not have to look far, however, to realize she had children. Indeed, one would only have to look at her.

Her two-year old daughter, Megan, was in Jill's toned left arm, hugging her neck, and her four-year old son, John, Jr., clung to her long shapely legs and stood on her foot. She held a recently opened letter in her left hand. Her striking blue eyes were wide.

"Colonel, there must be something you can do." She had already talked to Colonel Ward earlier that day when he'd told her that Paxton had to leave on a last-minute TDY assignment.

"I'm sorry, Jill, at this moment, there's nothing I can do."

"I need to talk to John. It's important." Jill waved the letter as if Ward could see it through the phone.

"I wish I could help, but unfortunately, as I told you, he's gone TDY. For the time being, your husband isn't in a position to take calls," Ward said. "Could you tell me the news, and I can see to it that it gets relayed to him?"

Jill paused. "No, I want to tell him myself. Please have him call me as soon as he can."

"I will."

"Thank you." Jill hung up. She looked at the letter one more time, and then placed it on the countertop.

• • •

Resigned to his fate, Paxton returned to his bench seat at the back of the Jayhawk. He unbuttoned his crisp Air Force fatigues and grabbed the rumpled mercenary uniform out of the nylon bag. He took his wallet and keys out of his pocket and tossed them on the seat next to him. There wasn't much room to maneuver, but he was able to put on the plain uniform, noting that whoever ordered it managed to get the size correct. Still seated on the bench seat, he buckled the web belt containing his pistol around his waist.

After he finished tying the scuffed jump boots, he rolled up his Air Force uniform intending to place it in the nylon bag. He noticed a towel covering other objects. He lifted the towel and pulled out the most interesting of those items—a Soviet-made AKS-74 assault rifle. He opened the bolt and confirmed that the weapon was unloaded. Paxton knew that the rifle was chambered in 5.45 x 39 mm, a smaller caliber round than the 7.62 mm utilized in the older and more prevalent AK-47 Kalashnikov rifles.

The 5.45 x 39 mm round was developed in the 1960s by the Soviets as part of the trend of modern armies moving toward reduced-caliber, high-velocity ammunition for small arms. Instead of creating a whole new weapon for the round as the United States had done in developing the M-16 for the 5.56 mm ammunition, the Soviets merely re-chambered their existing AK rifle design to accept the new ammunition. Thus, to the untrained eye, the newer rifles look nearly identical to the older ones.

Paxton noted that this rifle featured a folding stock, which would make it easier to carry on his parachute jump. He laid the rifle on the bench seat next to him and continued digging in the bag.

• • •

Dressed in his Serbian mercenary uniform, Paxton settled in his seat on the Jayhawk and studied the papers that General Reed had handed him earlier. Attached to the United States Air Force orders were NATO orders. Paxton knew that

NATO orders, in conjunction with an active duty ID card, took the place of a passport.

It didn't matter, though. Where he was going, a passport would not do him much good.

General Reed turned around in his seat and said to Paxton, "I want you to remember the name Ahmet Jashari. He's a member of the Kosovo Liberation Army."

Paxton knew a little about the Kosovo Liberation Army, also known as the KLA in English or UCK in Albanian. Paxton was aware that the KLA was responsible for various bombings in Kosovo. Since most of the bombings were of Serbian police stations, the Serbian government branded the KLA a terrorist organization.

The KLA sought independence for Kosovo, currently a province of Serbia, one of the republics of Yugoslavia, and to unite the Albanian peoples of Kosovo, Albania and Macedonia. About a year earlier, the clashes between the KLA and Serbian police forces intensified, and in retaliation, the Serbian police forces raided Kosovar villages. Houses were burned, dozens of civilians were killed, and many thousands were driven from their homes. Since the Kosovars and ethnic Albanians were Muslim, the Serbs were whipped into an anti-Islamic frenzy. After large-scale fighting broke out during the summer of 1998, there were reports of ethnic cleansing. As many as 300,000 people were displaced from their homes as tensions that had simmered for a thousand years erupted. Mercenaries from many countries joined the fight on both sides.

Constant images on American televisions of the Albanian

refugees' terrible plight prompted action out of Washington. A peace conference was held in Rambouillet, France, but the parties failed to agree upon a peaceful settlement, despite threats of NATO involvement. So three days earlier, the president of the United States, without United Nations approval, ordered the United States military to begin a bombing campaign called Operation Allied Force in support of the KLA and ethnic Albanians. The aerial bombing was an effort to cease the ethnic cleansing that reportedly occurred. So, here sat John Paxton in the Jayhawk, with Reed and McMurphy, two men he had never met before, on his way to fight somebody else's war.

"As you know, we're working closely with the KLA. In fact, key KLA leaders have been provided satellite phones so they can help report the positions of Serbian military units to us," the general explained. "If for some reason we can't extract you and your team, contact Jashari and he'll assist in getting you to safety."

"How will I find Jashari?" Paxton asked.

"McMurphy knows how to contact him."

"Well, is McMurphy going to share that info with me?"

"No."

"What good does it do for only McMurphy to know how to contact him?"

"It ensures you have a personal interest in McMurphy staying alive."

"Sir, with all due respect, you're nuts."

"That'll be enough, Sergeant," the general snapped.

Paxton tamped down on his anger. "Does Jashari know

we're coming?"

"Yes, he's been told you may drop in." Reed looked down at the packet of orders Paxton had been studying. "You won't need those. I'll take them."

Paxton handed the orders to the general. "While you're at it, go ahead and give me your Military I.D. card, dog tags, and anything else that identifies you or links you to the United States. It's for your own protection."

"Bullshit. You're protecting your own ass."

Reed scowled. "Give me your identification, Sergeant."

Paxton regarded Reed and then reluctantly complied. He handed the general everything that identified him or linked him to the United States Air Force. The only identification he couldn't remove was the green footprints tattooed on his rump—the Jolly Green Giant's footprints. The PJ tradition honored the nickname of the helicopter they used in Vietnam. It was started by some drunk PJs on leave in Thailand and became their unofficial logo.

"What can I tell the rest of my team about this mission?"

Reed smiled. "Of course, you can't tell 'em anything I've told you. But here's what I do want you to tell them…."

CHAPTER 5

THE JAYHAWK LANDED UNEVENTFULLY AT HURLBURT Field in the panhandle of Florida and taxied near a gray Air Force Air Mobility Command C-17 Globemaster III. The Globemaster was the Air Force's newest transport plane. Designed to carry troops and equipment such as tanks or helicopters long distances, it was able to take off and land on short runways. The Jayhawk looked tiny next to the mammoth four-engined jet. The Globemaster was longer than half a football field, nose to tail, with a wingspan to match. With its giant T-tail, it stood taller than a five-story building. The tips of the wings had distinctive winglets canted upward and outward at fifteen degrees.

The Jayhawk's door was opened and the stairway lowered. McMurphy, Paxton, and Reed climbed down the metal stairway. Paxton carried his medical bag and the rifle, forced to leave the rest of his belongings onboard. An Air Force major dressed in a baggy beige flight suit met the men at the bottom of the stairs. The major had short black hair and appeared to be a few inches over five feet tall.

Paxton snapped off a smart salute to the major as he reached the bottom of the stairs. The major returned the salute and held it there for the general who was following Paxton and McMurphy down the stairs.

"Major, this is McMurphy and Senior Master Sergeant Paxton," the general said.

"Glad to meet you, gentlemen," the major said. "I'm Thompson." He shook hands with the men. "I'll be your pilot for the remainder of your trip."

Paxton reflected on the irony of such a small individual controlling a massive aircraft such as the Globemaster. But he knew, as was the case with Formula One race car drivers, some men of smaller stature had the quickest and surest reflexes. Thompson had that air of confidence possessed by all the best pilots.

Paxton also noticed that McMurphy seemed distracted and was peering over Thompson's right shoulder as they shook hands. Paxton followed McMurphy's gaze to a man dressed in a dark blue suit near the C-17 transport plane. The man wore a white shirt, red tie, and dark aviator sunglasses. He leaned against a black American-made sedan. Next to his shiny leather shoes lay an overstuffed green canvas pack, which looked the worse for wear. It was a strange contrast to his sharply dressed appearance.

"Excuse me, gentlemen," McMurphy said, touching Thompson's elbow as he did so. He then walked around the pilot and toward the man with the ratty backpack. Paxton's gaze followed McMurphy, but General Reed clapped his shoulder and distracted him.

"Sergeant Paxton's been fully briefed on the mission, Major. Has the rest of his team arrived?"

"Yes, sir," Thompson replied. "They're already aboard."

"Outstanding," Reed said.

Paxton, Reed, and Thompson walked across the tarmac toward Thompson's plane. The back of the transport aircraft was open and the cargo ramp deployed. As they walked toward the ramp Paxton watched McMurphy out of the corner of his eye.

"I'm sure I don't have to tell you, Major, the importance of mission security," Reed said.

"Of course not," the pilot replied.

"Good," Reed said. "So from here on out, Sergeant Paxton and his team of PJs are to have radio contact with no one but me."

Paxton shot a cold glance at the general, but did not break stride.

"I understand, sir," the pilot said.

The three men reached the bottom of the cargo ramp leading into the plane under the giant tail.

"This is the end of the line for me," General Reed said.

"Not joining us for the flight over, huh, sir?" Paxton asked.

"You have your orders. You don't need me now. Just make sure you keep me informed."

"I need to finish the pre-flight." Thompson saluted Reed. Reed returned the salute, as did Paxton, and then the pilot walked up the metal ramp into the back of the plane.

Paxton glanced at McMurphy who was engaged in a conversation with the man in the suit. Only now McMurphy held the green pack in his right hand. By the way McMurphy was holding it, the pack appeared heavy.

"Sergeant, good luck on your mission," Reed said.

"Thank you, Sir." Paxton's wasn't feeling any gratitude.

"And, Sergeant…"

"Yes sir?"

"Don't screw up."

"Sir?"

"I'm counting on you. Don't disappoint me."

"Sir, with all due respect, you picked me. Before today, I'd never even heard of you," Paxton said. "You're sending me on a mission that makes no sense. You've got me parachuting into enemy territory mercenary style, and bringing along some guy I've never trained with who is on his own special mission, and you're telling me not to screw up?"

"That's an order, Sergeant." The general turned and walked away.

Paxton dropped the automatic salute and uttered an expletive under his breath. He stood under the tail of the plane. Above him was the portion of the cargo door that folded upward and was tucked into the top of the cargo hold. The rest of the door folded down to the ground, forming a ramp. Paxton heard someone approaching and he turned.

McMurphy lugged the green backpack over one shoulder.

"Who was that?" Paxton asked.

"Nobody." McMurphy passed Paxton and started up the ramp into the aircraft.

"What's in the pack?" Paxton persisted.

"My clean underwear," McMurphy replied over his shoulder.

Paxton shook his head and repeated the expletive under his breath. Then he hitched up his bag and his rifle and followed McMurphy up the ramp into the plane.

• • •

"I want Daddy!" John, Jr. exclaimed, tears in his eyes.

"I want him, too," Jill Paxton said. "But Daddy had to go somewhere for work."

The four-year-old boy wailed. "I miss Daddy."

"I do too, sweetheart." She hugged and consoled her little man. "Don't be too loud or you'll wake your sister."

He sniffed and tried to be brave as his mother kissed his cheek. "When will Daddy be home?"

"Soon, I hope." Jill patted her son on his head and marveled at how closely he resembled his dad. She wondered how her family would be affected by the big changes that lay ahead for them.

• • •

The Globemaster's cargo hold was a maze of wires, piping, tie-downs, and netting illuminated by artificial lights and whatever sunlight managed to wash in through the open cargo door. The cold metal floor was covered with a pattern of anti-skid material intertwined with tracks and hard points to slide and secure palletized cargo. Along each wall were seats that could be folded up out of the way if more space was required. Overhead the metal skeleton of the plane was exposed, not unlike the ceiling of a warehouse. In short, the interior was utilitarian.

At the top of the ramp was a portable bench securely attached to the floor. It was centered with seats back-to-back down the middle facing outwardly toward the walls on both sides. A group of airmen in full battle dress stood just beyond the center bench seats. Past the airman, closer to the flight deck, was bulky cargo covered by blue tarps, which filled the inside of the hold.

"Master Sergeant John Paxton!" was the exclamation that met Paxton as he entered the aircraft at the top of the ramp. Paxton looked around for the source of the familiar voice. Then he saw him. The stocky black airman walked up to Paxton and extended his hand.

"Smith! How the hell are you?" Paxton shook his friend's outstretched hand.

"I'm just fine. You?"

"I'm surviving." Paxton grabbed Smith's arm and turned him partially sideways looking at the stripes and star sewn on the sleeve of Smith's uniform. "I see you made buck sergeant. Congrats."

"Thanks," Smith said. "I heard you're getting out."

Surprised, Paxton frowned. "Who told you that?"

"You know, word gets around. Is it true?"

"I'm thinking 'bout it. The life's hard on my family."

"What the hell are *you* going to do on the outside?" Smith asked.

"Oh, I don't know," Paxton lied.

"How many little Paxtons?"

"Two."

"No kidding! How old?"

"John, Jr. is four and Megan just turned two," Paxton said proudly. "Here, lemme show you some pictures." Paxton reached for his wallet only to find the pocket empty. He had handed all his things to General Reed. "Dammit!"

"What?"

"I'll have to show you some other time. I left 'em in my other pants."

"That's cool. Show me when we get back." Smith then turned to the others who were busy checking and stowing gear. "Hey everybody, I want you to meet Master Sergeant John Paxton."

"It's Senior Master Sergeant now," Paxton whispered to Smith.

"Oh, sorry 'bout that. Like I can tell." Smith patted the empty sleeve of Paxton's shirt where the rank patch should be sewn. Smith then turned to the group again. "Excuse me, it's Senior Master Sergeant John Paxton. I'm sure y'all met him before and remember him the same way I do. He kicked my ass in Superman School."

Superman School was the affectionate nickname given to the Pararescue Indoctrination School at Lackland. It was the first of a variety of schools called the "Pipeline" that had to be completed to become a Pararescue Jumper. Jump school, scuba school, free fall school, paramedic school, survival school, and others followed it. But a trainee had to make it through Superman School, which was widely regarded as the toughest school in the military. It was designed to weed out those who would not make it through the rest of the Pipeline.

Nobody ever flunked Superman School; it got so difficult that most candidates simply quit—called Self-Initiated Elimination (SIE). Or if the instructors felt a particular candidate was not a good fit, they made that candidate the focus of attention in such a relentless way that the candidate would eventually SIE. On average, ninety percent of the trainees SIE out of Superman School. There'd been classes where only one or two trainees finished. Indeed, legend had it that there had been classes where no one finished. But the Air Force didn't care. They didn't have a quota. The PJ candidates were not graded on a curve. They either had what it took, or they were gone. The PJs wouldn't lower their standards even though they were never fully manned. And in recent times, it had been up to Paxton as Non-Commissioned Officer In Charge (NCOIC) of the Indoctrination School to determine whether the candidate had what it took.

The other PJs gathered around, shook Paxton's hand and introduced themselves. The first was Senior Airman Mike Petersen, followed by Airman First Class Frank Dobbins and Airman First Class Justin Taylor. Senior Airman Blake Maxwell and Airman First Class Travis Robertson also stepped up and introduced themselves.

The last to introduce himself was Airman First Class Eric Jennings. Jennings was not a pararescueman—he was an Air Force Combat Controller. Combat Controllers, like PJs, were part of Air Force Special Tactics. Their primary mission was setting up Drop Zones (DZ) and Assault Zones (AZ), establishing ground-to-air communication, and providing air traffic control for a landing zone. They were oftentimes the first to parachute in during a large jump mission, usually to set up the DZ for the rest of the troops parachuting in. They checked wind and weather conditions and directed the planes accordingly.

"Nice getup, Sergeant Paxton," one of the airmen said.

"Thanks."

"What gives?"

"Those a lot smarter than I am think being in disguise will help me get closer to the downed pilot." Paxton smiled wryly. "Hey guys, I want you to meet a dear friend of mine, McMurphy."

McMurphy was on the other side of the aircraft stowing gear. As the PJs made greeting noises, McMurphy waved his hand once over his shoulder without turning around.

Smith saw McMurphy's gesture and turned to Paxton. "What's his problem?"

"He's an asshole."

Smith nodded.

Paxton looked at his watch, and then in a loud voice said, "All right, gentlemen. Let's get the rest of this gear stowed and get buckled up for takeoff. We've got a pilot to rescue."

CHAPTER 6

THE MASSIVE C-17 GLOBEMASTER TOOK OFF FROM THE small airfield in the Panhandle of Florida and headed east. Once the plane reached cruising altitude of 45,000 feet and leveled off, Paxton unbuckled and stood up. The rest of his team followed suit—except for McMurphy, who remained seated off by himself.

"Gentlemen, gather 'round," Paxton said. The interior noise was not as bad as on some planes, such as a C-130, so they could talk during the flight without the aid of headphones. Also, the plane was pressurized, so there was no need to wear oxygen masks. The PJs collected around Paxton and took a knee. McMurphy remained in the corner. He had put his stereo headphones on.

"Here's what we know," Paxton said. "An F-117 Stealth fighter on a bombing mission was downed by enemy fire outside of Belgrade, Yugoslavia. The pilot ejected, parachuted down and is, as of the last report, still alive. He's in contact with CSAR aircraft. His code name's Cue Ball. He's away from the crash site but his exact location is unknown. There're hostiles all over the place looking for him and for anyone trying to rescue him."

A hand went up.

"Smith," Paxton said.

"Sergeant, aren't we a little far away from the action for a rescue mission? It's going to take us a while to get there."

"Good point," Paxton replied. "Most rescues for this action are being launched from Brindisi Airbase in Italy. Evidently, CSAR personnel are stretched thin, and they're unable to reassign units."

"Sounds like someone screwed the pooch big time," Smith said. The other PJs laughed.

"Maybe," Paxton said, the serious tone of his voice stifling the laughter. "That's not for us to decide. Our job is to get over there, get on the ground without being noticed, find Cue Ball and get him out safely."

Paxton explained that since the danger of anti-aircraft artillery was so great, they would exit the plane for their parachute drop at a very high altitude. The planned jump altitude was 35,000 feet, which required them to breathe oxygen through masks. Instead of free falling to a lower altitude, they would open their parachutes at a high altitude. The procedure, known as High Altitude, High Opening, or HAHO, would allow the PJs to drift for great distances under parachute canopy and the C-17 need not fly directly over the drop zone. Thus, lessening the danger to the plane by avoiding the anti-aircraft artillery (triple-A) and allowing the PJs to arrive undetected. The specialty of PJs was stealth. Where other branches of the service might rescue a pilot by sending in a big show of force, the PJs snuck in undetected.

"Won't that make us sitting ducks as we float down?" Peterson asked.

"Possibly, but it'll be dark. And the Serbs are looking along the ground for the pilot and likely at low altitude expecting a helicopter," Paxton explained. "Certainly the Serbs will detect this plane on radar, but it won't pass closely enough to the crash site to raise suspicions that it's a rescue mission. Even if they do, they'll think we're way off course. Any questions?"

Peterson raised his hand and was acknowledged by Paxton. "What's the exit plan after we find Cue Ball?"

"This plane will continue to fly in theater, refueling in the air as necessary, and be available for our return. We'll capture a decent roadway so the C-117 can land, load us up and fly us out of there. Jennings, you'll direct the plane in for the landing. The short take-off and landing capabilities of the Globemaster will make for a quick getaway." Indeed the Globemaster was the only large transport plane that was capable of backing up on the ground under its own power. No tractor was required.

"Sergeant, in my personal opinion, your plan is nuts," Peterson said.

"It wasn't my plan, but we have our orders," Paxton replied.

"Any other questions?"

The PJs looked at each other. Smith voiced the unspoken thought on everyone's mind. "What's the deal with McMurphy?"

Paxton looked at McMurphy who was listening to his headphones with his eyes closed. "He's coming along for the ride."

"Who does he work for?" Smith pressed.

"Our Uncle, I believe," Paxton answered, "but I've never seen a copy of his paycheck, so I couldn't testify to that."

Smith grinned.

"Any other questions?" Paxton looked around. "We've a long flight ahead of us. Finish your preparations, triple-check your equipment, weapons and parachutes and then get some sleep. It may be a long time before we get to sleep again."

The PJs and the combat controller did as they were instructed. After a few hours, they were sprawled out on the floor of the cargo bay in their thick sleeping bags. All of the PJs—except Paxton. He was wide-awake surveying the scene before him.

Even McMurphy was sleeping, although away from the others. He evidently did not have a sleeping bag—at least he wasn't using one. He had, however, found a relatively cozy sleeping perch. He was lying near the tarp-covered cargo—on the left side on top of one of the benches that lined the cargo bay. He had put a jacket over himself for warmth. Lying on the floor near McMurphy's head was the peculiar green backpack.

The lights in the cabin had been dimmed to make sleeping more comfortable—as if comfort were even a possibility bouncing along on the cold metal-grated floor of the aircraft.

The Globemaster designers at McDonnell Douglas were clearly focused upon the task of transporting heavy equipment such as tanks and trucks, never letting the thought of creature comforts cross their minds. Paxton knew, as did his team, that the floor of the Globemaster would seem like a room at the Waldorf in comparison to the accommodations that awaited them in Yugoslavia.

Paxton could not make out the shapes of the tarp-covered objects, but he could see that they almost reached the ceiling and were nearly as wide as the cargo bay. In the dim light, Paxton saw the glint of the huge tie-down chains used to secure them. The loadmaster had weighed the cargo precisely and calculated the exact position to place it to properly balance the aircraft. Overloading, or improperly balancing, or inadequately securing the cargo could very well result in the loss of the aircraft and its crew, which included the loadmaster. In this case, the two items were loaded far forward in the cargo hold, one in front of the other. Just aft of that was the area where the PJs were sprawled out. The cargo was wide, but there was ample room to walk on either side of it. Paxton nodded in approval, for he had a good idea of what was under the tarps.

It had been a long stressful day. And Paxton knew that there were more long stressful days ahead of him. He wished he could curl up and go to sleep like the rest of his men. Even the bare metal floor looked inviting. But he could not rest. He had too much work yet to do.

• • •

Cue Ball's legs were killing him after crouching for so long in the brush. But he couldn't allow himself to sit down because he wanted to retain the ability to move quickly on a split second's notice if needed. So he crouched. Every once in a while, he would allow himself the luxury of placing one knee on the ground to rest that leg, but only for a short while. Then he switched. Despite his conscious efforts to force himself to not stay in the kneeling position for any length of time, he was aware that fatigue caused him to linger longer and longer on one knee or the other. His legs felt like he had been crouching longer than Johnny Bench had in his entire career as a catcher.

For what must have been the fortieth time since sun-up, he checked his 9mm Beretta pistol. He released the magazine, pulled it out of the pistol grip and verified that it was full of ammunition. Then he eased the slide back ever so slightly, just far enough to confirm that a round was chambered, but not far enough to eject the round. The hammer was cocked. He replaced the magazine into the grip and smacked it home with his palm. The only thing he had to do to fire off a round was tick the safety to the off position with his thumb and pull the trigger.

He logically knew nothing had changed with the gun since the last time he checked, but it helped pass the time and burn off nervous energy. Besides, it was somehow comforting to see that everything was in order. In his exhausted state, he looked upon those bullets as his friends. Here he was, in the backwoods of Yugoslavia, with what seemed like the entire Serbian army looking for him. No doubt they'd want revenge for the bombs that he and his fellow pilots had dropped on their country. Revenge for the death he had caused.

Even the CSAR aircraft had left him here, alone. But his thirteen steel-jacketed lead friends had not abandoned him. No, they were still by his side, ready for action. Ready to intervene if someone tried to harm him.

He knew he would be found before long. It was inevitable. Very soon, he was certain, men would come and take him away. He couldn't know at this point, however, *who* would get to him first. He prayed to God that the first to arrive would be the Americans and not the Serbs.

• • •

Paxton finished preparing his equipment for the parachute jump. Reed had not lied when he told him that everything he would need would be on the plane. Satisfied that everything was in order, Paxton sat down on the floor and pulled out a piece of paper and a pen from his pack. He located a hard surface to write on and composed a letter to his wife. He figured in a letter he could explain his need for leaving without saying goodbye, ask for forgiveness and tell his family everything he needed to say. He would ask Major Thompson to deliver the letter to his wife in the event that he was killed. Assuming that the Globemaster returned to base safely.

"My dearest Jill," he wrote. "I'm so sorry I wasn't able to say goodbye to you or the children before I left…"

"Sergeant Paxton!" yelled the plane's loadmaster.

Paxton looked up. "Yes?"

"There's a Major General Reed on the scrambled radio channel and he's asking for you," the loadmaster replied. "Come with me." The Globemaster was designed to operate with a crew of three: the pilot, co-pilot, and loadmaster. The pilots were busy flying the plane, so that left to the loadmaster all other tasks, including, at least in this case, the task of being a messenger.

Paxton sighed and then stood up. He still held the paper and pen in his hand as he followed the loadmaster toward the front of the plane. The two men walked right past the sleeping McMurphy who still wore his stereo headphones. Paxton noticed that the green backpack that lay on the floor next to McMurphy's head had a length of cord running through the top handle of the pack. The cord looped through a carabiner clipped to McMurphy's belt loop.

Paxton tried to surmise what could possibly be in the pack. What was so important that McMurphy felt the need to lash it to himself while he slept? Paxton had as much an idea of what was in the pack as he had about what General Reed wanted to talk to him about.

• • •

Rugova was pleased at the sight of the wreckage of the Stealth fighter. He had looked it over inside and out. It was a good sign that most of the main fuselage was intact. That would be very useful for his plans. His unit alreadyhad succeeded in shooting down one of the most advanced fighter planes on the planet. All they needed to do now was capture the pilot, obtain the special part, and *then* he would declared a hero. Yes, he would be a very wealthy hero.

• • •

General Reed rattled off GPS coordinates over the scrambled radio to Paxton who wore thick headphones and stood next to the C17's loadmaster. The cord to the headphones ran through the open cockpit door and attached to a receiver inside the cockpit. Paxton jotted down the information on the only paper handy—the letter he had started writing to his wife.

"These are the coordinates for the wreckage?" he asked Reed

"Affirmative."

"Do you have coordinates for Cue Ball?"

"Negative."

"Is he still alive?"

"As far as we know."

"Any word from my wife?"

"Everything's fine at home."

Paxton wasn't sure he believed the general. He could only hope that Colonel Ward had lied well and that Jill wasn't worried. He terminated the transmission and handed the headset back to the loadmaster. He looked down at the coordinates scrawled across the face of his letter. Obviously he could not send this letter to his wife. *I can start over on a fresh piece of paper.* He folded the paper and placed it in the top pocket of his shirt. He buttoned the pocket as he headed to the cargo hold.

He paused by the tarp-covered objects. He bent down and lifted the tarp on the first object. It was exactly what he expected. He dropped the tarp to check the second object. Again he lifted the tarp and confirmed his suspicions. Satisfied, Paxton walked toward the rear of the plane.

Paxton returned to his spot, sat on the floor and searched his pack for another piece of paper so he could re-write his letter. He looked at the sleeping McMurphy. Then he eyed the green bag. Obviously that bag had something to do with McMurphy's so-called special mission—and that meant it had something to do with Pax.

He assessed the situation. *What the hell.* He crept to McMurphy, who was lying on his left side with his head toward the front of the airplane and his feet toward the rear. His back was against the bulkhead as he faced the center of the cargo hold. A light jacket covered him from his shoulders to his hips. The bench had some padding so it probably was not entirely uncomfortable. His breathing was regular and his eyes were closed.

Paxton felt the movement of the aircraft through the bottoms of his boots. While standing there in the low light, he examined the bag and how the cord was looped through the bag's handle and then tied off on the carabiner that was clipped to McMurphy's belt loop. Clearly he would not be able to unclip the cord because to do that he would have to touch McMurphy's belt loop and that would surely wake him.

He would have to be careful—and fast.

There are already enough unknowns on this mission.

Paxton squatted down and placed his hands on the green bag. He turned it around so the front faced him. The bag was extraordinarily heavy. He had to be cautious while turning it to allow the cord to slide through the handle and not cause tension. Paxton heard muffled metallic noises inside as items moved around and banged against one another. He stopped, holding his breath, hoping he hadn't disturbed the sleeping man.

Nothing happened.

Two black straps held the top closed. The straps were tightened through two plastic buckles. Paxton examined precisely how the straps were positioned so he would be able to put them back exactly so McMurphy wouldn't notice that the bag had been tampered with.

Paxton unfastened the left strap from its buckle. Once he had the left strap entirely detached, he glanced at McMurphy. The man slept like a rock. He then turned his attention to the right strap. Slowly he pulled it out of the buckle.

McMurphy didn't stir.

Returning his attention to the bag, Paxton leaned closer, opened the top flap, and peered inside.

CHAPTER 7

MORE CAMERAS FROM VARIOUS INTERNATIONAL television news networks arrived at the wreckage of the Stealth fighter. Lt. Col. Nikolic led them to the remote location and directed their set-up. With military-like precision, the crews arranged equipment to get the best vantage point for their broadcasts. The first satellite trucks had yet to arrive, but when they did, they would beam live images of the wreckage around the world.

The plane's fuselage sat on its belly in a grassy field. On one side was a deep old-growth Serbian forest. On the other was an open meadow by the muddy road. The fuselage's flat black finish was marred and dirty, but the white-stenciled words United States Air Force were clearly visible. Across the American flag that adorned one wing someone had spray-painted a red circle with a slash—the "international no" symbol. The plane, although mostly intact, was heavily damaged. It wasn't immediately clear, however, how much of the damage was a result of being shot down and how much was caused by the curious civilians. The canopy was missing, jettisoned so the pilot could eject, so the cockpit was wide open. People waited to sit in the cockpit and play with the controls. A Serbian police officer posted on top of the plane kept order and reminded civilians when their time in the pilot's seat was up. Several Serbian soldiers stood around with their rifles in hand, but pointed downward, watching the crowd. The news crews had parked their vehicles in a line along the edge of the dirt road. Several military vehicles were parked there as well.

Satisfied, Nikolic watched the activity. Rugova had returned to headquarters, so for the time being, he was in charge of the scene. All was going smoothly so far. But his work was far from done. He still had an important item to deliver.

• • •

What was so special about a plain metal box? Paxton peered inside the bag. He couldn't see a way to open the box, which was on its side. The damned thing barely fit inside the pack.

Paxton's heart pounded as he reached in and slowly slid the box out. Metallic objects banged together. Shit. Paxton froze and glanced at McMurphy.

McMurphy didn't flicker an eyelash.

Maybe the sound of the airplane drowned out the clinking. Although loud, the hum of its engines was regular and somehow soothing, not unlike the relaxing resonance of ocean breakers on a cool summer night at the beach.

But Paxton wasn't at the beach, he was tens of thousands of feet above the ocean, hurling toward an unknown future with too little information with which to make command decisions. The lives of the members of his team depended upon him. So he placed the heavy metal box on the floor next to the empty pack.

It was a red metal toolbox like you could buy at any hardware store. A metal handle was on top and two metal clips kept the lid closed. Paxton glanced again to his left at McMurphy who was lying right next to him looking for the slightest hint of a reaction. He felt like a thief, but it wasn't like he was stealing it. Curiosity drove him on. Paxton unclipped both latches at the same time and opened the lid. He peered into the toolbox and saw … tools. Ordinary tools. The top tray, which could be lifted out, had an assortment of screwdrivers, an adjustable wrench, a small hammer, a socket wrench with various diameter sockets, and other tools. Paxton was puzzled. *Why would they go to so much trouble over a set of tools?*

McMurphy's kick struck Paxton solidly behind his left ear.

Paxton pitched forward and sideways from the force of the strike. His left knee struck the corner of the toolbox before he thudded onto the floor.

"Shit!" Paxton felt as if his head had been loosened from his spine. Dizzy and sick to his stomach, he was vaguely aware of the pain surging up his left leg.

McMurphy propelled himself off the bench and onto his

feet. He pounced on the Paxton's back and wrapped his right arm around his neck. Paxton grabbed McMurphy's forearm with his right hand and turned his head into the crook of Mc-Murphy's elbow. The pressure on his larynx lessened, allowing him to breathe again.

Then McMurphy squeezed harder, pinching off the blood supply to Paxton's brain. Paxton knew he had to act quickly or he would lose consciousness. McMurphy's breath fanned the back of his head. He jerked his head backward, smashing into McMurphy's nose and teeth. Warm liquid splattered the back of Paxton's head.

McMurphy loosened his grip.

Paxton wrenched McMurphy's arm as hard as he could with his right hand while he twisted his body to the right. Lifting his left knee off the floor, he braced his foot and pushed hard, still twisting his body to the right.

With sheer brute force, Paxton lifted himself and McMurphy off the floor. They crashed down, this time on their backs, with Paxton on top. Paxton knocked the wind out of McMurphy by jabbing his left elbow into his side.

McMurphy released Paxton's neck and Paxton took advantage of his momentary freedom. Lying across McMurphy's chest, he balled up his legs and thrust them to the ground, propelling himself forward and onto his feet.

Paxton whipped around. McMurphy, blood dripping from his nose and mouth, rolled away from Paxton and jumped to his feet.

Pain burned in Paxton's left knee. The metal edge of the

toolbox had torn his uniform and dark red blood covered the whole lower pant leg. *No time to worry about that.*

McMurphy moved toward him, his hands in front, ready for action. Paxton squared off in a Tae Kwon Do sparring stance: left leg in front, on the balls of his feet, balanced, open palms.

"Stay out of my shit," McMurphy growled as he advanced toward Paxton. Paxton thought how odd McMurphy looked, stepping toward him, dragging the empty backpack still tied to the carabineer clipped to his belt loop.

"What's with your tools, McMurphy?"

"None of your business."

"Everything on this mission is my business." Paxton positioned himself to repel the attack. "Why are you here?"

McMurphy lunged.

Paxton hopped backward, out of range, lifted his left leg and shot out a stopping side kick into the man's midsection. Paxton tried to use his kick to push off and increase the distance between himself and McMurphy, but the pain in his knee weakened his effort. McMurphy, only slightly slowed by the kick, continued advancing.

"How do we find Jashari?" Paxton demanded.

McMurphy charged. Paxton twisted away, but McMurphy hit him low in the center of gravity and wrapped his arms around Paxton. He drove Paxton backward into the closest tarp-covered object. Off balance, Paxton smashed into it, driving all the air out of his lungs. He crumpled, sliding down the tarp to the floor.

McMurphy lifted himself off Paxton and kneeled. McMurphy looked Paxton right in the eyes and whispered, "Stay away from my stuff and stop asking questions. Understand?"

Paxton did not reply. His gaze never left McMurphy as the man got up, brushed off his hands and knees, and walked to the bench. He crouched down and closed the red toolbox.

Paxton looked down at his bleeding leg; he tried to focus his flurry of thoughts. He had no choice. He knew what he had to do. Paxton steeled himself and slowly got up. Once on his feet, he brushed himself off and looked around the cabin. Amazingly, all the others were still asleep. The sound of the engines had drowned out the sounds of their altercation.

Paxton walked to the crouching McMurphy and picked up the backpack, which was still tied to McMurphy. Paxton stepped toward the man, who was closing the last latch, offering the backpack to him.

He reached for the pack.

Paxton took another step closer. In one swift motion, he whipped the pack around McMurphy's head several times in a clockwise direction, wrapping the cord around McMurphy's throat. McMurphy's eyes widened and his hand went uselessly to his throat. Paxton drove his bleeding knee into McMurphy's back, pulled the pack back over his right shoulder with his right hand and tugged. McMurphy silently gagged, the whites of his eyes showing all the way around his pupils.

"I've got a team of PJs to protect. You have information I need for their safety. If you don't tell me right now how the hell to contact Jashari, I swear I'll kill you and throw your body out of this plane. Reed can go fuck himself."

McMurphy's face reddened, though it was impossible to tell how much was a result of rage and how much was a result of the lack of oxygen. He desperately grabbed at his throat.

Leaning over McMurphy, Paxton loosened the cord slightly with his right hand so the man would not lose consciousness, but maintained the hold on his head.

McMurphy's right elbow struck Paxton's exposed ribcage.

Sharp pain ricocheted across his ribs, but Paxton did not loosen his grip.

It didn't matter.

The instant his elbow made contact with Paxton's right side, McMurphy's hand dropped to the holster on Paxton's right hip. In one fluid motion, McMurphy ripped Paxton's pistol out of the holster, racked the slide with the other hand and swung it over his shoulder upside down toward Paxton's face.

As the weapon came to bear on his right eye, he dove left.

The first shot rang out.

Paxton's face burned as white-hot heat sprayed his right cheek, but the bullet zipped over his right shoulder, just missing him. The sound exploded through his head. The ringing in Paxton's ears prevented him from hearing the second shot, but he saw the flash.

He released the backpack and smacked the pistol away with his right forearm. The second shot whipped past, but the ejected metal casing seared Paxton's neck. It caught his collar and slid down the inside of his shirt, burning flesh all the way down his chest.

McMurphy stood up and turned around, pointing the Kimber .45 at Paxton who lay on the floor.

Shit! The fucker's really going to kill me.

Paxton gritted his teeth as pain surged through him. Thoughts of his wife and kids floated through his mind as he stared down the barrel of his own gun.

"Drop that weapon!" shouted a voice from the rear of the plane. Smith advanced toward McMurphy, crouching slightly, looking down the sights of the M-4 pointed at McMurphy's head. "Now!"

McMurphy lowered the pistol, letting it drop.

Two other PJs joined Smith, bringing their rifles to bear on McMurphy.

"What the hell is going on?" shouted Thompson as he and the loadmaster hurried from the front of the plane—the latter was armed with an M-16 rifle. The loadmaster pointed his rifle at the PJs.

Paxton watched Thompson assess the situation. He looked at the pistol at McMurphy's feet, at the cord draped around his neck, and at the bleeding Paxton on the ground. "One man shot is enough! Put your weapons down," he commanded.

"Yes, sir," Smith replied as he lowered his rifle. The other PJs followed Smith's lead. The loadmaster, standing next to Thompson, kept his rifle up and ready to fire, but his finger was out of the trigger guard.

Thompson's gaze flicked over McMurphy's blood-covered face. Then he looked at Smith. "What's going on, Sergeant?"

"I don't know, sir. I heard two gunshots and saw McMurphy

pointing a pistol at Sergeant Paxton."

"Who fired their weapon?" Thompson demanded.

"I did," McMurphy said without emotion. He removed the cord from his neck, then he gestured to Paxton. "He tried to kill, me, Major."

"Is that true, Sergeant?" Thompson asked Paxton.

Paxton's ears buzzed from the aftereffects of the pistol shots so close to his unprotected ears. He rose slowly. "Sir, if I had wanted McMurphy to be dead, he would be dead."

"Why you were strangling him?" Thompson sounded like he was talking through a pillow.

Paxton looked at McMurphy. "I didn't like the way he looked at me."

"Are you mocking me, Sergeant?"

"No, sir."

"Then tell me why you were strangling him."

"I can't tell you," Paxton answered.

"Why not?"

"Mission security, sir."

"Mission security, my ass. I'm the pilot of this plane, and you will tell me what's going on."

"No, sir," Paxton replied. "I will talk to no one about this except General Reed."

"To hell with that!" Thompson snapped. "Take them *both* into custody, Airman," he said to the loadmaster. "I want them both secured. Remove all their weapons. Then get them medical attention."

"Yes sir," the airman said.

"But, sir, I have a mission to complete," Paxton protested.

Thompson looked at Paxton then at McMurphy. "I will release you from custody right before we hit the drop zone."

Thompson returned to the cockpit and the loadmaster went to work. He was very good at his job. After he searched the men for additional weapons, removing even Paxton's web belt containing additional magazines for the Kimber, he secured their hands behind their backs with zip ties. Then he sat both men down next to each other, McMurphy forward of Paxton, on the bench on which McMurphy had been sleeping earlier. He took some tie-down straps and secured the men to the one of the many anchor points on the side of the aircraft. Neither man was going anywhere.

After the loadmaster finished his handiwork, he picked up the Kimber .45, holding it by the barrel, placed it in a plastic bag that he had taken the zip ties out of and carried it with him as he returned to his seat. Then two PJs went to work treating the men. Petersen examined McMurphy and Smith looked at Paxton's leg.

Petersen stemmed the bleeding of McMurphy's nose and mouth with cotton. It appeared that his nose was broken, but there was not much to be done about that. He cleaned the blood off McMurphy's face.

Smith looked at the two-inch gash in Paxton's knee. He thoroughly cleaned the wound and stitched it closed. "I hope your tetanus shot is up to date." After he finished, he admired his work. "That's so tight it won't leave a scar."

"You have always thought highly of yourself, haven't you, Smith?"

"Hey, it ain't braggin' if you can do it." Smith cleaned the burn on Paxton's cheek and applied a bandage.

The PJs cleaned up and left Paxton and McMurphy sitting by themselves. Paxton, ears still ringing, looked at McMurphy. McMurphy looked back. Paxton broke the silence. "This sucks."

A faint smile twitched on McMurphy's lips. He nodded. "Yes. It does."

"We'll probably get court-martialed for this."

"The UCMJ doesn't apply to me," McMurphy said, referring to the Uniform Code of Military Justice.

Paxton turned away, silent.

The plane jetted toward war-torn Yugoslavia. Unfortunately, no one thought to wonder about the expended bullets.

The first bullet imbedded into the thick metal of the tarp-covered object, but the second round had not been so benign. Its downward trajectory had sheared off most of the tie-down, which attached the aft securing chain. The damage was hidden from view by the tarp.

The loadmaster's quality work securing the load was rendered ineffective by one 230 grain .45-caliber slug.

CHAPTER 8

THOMPSON'S VOICE CRACKLED OVER THE C-17'S INTERCOM and announced that they had crossed into Serbian airspace. Paxton viewed it as a mixed blessing. On one hand, they were now exposed to the ever-present danger of Serbian anti-aircraft batteries. On the other hand, it meant he would soon be released from his medieval truss. His hands had long since gone numb. Paxton estimated it had been several hours since the loadmaster anchored him and McMurphy to the fuselage. He passed the time mostly by staring at the crinkle pattern in the blue plastic tarp directly in front of him.

McMurphy managed to fall asleep sitting up. Even Paxton's crew had taken the opportunity to get some additional sleep. After the announcement, they stirred and prepared for the upcoming mission.

As tired as Paxton was, however, the pain in his lacerated

knee and his anxiety about the mission prevented him from dozing off, even for a few minutes. All he could think about was his family. *They must be worried.* Frustration battered him. If only he had figured out some way to talk to Jill and their children. He watched all the activity, wishing he had something else to occupy his mind.

The loadmaster cautiously approached Paxton. He passed McMurphy, leaned in close and said, "Sergeant Paxton, you have a call."

"Who is it?"

"General Reed," the airman replied.

"What the hell does he want?"

"I don't know, Sergeant. He says it's very important that he speak with you. I'll have to untie you so you can get on the radio."

Things were looking up. "Well, Airman, let's go. The general is waiting."

The airman produced a large Gerber folding knife, reached behind Paxton and cut the tie-wraps from the tie-down straps. Paxton's brain sent the signal to his arms, but they were so numb he couldn't tell for sure if they were moving until he saw his hands in front of him. He shook them in attempt to restore circulation. The tie-wraps had left red creases on his wrists. The airman closed the knife. "This way, Sergeant."

Paxton stood up and followed him. They walked to the left of the two massive tarps. Only four feet separated the front object and the rear object. They approached the flight deck and Paxton saw Thompson asleep on a small cot to the right of the steps that led to the flight deck door. He was on his back, covered by a thin green blanket. *He and the co-pilot must take turns napping and flying the plane.* Not an unusual arrangement on such a long flight. Paxton climbed the stairs and knocked. A muffled voice granted permission, so he opened the door.

Paxton had to lean partway into the cockpit to retrieve the headphones. He politely acknowledged Captain Weil, the co-pilot, who was in the cockpit alone and busy studying the computerized instruments on the C-17. Weil nodded, focused on the operation of the aircraft. The loadmaster remained standing behind Paxton, just outside the cockpit. Paxton looked at the loadmaster, who watched every move Paxton made, and then he put on the headphones. He aligned the microphone to his mouth and clicked the transmit button. "General Reed, this is Paxton."

•   •   •

"Lieutenant Petrov! Get up!" the young soldier shouted as he burst into the tent.

Lieutenant Petrov grunted and rolled away from the source of the sound. "Sir, please get up!" the excited conscript repeated as he shook his superior.

The Serbian officer grunted again and rolled toward the excited teenager. The cot creaked with the strain of his considerable girth. He opened one eye and grumbled, "What is it?"

"Sir, we've picked up something on radar. You should see

this," the young private replied.

The lieutenant sighed heavily. "This intrusion better be worth it."

The nervous private backed off. "Sergeant Jovanov said I should wake you."

"Can't he do anything on his own?"

The young soldier, torn between his superiors, shrugged. "I don't know, sir. I'm just following orders."

"Orders. Yes. Of course." The lieutenant rubbed his forehead. He still felt the head-pounding effects of too many Slivovitzs, strong plum brandy, before bed. One of these days he was going to give up the bottle—but not before the end of this war. He steadied himself, lamenting his life, and slowly pulled on his pants. Then he put on the shirt. His collar still bore a mark from removed insignia of the higher rank he once held but unfairly, at least in his mind, lost.

As soon as Petrov stood up, the private headed for the opening in the tent.

Thick cables ran from the command truck to the Surface to Air Missile (SAM) system mounted on the back of a truck trailer parked about fifty meters from their position. The cables housed sophisticated fiber optics that transmitted control signals and were less susceptible to interference from NATO wonder-weapons.

The lieutenant lumbered from his tent, following the antsy private. He did not look like he would make it up the steps to the command truck. As he wobbled, the private grabbed his arm and tugged him up and into the open doorway.

Inside the truck was cramped and dark, except for the green glow of a radar screen. The glow reflected off the face of a young bearded sergeant who studied it intensely.

The lieutenant stumbled across the short distance to the radar equipment. He leaned on the sergeant's back with one forearm and the radar table with the other hand. "What is it, Sergeant?"

Overwhelmed by the lieutenant's foul breath, the sergeant fought the urge to recoil. "Sir, I picked up a large aircraft at a very high altitude that crossed into our airspace about ten minutes ago."

"So?"

The sergeant turned away from the screen and looked at the lieutenant. "Sir, it's huge. This aircraft is bigger than any of the fighters or bombers that we have tracked so far. I believe it is a cargo plane—perhaps an American C-5 or C-17."

The lieutenant looked at him blankly.

"Sir, is this the start of an invasion? Paratroopers will land, perhaps? Maybe we should contact headquarters for further instructions."

"Sergeant, you think too much." The lieutenant shook his head in disgust. "I'm going back to bed. Turn off that damn radar before we get bombed." He knew American missiles were designed to seek out and destroy significant sources of microwave radiation such as radar antennae. "And don't bother me again!"

"Yes, sir!" The sergeant watched the lieutenant turn and stumble for the door. "Sir?"

The lieutenant stopped, bristling, his back to the sergeant.

"Yes, Sergeant?"

"What do you want me to do about the cargo plane?"

The lieutenant stood in the doorway of the truck swaying noticeably. Without turning around, he said, "Shoot it down."

• • •

Paxton wrapped up his radio conversation with General Reed. "Yes, sir. Understood, sir. Over and out."

He hung the headphones on the designated rack, politely said his goodbye to Weil and stepped back from the cockpit doorway. He turned toward the loadmaster. "You going to tie me up again or are you going to let me get ready for my jump?"

• • •

The Soviet-made SA-10A SAM was a radar-guided anti-aircraft missile.

NATO gave the SA-10 the code name "Grumble."

The Grumble was the rough equivalent of the American Patriot missile used in the Gulf War, but it was a much larger system with bigger, longer-range missiles. Like the Patriot, the Grumble was capable of shooting down tactical ballistic missiles as well as aircraft. Its mobile launch system was composed of several vehicles. The launch complex included a battery command post and engagement control center inside a truck, the large CLAM SHELL 3D continuous wave pulse Doppler target acquisition radar, and the FLAP LID A I-band multi-function phased-array trailer-mounted engagement radar.

The missiles were seven meters in length and sealed inside long tubes, four of which were mounted on the back of a large erector-launcher trailer pulled by a Russian-made six-wheeled tractor truck called the KrAZ-260V. The launch tubes were transported horizontally but were raised to the vertical position for launch, allowing the quickest possible engagement of targets approaching from any direction. When in the vertical launch position, the bottoms of the launch tubes touched the ground behind the trailer. The four tubes were painted dark green and mounted two-by-two—marking the four corners around the frame to which the erection apparatus was attached. Reinforcement rings encircled the tubes at various places along their lengths. Ready for launch the tubes resembled twenty-foot high smoke stacks.

In the late 1980s, the Soviets ringed Moscow with the later version of the Grumble designated the SA-10B. The SA-10B was mounted on a specialized 8-wheeled transporter that included the target acquisition radar and control unit. The cash-starved government was happy to sell off the older SA-10A models to any country willing to pay. Eager buyers included the Chinese, the Syrians and, unofficially, the Serbs. Thus the Serbs were equipped with the makings of a fairly sophisticated air-defense system to protect Belgrade.

The heart of that system was triggered when Sgt. Jovanov pressed the launch button in the mobile command truck.

A single missile catapulted clear of its tube.

It rocketed five times the speed of sound ... toward the passing C-17 Globemaster carrying Paxton and his team.

• • •

The cockpit alarms blared. Thompson bolted up and scrambled up the stairs. As the pilot brushed past Paxton, he ordered, "You two, back to your seats and buckle up. Now!"

Paxton and the loadmaster didn't hesitate. Paxton shut the door, clapped the loadmaster on the shoulder and said, "Let's go."

Both men scrambled down the stairs. The loadmaster stopped at his station at the bottom, sat down, and pulled the buckle over his lap. Paxton hurried on, past the tarp-covered objects and past the tied up McMurphy, who was now wide awake. "What the hell is going on?"

"Missile launch." Paxton joined his men in the rear of the plane. "Everyone buckle up! Somebody's shooting at us!"

Paxton's men switched gears instantly. Most already had their parachutes on. They scrambled into seats on the right side of the cargo hold, their backs to the wall facing the left side of the plane. McMurphy sat forward of the PJs, on the left side of the plane, facing the rearmost tarp-covered object. Paxton ran to his own gear and grabbed his parachute. Not having time to put it on, he sat on an empty bench in the center of the aircraft—facing his men. He buckled the seatbelt, held the parachute on his lap, and braced for disaster.

• • •

In the cockpit, Thompson sat down in the pilot's seat and assessed the situation. Not knowing whether the missile was heat-seeking or radar-guided, he ordered Weil to deploy coun-ter-measures inan attempt to defeat both possibilities. The co-pilot deployed thousands of strips of radar-reflecting Mylar, called chaff, to confuse any radar tracking the aircraft. If the missile were heat-seeking, the on-board electronics of the mis-sile would be designed to do one thing and one thing only: head for the hottest point its instruments could locate.

At the moment, that hot spot was the white-hot exhaust of the four jet engines propelling the C-17 through the night sky. To counter the heat-seeking missile threat at the same time the chaff was deployed, the aircraft jettisoned numer-ous magnesium flares in various directions, the heat of which was greater than that of the jet's engines. The hope was that a heat-seeking missile would follow one of the flares instead of flying up the tailpipe of one of the jet engines and exploding.

The Grumble was not heat-seeking. Its guidance system was Track-Via-Missile (TVM). The FLAP LID radar on the ground beamed microwave radiation at the target. A certain amount of that radiation was reflected off the target and picked up by sensors in the nose cone of the missile. Electron-ics aboard the missile then made calculations and constantly adjusted the missile's flight through the use of fins and vector-ing the thrust from the single-stage solid propellant rocket motor. The TVM system was difficult to spoof because the distance the reflected radar waves had to travel was greatly reduced in comparison to ground-based tracking systems.

The C-17's radar reported the bad news: The missile was not fooled and still tracked toward them. Unfazed, Thompson said, "Okay. We're going to deploy again, but this time with a little fancy footwork." Thompson sounded as if he was describing how he planned to rearrange furniture in his living room.

The data point representing the missile on the cockpit radar screen moved closer to the data point representing the plane.

"On my mark."

On the radar screen the missile blipped closer to the plane.

"Steady."

Thompson's eyes were locked on the radar screen watching death approach from the rear. Weil's eyes were locked on the radar as well, trusting in Thompson's judgment, but every muscle in his body tensed just the same.

The missile blipped closer. The air inside the cockpit was saturated with apprehension.

Weil's left index finger hovered over the countermeasures button. He flexed the other three fingers.

"Not yet."

Another blip. The missile was almost on top of them.

"Here it comes."

The missile seemed to accelerate. Blip.

"Now!"

Weil jammed his finger down on the button. The Globemaster spat out its countermeasures again, but this time Thompson simultaneously stomped on the left rudder peddle, jerked the stick to the left and shoved it forward, causing the aircraft to dive.

With surprising maneuverability, the large cargo plane dove

sharply down, banked and turned left. The C-17 groaned and shuddered as it performed a maneuver ordinarily reserved for agile fighter aircraft. The operation was so drastic that Thompson and Weil "got some air." They felt almost weightless in their seats. Thompson braced his right knee against the instrument panel to avoid losing his seat entirely — he hadn't buckled in.

"Come on, baby," Thompson said as the two men tracked the missile on the radar screen. The data point representing the projectile on the screen converged with the point representing the plane. Weil swallowed hard.

The pilots saw a flash through the right side windscreen outside the aircraft and simultaneously turned their heads toward it. The flame from the missile's rocket motor jetted as it streaked by, passing harmlessly on the starboard side of the aircraft. The C-17 still groaned and shuddered as it continued its diving turn. Thompson and Weil both rejoiced the near miss. "Yeah, baby!" they shouted.

Then the large aircraft shook more violently.

A thud sounded in the rear of the plane.

Both men looked at each other in bewilderment.

• • •

Paxton couldn't believe his eyes. He hung onto his parachute, his seatbelt the only thing keeping him in the seat on this roller coaster ride, as he watched the rearmost tarp-covered object shudder and lurch toward the left side of the plane. The aircraft banked so sharply that it caused the item to shift under its own weight, shearing off the rearmost tie-down that had been damaged by the .45-caliber slug. Ordinarily the chains securing the cargo would hold it firmly in place, but not this time. The chain attached to the failed tie- down dragged along the floor of the cargo hold. It moved more with each jolt of the plane.

McMurphy sat there, his hands tied behind his back, unable to move, trapped by tie-down straps, eyes wide, watching the large mass shake directly toward him. The tarp completely filled his field of view. The object jiggled so far left that the tarp, which was still attached to the cargo hold tie-downs, ripped. The weight of the item moving off its perfectly balanced position interfered with the stability of the aircraft, causing the shudders to worsen.

Then the object lurched so violently that it shredded open the tarp, revealing a large construction bulldozer. Painted olive drab, it had four mammoth rubber tires, a glass-enclosed cab, and front-end loader—a large metal scoop with sharp teeth. The scoop was in its lowest position, facing the rear of the plane. It was angled upward, likely to prevent damage to the cargo hold floor, and the teeth were at chest level—aimed right at McMurphy.

A single chain attached the dozer's rear engine compartment to the floor of the cargo bay. As the dozer creaked ominously and gyrated toward him, it was impossible to tell if McMurphy would be crushed under the large right front tire or if he would be shredded by loader's serrated teeth.

"Shit!" McMurphy screamed. But it was too late for anyone to do anything.

• • •

Thompson fought to regain control of the aircraft. His consummate skills and experience were no match, however, for the 33-ton weight that had violently shifted the center of balance. Not entirely sure what was happening, he realized that some, if not all, of the cargo had broken free and was moving around with every maneuver of the plane. The C-17 was quickly losing altitude. *How ironic to successfully avoid the surface-to-air missile only to be brought down by shifting payload.*

Never in all his years as a pilot had Thompson ever had a mishap involving loose cargo. *How the hell did the loadmaster screw this one up?* He was determined not to lose this plane and continued to battle the controls as the Globemaster resisted and slowly rolled left.

• • •

The tilt of the plane accelerated the bulldozer's erratic movements. It pivoted in a large arc, straining against its front chain. The plane pitched over and forward so far that Paxton noticed the other large object forward of the dozer strained at its tie-down chains.

Paxton watched in horror as the machine bounced toward McMurphy. With an unearthly shriek, the rubber tires scraped across the metal floor. The metal bucket swung right toward McMurphy, who was jerking violently back and forth as he desperately tried to free himself. Paxton felt helpless as the events unfolded in a flash.

The C-17 was almost in a nosedive, with its left wing pointed toward the ground far below. The sudden alteration caused the bulldozer to slide toward the cockpit. The dramatic angle of the aircraft saved McMurphy's life as the bucket swung past, missing him by inches.

Then the aircraft turned completely on its side. The bucket swung to the left of McMurphy and crashed into the side of the fuselage.

It pierced the casing of the C-17.

Air exploded out of the pressurized cabin. The sharp teeth of the front-end loader tore through the thin skin of the aircraft like it was aluminum foil. Everything not tied down flew through the air, sucked toward the opening.

Paxton clung to his parachute to keep it from being blown outof his hands. Objects pummeled McMurphy before rushing out the hole not two feet from where he sat. He couldn't even protect his head because his hands were still secured behind his back.

Cacophonous sounds vibrated throughout the plane. Then the cabin lights flickered. As moisture condensed due to the rapid loss of pressure and temperature, fog filled the interior of the aircraft.

The men onboard experienced the sharp painful sensation in their ears known to SCUBA divers as a middle-ear block, which happens when the pressure in their inner ears greatly exceeds that of the atmosphere around them. Years of diving allowed Paxton to instinctively clear his middle-ear block by moving his jaw to open his Eustachian tubes.

As the pressure inside the aircraft equalized with the pressure outside, Paxton looked around and assessed the situation. The fog dissipated. Shit! Paxton knew that he had better get some air, and he had better get it quickly. The air at that altitude was so thin that it was impossible to properly oxygenate his blood. He would blackout in a matter of seconds. Fumbling around with his parachute harness, he located his breathing mask.

Paxton shouted, "Air!"

All the paratroopers onboard had small pony bottles of oxygen attached to their harnesses so they could breathe during the parachute descent until they reached a lower altitude. Most of them were donning oxygen masks. He was already feeling lightheaded as he pulled the straps over his head and fitted the mask over his nose and mouth. With the mask in place, Paxton turned the valve on his pony bottle all the way open and then back a quarter turn. He gulped a few breaths of pressurized oxygen and then got to work.

The C-17 pitched and jolted wildly. Paxton looked at McMurphy, who bounced around like a rag doll. His seemingly-lifeless form hung precariously over the teeth of the bucket. Paxton turned toward his men who were still strapped to their benches on the other side of the aircraft. They were on the right side of the plane, so they were actually above Paxton because of the steep leftward bank. He pulled down his mask and shouted, "Smith, your knife!"

Now that the pressure had equalized, the wind rushed into the hole, creating a loud din. Smith cupped his ear with his hand and shook his head.

"Your knife!" Paxton repeated as he made a slashing motion with his hand. He then replaced his air mask.

Smith slid his boot knife out of its sheath and leaned down to place the knife on the floor of the plane. With a gentle push, the six-inch double-edged knife slid downhill toward Paxton. He stomped out with his right boot and stopped it before it slid past him.

Paxton unbuckled, retrieved the knife from the floor and did his best to stand up. He had to put one foot on the back of the bench and the other on the lip of the seat. It would have been impossible to stand up on the floor because the floor had, for all practical purposes, become the wall.

Paxton needed both hands to keep his balance, so he took a deep breath, pulled his mask down by his chin, and put the knife in his teeth pirate-style. He then put his parachute on his back, but he didn't take the time to step into the harness that would secure him to the parachute. He walked to the end of the bench and leaned over until he was lying on the floor. He pushed off and slid toward the left side of the plane, hitting the row of benches. His injured knee banged into one of the bench supports. Pain shimmied down his leg. *Damn.* The knife bit into the corners of his mouth. He then stepped on the back and lip of the benches as he had done with the center row of seats and made his way to the limp McMurphy. He stopped his forward momentum by grabbing the bucket of the front-end loader.

Paxton took the knife out of his mouth and replaced his oxygen mask so he could breathe again. The blade was covered in blood. Stabbing the knife into the padding of the bench, he left the handle sticking out so it would be handy. Paxton reached under the bench and fished out McMurphy's parachute. Its straps were tangled in the other gear under the bench, but Paxton managed to locate McMurphy's oxygen mask. He unclipped it from the harness and extended its hose until it reached McMurphy's face. He twisted the valve full blast open and placed the mask against McMurphy's nose and mouth. Paxton held the mask tightly to McMurphy's face with his right hand and pressed the fingers of his other hand to check the unconscious man's carotid artery. There was a faint pulse. Satisfied that McMurphy was still alive, he pulled the straps over McMurphy's head so the oxygen mask would stay in place.

For the size of the C-17, the three-foot hole made by the bulldozer was not that large, but there was no such thing as a *small* hole in an aircraft at altitude. Had McMurphy not been tied down, he would've been sucked out by the violent change in pressure. The hole had been punched into the left side of the plane, which had become the floor. Paxton felt the wind whistling through the hole and leaned over to look out. All he saw was darkness.

McMurphy stirred. When he awoke, it was clear he had no idea where he was or what was happening. He fought the straps that tied him down. Paxton grabbed his shoulders to steady him and shouted, "Calm down!"

When McMurphy stopped struggling, Paxton pulled the knife out of the bench padding and sliced through the cloth straps and tie wraps.

Smith slid down to the benches and maneuvered to Paxton.

"Here," Paxton said, his voice muffled in the oxygen mask, "help him and make sure he doesn't fall out." Paxton handed Smith the knife, then he then pulled down his mask. "Make sure everyone is ready to parachute out. We might need to abandon ship."

Smith pulled off his mask. "Okay, Sergeant Paxton." Smith took the bloody knife, slid it in its sheath and then reached out to steady McMurphy. "Where are you going?"

"I'm going to get my gun," Paxton shouted. He put on his mask, stepped up and over McMurphy and stood on the back of the bench. He hesitated, his boots right on the edge of the new opening. Then he leapt over the gaping hole, landing on the other side of the bulldozer's bucket, and quickly worked his way forward toward the cockpit.

CHAPTER 9

BORISLAV DELEVIC AND MILO LABUS WALKED INTO THE dimly lit neighborhood bar. The fading Florida sunlight washed in through the tinted windows, splashing across the bar that formed a large rectangle in the center of the room. Stools lined all four sides. To the left of the bar was an assortment of high-top tables. Along that wall was an array of big-screen televisions set to various channels ranging from sports, to news, to talk shows. The low volume of the TVs allowed the latest Kid Rock single to blast from the jukebox. To the right of the bar was another row of tables against the wall. Beyond the rectangular bar were two pool tables; one was occupied by two bikers. The only other patron was an elderly man sitting at the bar, his back to the televisions. He flirted with the perky young bartender.

Delevic took one look at the tight blue jeans worn by the

bartender as she leaned over the bar, feigning interest in the old man's words, and he knew he had found his kind of place. He looked at Labus who stood just behind him. The larger, softer man was looking in the same direction. Delevic nodded. They walked to the right side of the bar and picked out two stools directly behind the bartender, facing the television screens mounted on the opposite wall across the bar. The bartender excused herself and turned to the two new faces at the bar. She flipped her auburn hair and smiled as she sauntered toward them.

"What can I get you gentlemen?" she asked with a cute Southern drawl.

Delevic smiled as his gaze alternated between her green eyes and her spaghetti-strap top with The Dugout, the name of the bar, printed on it. He wondered if this hole-in-the-wall bar in Lake Mary, Florida had any decent single malt scotch whisky.

"I'll take a Glenfiddich straight up, please," he said still smiling. Obviously they carried his favorite brand because she offered no substitute. Delevic's approval of this place was growing by the moment.

"What about you?" she asked his companion.

"I'll take a gin and tonic," Labus replied.

"Any particular brand?" the darling behind the bar asked.

"Whatever you have is fine."

Delevic grunted at his companion's obvious lack of taste. It had long been a pet peeve of his, but Labus never learned. If he wasn't so good with a gun, he would be useless.

"Ya'll want something from the kitchen?"

Delevic had a very nice expense account, and he wasn't about to waste it on bar food. He was planning on a nice steak later, and he thought how wonderful it would be for him to have this delicious bartender join him for dinner instead of his oafish companion. "Nothing right now, darling," he said.

"Okay."

As she turned and busied herself making the drinks, Delevic's eyes dropped to her nicely shaped behind with the bottle opener sticking out of her back pocket. Delevic liked hanging out in the Orlando area. The town of Lake Mary was just up Interstate 4 from Orlando and several world-class tourist attractions. The local attractions assured a steady stream of foreigners such as himself, so he blended right in. Other benefits included access to transportation at two local international airports, pleasant weather and the numerous hotels, restaurants and shopping centers. But the best benefit of all was the spectacular women.

Delevic unclipped his cell phone from his belt under his light jacket and placed it face up on the bar in front of him. March in Florida was almost too warm for a jacket, but he needed to wear one to conceal the Ruger 9 mm automatic pistol. He carried it in a holster clipped to his belt and tucked inside his pants. The ready light on the cell phone blinked steadily red indicating a lack of signal. He held the phone in place with one hand and extended the antenna with the other to improve reception. The flashing light turned from red to green indicating sufficient signal strength. Delevic was satisfied. He didn't want to be forced to move from his position so close to the bartender. It was important, however, that he havea signal for his phone. He never knew when it might ring, and he had to be ready at a moment's notice.

The babe returned with their drinks, arranging them on beverage napkins. Delevic smiled again and she smiled back. "Can I get anything else for you gentlemen?" she asked pleasantly.

"You could tell me your name," Delevic said.

"Amanda."

"Amanda. That's a beautiful name." *She couldn't be more than twenty-five years old,* thought Delevic.

"Thank you."

"I'm Boris and this is my friend Milo."

"Glad to meet you," she said. "I've never seen you two in here before. Then again, I'm new."

"We've never been in here before. We are from out of town," Delevic explained.

"Really? Where are you from?" She leaned directly over the bar and Delevic liked the view.

"We are from Europe." Delevic sipped his Scotch. Labus ignored his gin and tonic and stared at the bartender's cleavage.

"No kidding! Where in Europe?"

"We're Italian."

"Boris and Milo don't sound like Italian names."

Smart. A woman with looks like hers could make it on beauty alone. He grinned. *I enjoy a challenge.* "I'm named after my grandfather on my mother's side who was from Eastern Europe," he lied. "Are there any good steak houses around here?"

"There's an Australian steakhouse up by the mall. It's my favorite."

"*Your* favorite, huh?"

"Oh yes," Amanda said. "I love the warm fresh bread they bring out with your food." She closed her eyes as if she imagined the warm bread melting in her mouth.

Now to bait his trap. "Sounds delicious. Why don't you join me?"

Amanda straightened and shrugged. "Oh, I don't know," she said. "My shift here doesn't end for another hour."

Ah. She wanted him to press. Yes, she was definitely a challenge.

"An hour is perfect. That will give me plenty of time for another drink." He paused to read her reaction. She was smiling and toying with her hair. "Please join me. My friend has another engagement, and I don't wish to dine alone in a strange town. Besides, I don't know the way."

Labus looked at Delevic, frowning.

Amanda bit her bottom lip obviously assessing him. Delevic knew he was handsome and that he appeared wealthy. Still, she was hesitating.

"They have warm fresh bread." Delevic said, chuckling. "Think about it, okay?"

She nodded. "Can I get you another drink?"

"Yes, please."

Labus sloppily gulped down his drink. "Me too."

Amanda turned and walked away to make the next round. Labus leaned close to Delevic and whispered, "What 'other engagement' do I have?"

"Something … anything away from us." Delevic reached into his jacket pocket and fished out a wad of bills. He peeled off five $100 bills and stuffed them in his companion's shirt pocket. "Go find yourself a strip club and a cheap hotel. I'll call your cell in the morning. Keep it with you all night in case I need you."

"Can I use the car?"

Delevic peeled off another hundred bucks. "Call a cab and go rent yourself a car for the night. Finish your drink and disappear," Delevic whispered as Amanda walked toward them, fresh drinks in hand.

"Here you go, Milo," Amanda said as she placed the tumbler in front of the larger man. "And here is yours, Boris." She lightly brushed the back of his hand with her fingertips as she placed his drink.

"Have a drink with me, my dear."

"I can't. I'll get into trouble."

"Put it in front of me and sip it when you come around to chat with me. No one will be the wiser."

"Is that how they do things in Italy?" Amanda asked, matching Delevic's playful tone.

Delevic chuckled. "In Italy, *no one* cares if you drink!"

Amanda walked away to fix a drink for herself. Delevic turned to Labus. "Keep your phone on. And don't drink too much. We might be needed tonight." His eyebrows rose. "Why are you still here?"

"Okay, okay, I'm leaving." Labus tilted his glass and finished off the gin. Then he clapped Delevic on the shoulder and left.

Delevic scanned the big screen televisions. The one on the far right was tuned to one of the many 24-hour news networks, which was covering the American Stealth Fighter that crashed outside of Belgrade. There was tremendous media attention because it was the first Stealth plane ever lost in combat.

Amanda returned with her drink, putting it in front of Delevic, but closer to her side of the bar. With a furtive glance, she picked up her glass and took a sip. "Mmmmm."

"Aren't you having fun?" Delevic asked.

She nodded, smiling.

"You and I could have even more fun if you'd join me for dinner."

She smiled again. "Sure."

Delevic held up his glass for a toast. "Here's to the start of a memorable evening."

Amanda clinked her glass against his and drank.

• • •

Ahmet Jashari sat on a creaky wooden chair on the safe house's balcony in the town of Drenica, Yugoslavia. He was dressed in faded green fatigues and wore mud-encrusted black leather boots. Around his waist were a leather belt and holster. They were so worn that they looked as if they were hand-me-downs from his father who had gotten them from his grandfather who must have been a young boy when he bought them secondhand.

Three other men, also dressed in matching faded green fatigues and armed with slung MP-40 machine guns, stood between Jashari and the balcony's railing, effectively blocking his view. The MP-40's, often incorrectly referred to as "Schmeissers," were World War II-era German relics. Someone likely took them from the bodies of fallen Nazi soldiers who had fought in the Balkans back in the early 1940s. It would be impossible to determine how many times since then the weapons had changed hands, either in exchange for money or a hail of bullets. Nonetheless they were reliable and deadly, capable of firing 9 mm rounds at a rate of 500 per minute.

The three men were there to protect Jashari from snipers as well as to block the sound of Jashari's voice from potential eavesdroppers who might employ a parabolic microphone. This was particularly important because Jashari was engaged in a private conversation on the scrambled satellite phone, the receiver of which he held in his left hand. The antenna for the satellite phone was set up on a tripod assembled on the floor of the balcony to Jashari's left. The satellite phone's antenna required line-of-sight alignment with the appropriate quadrant of the sky, hence the requirement that Jashari conduct his conversation on the balcony on this chilly March evening. It was quite the impressive set up—a gift from the Americans.

"We are ready for every contingency, General," Jashari said into the receiver in perfect English. "You can count on us."

The voice on the line was slightly garbled due to the scrambling process and the great distance. Jashari replied, "As I told you before, I will be happy to assist in any way I can. I will call again in three hours for another update." He ended the transmission and mulled over what the General had said. Then, in Serbo-Croat, he said, "I don't believe we are being told everything."

The man in the center of the balcony turned to face Jashari. "You don't?"

"Our dear friend General Reed is withholding something from us—something very important."

"Are you still going to help him?"

"Of course," Jashari answered without hesitation.

"Why?"

"A little favor, my friends." He grinned. "The Americans are considerate enough to fight our war for us."

"What is it that you think he is not telling us?"

"I don't know," Jashari said thoughtfully, "but I intend to find out."

CHAPTER 10

THOMPSON STRUGGLED WITH THE CONTROLS TRYING TO regain command of the C-17 aircraft. It was pitched almost entirely on its left side due to the incredible weight shift of the tractor to the port side. Fighter pilots would call this "knife-edge" flight. At this attitude, the wings generated little lift. Thompson kept the mammoth plane aloft with only the massive thrust of the engines and his extraordinary piloting skills.

To make matters worse, the hole in the fuselage created by the bulldozer's bucket caused extra drag on the left side of the plane—the same side burdened with the unbalanced weight. As the plane descended to a lower altitude, the flight controls became slightly more responsive as the density of the air passing over the control surfaces increased. This enabled Thompson to stem the rapid altitude loss and regain somewhat level flight, albeit on the plane's side. The same increased density of atmosphere that gave Thompson some semblance of control also increased the turbulence. The bumping and shuddering grew exponentially. It was a tribute to the Boeing engineers and craftsmen that the plane didn't shake apart.

While Thompson tried to keep the plane aloft, Weil did his best to determine exactly where the plane was in relation to where it should be. The last thing they wanted at this point was to level the plane off only to fly straight into a mountain. All that he could see out the windows was inky blackness. Either the Serbian authorities had ordered a blackout in fear of an air raid or NATO had knocked out the local power grid with a graphite bomb. Regardless, the blackout coupled with the moonless overcast night made it impossible to tell where the sky ended and the ground began. There was no horizon. There was only black—a black so dark that he felt it on the surface of his eyes.

Their flight plan called for a high-altitude airdrop that would have been conducted entirely on instruments, so neither he nor Thompson wore their Night Vision Goggles (NVG). Indeed their NVGs were safely packed away. It would be too difficult under the circumstances to unbuckle and try to crawl around the shuddering plane and retrieve them. Only a fool would try to move about the aircraft as it pitched and rolled uncontrollably.

He also knew from experience that he could not rely upon his other senses to divine level flight. The graveyards were full of pilots who augured into the ground because they ignored their instruments. He double-checked the altimeter and the artificial horizon. Then he checked the GPS receiver and attempted to translate the coordinates to the map that was clipped on a foldout clipboard near the stick in front of him. He placed his finger on the map at what he believed was their approximate position and scanned the map for nearby mountain ranges.

He also had to worry about anti-aircraft fire. They were at a lower altitude now, thus making them vulnerable to a greater variety of weapons. Both Thompson and the co-pilot wore the oxygen masks they had donned immediately after the cabin depressurized because, although they were still flying—if what they were doing could technically be called flying—they were too high for normal breathing. The co-pilot wore his mask in conjunction with his flight helmet. Thompson had left his helmet next to the cot where he had taken it off to nap more comfortably, so he wore his oxygen mask strapped to his face without a helmet.

Thompson chose not to bleed off more altitude, even though he doing so would render the oxygen masks unnecessary. He had quickly weighed the added risk of low-altitude flight, which would expose them to even greater dangers bothof ground fire and controlled flight into terrain —that is, flying into a mountainside—against the minor inconvenience of wearing an oxygen mask. He angled the Globemaster and the plane ascended.

Even as Thompson feathered the controls, he was already thinking about his next move. Would he be able to locate the drop zone, drop the paratroopers and then fly to Italy? Surely he would not be able to orbit, refuel, land and pick up anyone as the mission plan stated. Should he abort the mission and fly directly to Italy? Or could he re-direct to a U.N.-controlled airfield in nearby Bosnia? Thompson refused to consider any option that involved an emergency landing in Serbia. *Any landing you can walk away from is a good landing—and any landing that allows you to use the plane again is a great landing.*

Something hit the cockpit door three times. The two pilots looked at each other. What the hell had broken loose now? Something banged three more times, louder this time. Then over the din of the vibrations and jet engines they heard a muffled voice. Aggravated by the interruption, Weil reached back and unlocked the door.

Paxton stuck his head through the opening. He pulled off the oxygen mask attached to his bailout bottle. "Sirs, are you all right?" he shouted above the noise. Somehow Paxton had worked his way all the way forward. Along the way, he had checked on the loadmaster, who was still strapped safely in his seat breathing his emergency air supply. But he had not yet retrieved his pistol.

"We're fine," Thompson yelled through his oxygen mask. "What the hell happened back there, Sergeant?"

"The bulldozer broke free and smashed through the fuse-lage," Paxton said as he removed his mask again.

"Shit!" Thompson exclaimed. "How the hell did that happen?"

"I think the tie-down was struck by a bullet."

"A bullet!" Thompson exclaimed.

"I deflected McMurphy's arm just as he pulled the trigger. He missed me."

Both pilots turned to stare at Paxton. "You realize, Sergeant, what you've told me will be used against you at your court martial."

"Yes, sir," Paxton replied, resigned to his fate.

"Is everyone okay back there?" Weil asked.

"Yes, sir. McMurphy sustained some minor injuries, but he is being treated. Everyone else is strapped in. But there is one helluva hole in the plane."

"She can take it," Thompson said, confident. "Check with the loadmaster and see if there is anything he can do about getting that bulldozer moved back to center. We are proceeding with the mission."

"Sir, with all due respect—"

"We're proceeding, Sergeant."

"Yes, sir.'

"Where are we?" Thompson asked Weil.

He examined the GPS receiver display and consulted his map. "We're about thirty miles out from the drop zone."

"Sergeant, I suggest you and your men get ready for your jump. Good luck." Then Thompson switched on his microphone and made an announcement to the PJs in the cargo hold to stand clear of the rear cargo door because he was going to open it. The plane continued to climb toward their original cruising altitude.

• • •

"Thank you, sir." *You fucking idiot.* Paxton placed his oxygen mask over his face, retreated to the main cabin and shut the door to the cockpit. The handle of the sideways door was near eye-level to him as he stood there on a piece of equipment. It was like being in some sort of hellish fun house. As he climbed down to stand on the side of the fuselage, the plane pitched up and down wildly. He used a flashlight to make his way through the dim cargo hold.

He reached the loadmaster who was still strapped in. "Major Thompson wants you to see if there is anything you can do about the bulldozer."

"Okay," the airman replied through his oxygen mask as he started to unbuckle.

"I recommend you put on your parachute. There's a big hole to climb over. If you fall…"

The loadmaster grimaced, nodding. Paxton lifted the parachute onto the loadmaster's back. He then checked all the connections and clips. Paxton knew that, as a member of an aircrew, the loadmaster had much less experience with parachutes and he wanted to make sure everything was properly buckled and all lines were routed properly. Paxton then assisted the loadmaster in switching from his on-board air supply to his bailout bottle so he could move freely about the plane. "Okay, you're good to go," Paxton said as he slapped the loadmaster on the shoulder.

As the two men weaved toward the rear of the plane, Paxton heard the cargo door's hydraulics grind and squeal. The rear door yawned open and the ramp extended into the air.

The plane shuddered violently.

"That doesn't sound good," the loadmaster said.

"You think that's bad, wait till you see this." Paxton led him under the first large object. It was still covered by a tarp but hung precariously over their heads as they scrambled along the side of the plane. The loadmaster turned on his flashlight too. Above their heads, suspended by chains, was the engine compartment of the bulldozer. Its large wheels were still in contact with the metal floor of the cargo hold. But the whole tractor formed a wedge starting from over the loadmaster's head and ending in front of him at what was now the floor. The front wheel rested on the fuselage, but the bucket had pierced through. The loadmaster walked closer to the front wheel and examined the hole with the beam of his flashlight. The wall of the fuselage appeared to be wedged between the bucket and the front wheel with part of the bucket poking out of the plane.

"What do you think? Is there any way we can winch it back to the center?" Paxton looked over the loadmaster's shoulder.

"I might be able to rig the winch from the front of the other vehicle through a tie-down on the right side of the plane and pull it up toward the center." He pointed to the way the fuselage was pinched between the bucket and the front tire. "But doing so might rip a bigger hole here. Besides, I don't know if the winch has enough horsepower to move this thing. I need to look at it from the front." The loadmaster climbed over the bucket and jumped over the gaping hole to land on the benches on the other side. He turned around, crouched down and examined the damage from that side.

Paxton waved his flashlight across the rear of the plane.

The cargo door was open and his team was making their final checks of each other's parachutes as they stood on the backs of the benches along the plane's left side. He saw Smith, who wore NVGs, overseeing the process and making last-minute adjustments to various team members' equipment.

But something was wrong.

Paxton swept his flashlight around the interior. He pulled off his oxygen mask and shouted, "Smith! Where's McMurphy?"

Smith was on the other side of the gaping hole caused by the bulldozer. He looked up at Paxton and then pointed his thumb over his shoulder toward the open cargo door.

"*What?*" Paxton said.

Smith took down his oxygen mask. "He put on his parachute, Pax," he shouted over the roar of the jet engines. "As soon as that door opened and the ramp extended, he grabbed that damned green pack of his and jumped." It was particularly hard to hear because the rushing air created a wind tunnel now that the whole back of the aircraft was open. The wind would enter the hole and exit the cargo door behind Smith with an awful whistling noise. That combined with the sound from the jet engines and vibrations made conversing almost impossible.

He didn't even wait for the rest of us, Paxton thought bitterly.

With the loadmaster pre-occupied it seemed a good opportunity for Paxton to retrieve his Kimber automatic pistol. He turned around and headed forward again.

The tremendous pressure of the wind continually pushed on the bucket protruding from the fuselage. The force was constant and combined with the bulldozer's weight to put additional tension on the chains weakened from continual violent vibrations.

POP.

Shit! Paxton dove aside as the forward tie-down, securing the engine side of the bulldozer, sheared off. Since the angle of the plane was so steep, the bulldozer slammed down. The front grill brushed the bottom of Paxton's boot as it whipped by.

The bulldozer crashed right through the fuselage and hung there by its bucket and front tire, the entire engine compartment outside the plane.

Paxton lay on his belly, the wind knocked out of him, with his head toward the cockpit and his feet toward the tail of the plane. Near his feet, a jagged hole widened. The weight of the machine was making the rear portion of the plane sag down, further ripping the fuselage.

The plane continued to climb and Thompson tried to achieve level flight. Since the wings were attached forward of the big tear created by the bulldozer's engine, its weight was no longer as big a factor on the forward portion of the plane. So Thompson's efforts twisted the front of Globemaster to the right as the rear of the plane sagged on its left side.

That was all the structure could take.

The whole rear of the C-17 ripped off with a metallic groan.

The bulldozer, Smith, the loadmaster and the rest of Paxton's team fell into the darkness.

CHAPTER 11

A WALL OF ICE-COLD WIND SLAMMED SMITH BACKWARD. He flattened onto the floor, arms and legs spread-eagled. Because of the curvature of the fuselage, his hands were slightly higher than the center of his body. The fuselage's aluminum ribs pressed painfully against him. He held up his head and strained to see any sign of Paxton.

In the ghastly green light of his NVGs, he spotted the loadmaster teetering on the edge of the original hole. He crawled crab-like toward him and grabbed his right boot at the ankle. Then Smith pushed himself and the loadmaster away from the gaping hole.

Smith watched in horror as the last connections between their portion of the plane and the front section shredded. Smith wanted to bolt up and leap to the perceived safety of the forward section. But such a feat would be impossible and, worse, pointless. With the plane disintegrating, those trapped in the front were just as dead as the rest of them.

Smith's stomach clamped into a knot as he saw the jagged rough oval outline of the open forward fuselage hover and then streak away from him, the scream of the still-running jet engines blending into the howl of the wind as they flew farther and farther away. Smith tried to see, before the front fuselage disappeared in the distance, whether Paxton had made it or if he had been crushed under the falling bulldozer. But it all happened so quickly, and the bulldozer, which was still hung up on his portion of the fuselage, blocked his view.

Concerned about Paxton's fate, Smith climbed over the loadmaster and toward the bulldozer as his stricken segment of the C-17 wreckage glided forward through the air. He grabbed the cold steel of the bulldozer, pulled himself past the hole, and peered around the bucket.

The rear segment of the plane, with no engines, no wings and lacking any semblance of aerodynamics, was buffeted as the friction of the air scrubbed off the last of its forward momentum. The tremendous weight of the bulldozer, which still hung half out of the wreckage, caused it to pitch over. The dive rolled Smith into the bucket. He looked over its lip, but instead of the dark nothingness of the sky, he recognized green-tinted features of the ground. *Holy shit. I'm looking straight down.*

Smith felt the familiar sensation of his guts pushing up into his diaphragm as gravity accelerated his body toward the Earth. *Escape!* Smith's mind operated in survival mode, generating no reasoned thoughts—only instinct. He had to get out of the wreckage. *But how?* He looked over his shoulder into the remainder of the cargo hold. The loadmaster sprawled above him, head-first, hanging on for dear life to the metallic ribs of the fuselage. He looked past the loadmaster and saw only two other forms. They were sprawled out as well.

Where was the rest of the team? Thoughts were coming only in snippets, reduced to animalistic impulses. Then one man pushed himself up off the fuselage. He spread out his arms and was caught by the onrushing wind that carried him backward out the wide-open rear cargo door above him. The rear door! He watched the second figure exit out of the top in the same manner as the first. All he had to do was push himself out into the middle of the air stream flowing through the center of the open cargo hold, spread out his limbs to create as much drag as possible and the wind would slow him down in relation to the speed of the falling wreckage. The remainder of the plane would then literally fall out from around him and he would be free. Then he would deploy his parachute. But time was short. The wreckage was plummeting to earth at terminal velocity. He pushed himself up and braced to spring out from the bottom of the bucket into the air stream. Out from confinement into freedom. Out from death into life.

The loadmaster! Smith stopped himself and looked up. The loadmaster was still sprawled out clinging to the fuselage with his head buried in his armpit. He wore a parachute. "Let go!" Smith shouted through his oxygen mask. The loadmaster didn't move. Smith pulled down his oxygen mask and screamed, "Goddamn it! Let go!"

The loadmaster didn't look up. He just shook his head; obviously he was frozen with fear.

"Let go or die!" Smith screamed, trying to shock the loadmaster into action.

The loadmaster wouldn't budge. Smith had no idea how long until impact. He could look at his wrist altimeter to find out, but he did not.

He didn't want to know.

Smith put his oxygen mask back over his face and took a deep breath. Instead of propelling himself to freedom as he had originally planned, he climbed out of the bucket and crawled up the ribbed fuselage toward the loadmaster. Since the fuselage was plunging straight down, the loadmaster was above Smith. Each aluminum rib acted as a step on a ladder. The only sound was the eerie whistling of the wind. Smith stepped carefully because he did not want to entangle his foot in any of the wiring or conduits. Foot entrapment meant certain death.

Smith reached the loadmaster. They were face to face. The loadmaster was upside down, plunging head first, his feet pointing toward the sky. Fear was etched on the young man's face. There was no time to reason with him. Smith felt the ground approaching the bottoms of his own boots. He took one more step up until his face was at the loadmaster's belt level. His uniform was whipping around wildly in the wind. With his right arm he reached under the loadmaster's belly. There wasn't much room for Smith to maneuver his hand because the loadmaster clung to fuselage for the fleeting and false sense of security it offered. Smith felt around the loadmaster's chest and located his ripcord. Smith pulled with all his might.

The ripcord moved and the parachute pack popped open, ejecting the drogue chute into the rushing air stream. The small drogue chute immediately filled with air, created drag and yanked the main chute out of the loadmaster's pack and up past his boots toward the open rear cargo door. The large parachute bloomed inside the cargo hold and jerked up the loadmaster, breaking his death-grip on the aluminum ribs. Smith tried to move to the side, but the loadmaster slammed into him as he popped off the wall and was snapped upright and upward by his opening parachute. It happened so quickly that it looked as if the loadmaster had been sucked out of the top of the plane.

Smith sailed to the other side of the fuselage. The air struck Smith like a tsunami and carried him head first into the top portion of the rear cargo door. Smith's Kevlar helmet clunked into the doorway and he went tumbling out of the plane.

Smith cart wheeled three times before he was able to spread eagle and regain control. Freedom! All of his senses registered the lack of confines around him. Instinct took over and he immediately pulled his ripcord. His body was jolted as it slowed almost to a stop. He looked up. Above him was a beautiful sight. In the artificial green light of the NVGs was his fully deployed parachute.

He scanned the sky above him and saw the fully deployed

parachute of the loadmaster. Satisfied the two of them were safe, at least for the moment,he searched the sky above and behind him. With his NVGs, he could see yet another beautiful sight. Far above he could clearly see six other fully deployed parachutes. The rest of the team—all except for Paxton.

Sorry, Pax.

He pushed his friend out of his mind. He hung in his parachute harness gliding gently to earth. He found some comfort in the green image of the beautiful blossoms of his team's parachutes high above him.

Then reality struck him. *Shit.* Just as he could clearly see his entire team in the darkness with his NVGs, he knew without a doubt that down below there would be men waiting to kill them who had NVGs of their own.

• • •

Miraculously, the fuel system remained intact, so there was no flash fire when the tail fell off. The wings remained attached and the four jet engines continued thrusting. But the plane no longer had its tail section and thus lacked its giant vertical stabilizer.

Thompson fought to raise the left wing and lower the right wing to achieve level flight and now, all of a sudden, there was nothing to fight. The 33-ton unbalanced weight of the bulldozer tipping it to its left side was gone. The C-17 performed a 360-degree-plus clockwise snap roll.

Everything not tied down was tossed around—including

Paxton. He had been lying there, stunned, head toward the cockpit, on the left side of the fuselage where he had landed after diving out from under the falling bulldozer. When the plane rolled suddenly to the right, Paxton tumbled along the floor of the cargo hold. He was flung helplessly into the large tarp-covered object that had been in front of the bulldozer and still attached at the very rear of what remained of the plane.

As the C-17 pitched right, Paxton rolled up the left side of the object. He flung out his arms in a futile effort to stop himself. His left arm slid under the tarp's edge and he instinctively slammed his arms together, trapping it between his forearms. Paxton was spun onto his stomach, clutching the tarp to his chest. It wrapped up around him. Momentum flung him off the top of the object and he crashed into the fuselage's other side, ripping off part of the tarp.

Paxton caught a glimpse of a dump truck chained to the cargo hold floor. Like the bulldozer, it was painted green. It faced backward, toward the night sky.

The plane leveled off and the engines throttled down.

Gravity returned.

Paxton slid down into the corner and fought to unravel himself from the tarp. His feet were only a yard from the opening in the back of the plane. With the engines powered down, the plane's forward speed dropped at an alarming rate. That reduced the lift generated by the wings and the tremendous weight of the dump truck caused the rear to sink lower. The flat bottoms of the massive wings dug into the air as they dipped backward slowing forward airspeed to a halt. The

C-17 pitched backward like a skateboard, its nose pointing straight up. The fuselage seemed to hang there for an instant, and then, in a full stall, it began its slide down, picking up speed as Earth tugged it home.

Paxton couldn't see a damned thing, but the falling sensation was unmistakable. As the downward speed accelerated, so did the wind blowing through the bottom of the plane. Paxton was shoved up inside the fuselage like wadding being shoved into a cannon by a ramrod. He was thrust straight upward until he plowed headlong into the ceiling, which was actually the front bulkhead separating the cockpit from the cargo hold.

The enormous opening at the bottom was gobbling massive amounts of air as it fell toward the earth. The air quickly filled the cargo hold and created drag, slowing the plummet of the wreckage like an enormous metallic parachute. The blast of wind served to pin Paxton, still entangled in the tarp, against the forward-most bulkhead. He was squeezed between the upward drive of the wind and the downward push of the falling bulkhead.

Paxton struggled with the tarp, flailing his arms and kicking his legs until he freed himself. The icy cold air felt like a thousand needles piercing his exposed skin, and its strength made it difficult to open his eyes.

Some of the emergency lights still worked. For the first time, Paxton realized that the rear of the plane was missing. The jagged edge of the fuselage, lighted by the emergency lamps, framed the blackness below. The bulldozer was gone.

Smith, the loadmaster and the rest of his team were gone, too.

I have to get out!

He dove for the jagged opening below him, but the rushing wind slammed him against the bulkhead. He tried to quell the panic. How could he get out? He desperately looked for another exit, but he saw no other way to escape. How much time did he have? Above him was completely blocked off by the bulkhead. The only doorway through that led to the cockpit—which was a dead end. He was trapped. The plunging wreckage had swallowed him up, like the whale swallowed Jonah.

The air rushing backward over the wings caused the plane to spiral, like it would drill into the ground. The centrifugal force pushed Paxton out to the wall of the fuselage. His eyes darted around looking for an exit. *There has to be a hatch up here!* Disoriented, Paxton tried to focus. *Where is the damn thing?* Time was running out. He looked at his wrist, where he would normally wear his altimeter. It was empty, except for the marks left by the tie wraps. He never had a chance to finish preparing for his parachute jump. His wrist altimeter was still in his pack, which was gone along with his AK-74 rifle, his helmet and the rear of the plane. Gone like Smith and the others. He looked down again. All he saw was blackness. He did not have the benefit of his NVGs, which were also in his pack. His mind filled with images of Jill and the kids. He no longer cared about his altitude—he had to get out no matter what—for the sake of his family.

He found the exit hatch twenty feet below him. But how would he get down to it? Terror clamored through him, but he turned himself around by pushing off the bulkhead and reached out for the first rib. As his bare hand touched the cold aluminum, an alarm sounded in his head.

Wrong. This is wrong.

Death sped toward him at terminal velocity. He was wearing his parachute. If he could get free, he'd be safe.

What was he forgetting?

Oh my God! The pilots! Paxton looked at the cockpit door, which was behind him, in the center of the bulkhead. It was still closed. He knew that the C-17 lacked ejection seats. Maybe they were in no condition to open the escape hatch. The pilots might be trapped in the cockpit. Maybe they were already dead.

Paxton looked down again at exit hatch below him. The rest of his life was through that hatch. His family was on the other side of it. *Damn it.*

How much time had elapsed? How long before they crashed into the ground? His parachute needed a certain amount of altitude to properly open enough to slow his descent to a survivable speed. He looked again at the closed cockpit door and back at the exit hatch.

He wanted to see his son's smile again and hold his baby daughter in his arms. He wanted to hold his wife, to kiss her. Jill. *My family needs me.*

Paxton glanced at the cockpit door. *If they're alive, they'd climb out on their own.* Why hadn't they done that? Maybe they were injured. Maybe they were incapacitated. Or maybe they were confused. Paxton looked at the blackness below and inhaled deeply through his oxygen mask. *So others may live.* Paxton struggled to turn himself around and clawed at the bulkhead, pulling himself toward the cockpit door. He fought the buffeting of the wind and the rotation of the wreckage. After much effort, Paxton reached the cockpit door, grabbed the handle and pulled. It was locked.

Paxton pounded on the cockpit door with his fists and screamed at the top of his lungs. No one answered.

It was time to get the hell out.

Paxton headed for the exit hatch.

The cockpit door handle jiggled. Someone was still alive in the cockpit. The door started to push open, but the force of the wind blasted it shut. Paxton spun back toward the door and grabbed the handle. He jammed his boots into the bulkhead on the opposite side, crouching, his arms between his knees, his back bowed, upside down and he pulled on the door.

He felt someone pushing out on the door from the inside. Once the door was open part of the way, the wind intruded and slammed it back on its hinges, wide open, ripping the handle violently from Paxton's grip. The blast of air entered the cockpit, slamming Paxton into Weil.

"Thank God!" Weil shouted. "Help me! The escape hatch is jammed! I can't get his parachute on!" He gestured at the other side of the cramped cockpit. Thompson lay there, unconscious.

Paxton pressed his fingers into Thompson's throat looking for a pulse. The pilot was alive, but unresponsive. Paxton expertly completed connecting all the straps and links for Thompson's parachute and made sure they were all snug and secure.

As he tightened the last strap, he remembered that he had not strapped on his own parachute. If he had jumped out of the plane with his parachute unfastened, it would have been ripped right off his body the moment the parachute opened, and he would have plunged to the ground.

Heart pounding, he quickly and expertly strapped on his own parachute and then checked Weil's parachute. All was in order.

"Let's get out of this coffin," Paxton shouted to the co-pilot as he grabbed the limp Thompson, pulling him toward the open doorway.

"How are we going to open his parachute?" Weil yelled

"Automatic reserve." Paxton indicated Thompson's Automatic Activation Device (AAD) designed to deploy the reserve parachute at a predetermined altitude. Paxton had to get the pilot out of the plane first before the device deployed the parachute.

Weil exited the cockpit. Paxton hefted Thompson onto his back and climbed down through the cockpit door. He held onto the unconscious Thompson's forearms around his neck with his left hand as he used his right hand to pull himself along the bulkhead.

Weil was already pulling himself down, rib by rib to the escape hatch. As Paxton reached the ribbed sidewall with Thompson still securely on his back, his bailout bottle went dry. Empty. No more oxygen.

Paxton, already breathing hard from the exertion and the excitement, caused his oxygen mask to collapse around his nose and mouth. *Is there enough oxygen in the air to breathe?*

He trapped Thompson's right forearm between his shoulder and his neck and ripped off his mask, gulping in air so cold it burned his lungs. He wasn't feeling faint, so there were sufficient levels of oxygen to support life—which meant they were getting close to the ground.

Paxton scrambled down the wall. The co-pilot swung the lever and pushed the escape hatch open into the darkness. Weil pushed through it, out to safety. Paxton pulled himself down, against the wind, until he was level with the opening. He bent at the waist, held on to the doorframe, and shoved Thompson. The unconscious man popped out of the escape hatch and tumbled away from the falling wreckage. Paxton, still inside the hatch, hoped Thompson's AAD worked.

Just then Paxton's vision went black. His face was completely engulfed in nylon. *What the hell?* Paxton's own reserve chute had activated. One thousand feet! Shit! He desperately tried to catch as much of the parachute as possible, thanking God that damned thing had gotten caught on the conduit. If the reserve bloomed inside the plane, he was dead.

Paxton violently heaved himself through the escape hatch.

He jolted then viciously flipped over, upside down. His reserve chute, attached to his harness, was still caught inside of the plane.

He was going down with the wreckage.

Paxton's training kicked in. He jettisoned the reserve chute and then pulled the ripcord for his main chute. He felt the familiar jerk on his harness as his parachute inflated over his head, slowing his descent.

Seconds later, the C-17 Globemaster III crashed into the Serbian countryside. The fiery explosion lit up the surroundings like the morning sunrise. The tremendous heat of the flames reached him. In the bright light, he saw that he was uncomfortably close to the ground, but he was also higher than expected. Evidently the anomalies of the air pressure inside the plane caused his AAD to deploy prematurely. He looked up. In the light from the fire below, he saw two other fully deployed parachutes, one higher than the other: Thompson and Weil.

What happened to Smith and the others? Had they gotten out? Were they able to parachute to safety? If so, where were they now? And what had happened to that asshole McMurphy?

Paxton took inventory of his circumstances. He was on a mission that did not officially exist and made no damned sense. He was about to land in enemy territory with no identification and wearing the uniform of a spy. He had an injured flight crewmember, but no medical supplies. He had no means to locate or to contact his team, much less American rescue forces.

Soon, half the Serbian army would be looking for them thanks to the huge, burning beacon of the crashed C-17. *I have no weapons.* Everything had been taken from him after the fight with McMurphy.

His wife had no idea where he was, and if he didn't get out of this mess, he'd never see her or their children again. And that brought him to number one on the shit list:

The whole damned thing was his fault.

Part II

CHAPTER 12

DELEVIC AND AMANDA SAT IN THE DARK CORNER OF THE restaurant chatting, the remnants of dinner still in front of them. Delevic had enjoyed watching Amanda devour her steak and baked potato. He'd been unable to take his eyes off her pouty lips as they closed around a bite of food.

The waiter cleaned off the table and Delevic ordered another round. He'd kept the alcohol flowing all night. Amanda appeared to like drinking as much as eating. The waiter headed off to fulfill the order, arms full of dirty dishes.

"Thanks for getting a double order of bread." She smiled.

Delevic smiled back. "I like that you are a woman who enjoys food."

Giggling, she looked at him, her eyes sparkling. "You never told me what you do."

"I'm in sales."

"Really? What do you sell?"

"I am more of a … broker. I represent various European manufacturers."

"What do they manufacture?"

"Heavy construction equipment."

"No kidding?" Amanda shook her head. "I wouldn't figure you for someone in sales. You seemed more like someone in the military to me. You've got that vibe, y'know? You're intense, even when you're relaxing."

"You are a perceptive woman. Many years ago, I *used* to be in the army,"

"What did you do?" She grinned at him. "Sales?"

Delevic chuckled, though he wasn't entirely comfortable with the conversation. *This woman asks a lot of questions.* "I drove a big truck."

"For the *Italian* army?" Amanda's tone indicated she wasn't buying the "Italian" part.

Delevic smile turned wooden. "Yes."

The waiter returned with their drinks. Delevic picked up his glass and said, "To good food and beautiful women."

They clinked glasses and sipped. The alcohol was doing its job—at least on Amanda's inhibitions. Delevic felt her toes tickle his shin under the table, then her foot glided up and down his leg. As her lips curved into a seductive smile, Delevic discarded his suspicions. She had only been making small talk. *I'm being paranoid. She's only a barmaid.*

He leaned forward, taking Amanda's hand in his. "What do you say we finish our drinks and you come with me back to my hotel room?"

• • •

At 9:48 p.m. General Reed finished coordinating things from Hurlburt Field in Florida. Now it was time to get *closer* to the action. The sedan in which he was riding zipped along the tarmac. Its headlights illuminated the side of a plane. The top half of the fuselage was painted white and the bottom half was painted light blue.

It was an U.S. Air Force C-37A twin-engine jet aircraft. The civilian aviation world called it a Gulfstream V (G5) corporate jet. Reed felt smug satisfaction that he was able to procure one for his use tonight—there were only a handful in the Air Force's inventory.

The C-37A's primary function was worldwide special air missions for high-ranking Department of Defense officials. High-tech secure satellite communications equipment would ensure that Reed remained in control during the flight.

"Have a nice flight, sir," the driver said as the general exited the sedan.

Captain Marshall met Reed at the stairway. Marshall had been Reed's trusted aide for more than three years. Both the general and Marshall wore their Class A uniforms. Marshall saluted. "Sir, your luggage and your briefcase have already been loaded on board."

Reed returned the salute. "Thank you."

Reed climbed the stairs and Marshall followed.

The well-lighted interior of the cabin revealed twelve blue leather seats, which were as comfortable as cushioned recliners.

Two lines of aisle lights ran along the spotless beige carpeting. Oval windows on both sides of the cabin provided ample visibility for the passengers.

Reed selected a seat and settled into it. Marshall sat across the aisle. The two men buckled their seatbelts as the pilot fired up the jet engines. Reed looked at his watch. *Right on schedule.*

The plane taxied onto the runway and within moments, the C-37A glided into the clear Florida night sky. Soon the pilot announced a cruising altitude of 50,000 feet, which was well above the altitude used by most commercial airliners and usually above even the weather. At this altitude the jet engines were very efficient and required no refueling.

"Make us drinks, Marshall."

"Yes, sir." Marshall unbuckled his seatbelt and walked to the back of the cabin. Between the closet and the lavatory was a small but well-stocked wet bar. Marshall had to open several cabinet doors to locate what he was looking for and went to work fixing the drinks. He pulled out two heavy glass tumblers with the Air Force logo etched on them. One never knew what high-ranking official might be transported in this plane. It didn't hurt to have little reminders that the Air Force was providing them with comfort as well as fast travel. Marshall filled both glasses with cubes. He took out the expensive scotch and broke the seal, pouring the golden liquid into each glass.

"Here you go, sir." Reed reclined the seat and propped his feet on the footrest."Thank you," Reed replied and took the glass Marshall offered. "Might as well get comfortable. We have a long flight to Italy."

Marshall sat down, reclined his own seat, then sipped his scotch.

"Well, Marshall? How does it look? Does the Pentagon have any inkling about our plans?"

Marshall looked at his boss and grinned broadly. "Sir, I can say with confidence that they are clueless."

• • •

Jashari sat in a tattered leather chair beside the fireplace. He watched the crackling flames as he sipped the strong coffee.

"Sir, another plane has been shot down. A big one," his assistant said, holding his brick-sized field radio. "I don't know if it is American."

"Of course it's American," he said matter-of-factly. "The Serbians would not dare to launch any of their planes. The Americans would shoot them down in a heartbeat. I wonder if it was the rescue mission for the pilot of the Stealth fighter? You say it was a big plane?"

"Huge."

Jashari examined the room as he contemplated the situation. The space was lit by bare bulbs and heavy blankets covered the windows to prevent light from escaping. The floor was cold, bare concrete. A wooden table in the center of the room was covered with maps, documents and weapons, including knives, pistols, and grenades. Two guards stood at the doorway, slung machine pistols at the ready.

"I suspect it was the rescue mission ... the one we were asked to assist with."

"Maybe they need our help."

"The rescuers in need of rescue? Ah. But maybe they are all dead." He handed the empty mug to his assistant. "Please get me some more coffee."

His assistant hurried to the aluminum urn plugged into the wall opposite the fireplace and filled up the mug. He returned and gave it to Jashari who took the ceramic cup with both hands. "Send a man out to where the plane went down. I want to know if the Americans are dead."

"And if they are alive?"

"Have them observed, but don't let them know they are being watched." Jashari stared at the hot, black liquid. "I don't think their mission has anything to do with rescuing the Stealth pilot. After all, the Americans never asked us to help with finding him."

"You believe the Americans have another goal?"

"That's what we need to find out."

"Sir, I shall send a man at once. If the Americans are alive, he will watch them. We will find out their purpose." The assistant turned and marched toward the door. "Praise be to Allah,"

"Praise be to Allah," Jashari replied. He sipped the coffee and once again turned his gaze to the fireplace.

CHAPTER 13

PAXTON PLUMMETED INTO A FORESTED AREA THAT WAS uncomfortably close to the burning wreckage of Globemaster.

Had everything gone as planned, he and his team would've glided with their airfoil parachutes in loose formation for many miles through the night to pre-selected GPS coordinates on the ground.

Now that plan, as well as everything else, had gone up, literally, in flames.

He instinctively buckled his knees to absorb some of the impact and had to run because of his forward speed. His boots slipped on the wet ground and he fell flat on his back in the grass. Not exactly a graceful landing. His parachute floated to the ground in front of his feet.

Paxton lay there for a moment, not caring that cold wetness soaked through his uniform. The endless fall was over and he was on the ground again. Life was all around him … the trees, the grass, the plants—*living* things. And he was still part of the club. He was still alive. *Thank God!*

Panting heavily, he squeezed his eyes shut and then blinked them open. He focused on slowing his breathing and heart rate. He had to get a handle on himself so he could think clearly. *Whoa there, boy.*

Paxton couldn't afford to relax. The wreckage was still blazing. The Serbs had probably tracked the broken C-17 on radar; it would not be very long until they arrived.

Paxton heard wet leaves shake and branches snap. He bolted onto his right forearm and twisted around.

About 100 yards from him Paxton saw a parachute drape the lower branches of a large evergreen tree. The dark lump on the ground was either Thompson or Weil.

Pushing to his feet, he continued to crouch. He unclipped his parachute from his harness and pulled it across the ground, gathering it to his chest. Then he scooted to the cover of the trees to his right, carrying his wadded parachute.

The dense vegetation blocked the light radiating from the burning wreckage, though thin beams of firelight sifted through the branches. Nonetheless, Paxton stopped to give his eyes a moment to adjust. The Serbs would have to wait until the jet fuel burned itself out and the wreckage cooled before they could look for bodies. But if the Serbs discovered parachutes, they would relentlessly search for survivors.

He kicked the ground. *Damn. Too hard to dig a hole.* He couldn't bury it like he normally would. He had no survival tools. A folding shovel or even a knife would've come in handy about now. He had to find another way to dispose of his chute so he could administer aid to the other man.

Then he spotted a fallen tree about fifteen yards away. He carried the chute to the log and shoved it under the deadfall underneath. Hurrying, he gathered up as many branches and pine needles as he could and spread them over the portions of the parachute that remained exposed. Satisfied with his temporary solution, he returned to the edge of the clearing.

He paused to assess the situation. All he could hear was his own breathing and the steady rumble of the fire. He was thankful that he heard no trucks, footsteps or other nefarious sounds, such as slides being racked on firearms. The stench of the fire, a foul combination of burning fuel, wood, electrical components and insulation, burned his throat. He took a tentative breath and peered around the tree. A blanket of orange light covered the clearing. There were no signs of enemy troop activity.

He edged into the clearing and looked to his left. The figure on the ground was still lying prone, but rolling back and forth, flailing arms. He was alive. Above him, the parachute was draped on the branches of a tree, spread out like a giant billboard. The nylon might as well have had *This Exit for POWs* painted on it.

Paxton moved back behind his tree and looked at the terrain to his left. It appeared dense enough to help conceal him, so he worked his way through the trees toward the other man. The brush was thick and unwieldy. He was making more noise than he wanted. He could move fairly silently if he chose to cross to the downed airman on the clearing side of the trees, but that would have left him completely exposed in the light of the fire. Since his enemy could likely see farther than they could hear, he chose the noisy path that kept him out of sight.

He snagged his uniform several times crossing the distance to the moaning man. Then Paxton heard grunting and sliding. Paxton pushed aside some branches and peered out into the clearing.

Thompson was on his stomach, pulling himself along the ground toward the tree line away from Paxton. He had unclipped himself from his parachute. He was pushing with his right knee but dragging his left leg. The calf of his left leg was bent in a place God hadn't chosen to place a joint—an obvious compound fracture. Apparently he had heard Paxton muscling through the trees toward him. Thompson was doing what he was trained to do: evade capture.

Paxton called out in a low voice, "Major Thompson! PJ! United States Air Force!"

Thompson stopped and turned his head toward the sound of Paxton's voice. His face was covered in dirt.

Paxton spread the branches in front of him and stepped out. He knew the minute Thompson recognized him. He collapsed. "Thank God!"

Figuring stealth was useless at this point, Paxton sprinted the remaining few yards to the prone Thompson. He crouched down and asked, "Are you okay?"

"Do I look okay?" Thompson turned onto his right side and propped himself on his elbow. "I remember … you were in the cockpit talking to me … and…" Thompson squinted and shook his head. "Now I'm flat on my ass. Where are we?"

"Yugoslavia."

Thompson winced, obviously in pain. "What's on fire?"

"That would be your plane, sir."

"Shit!"

Paxton gestured at Thompson. "Other than your leg, what else hurts?"

"Got a hell of a headache."

"We need to find cover. Think you can walk if I help you?"

Thompson screwed his eyes shut and nodded.

Paxton lifted Thompson and draped his arm across Paxton's shoulders. "Up now."

As both men started to stand, Thompson screamed. Paxton stopped moving. "You okay, sir?"

"Let's go. I'll make it."

Paxton pulled Thompson up until he stood on his good leg. His left leg was bent at the knee to keep the broken lower leg from dragging on the ground. Because of the difference in height, Paxton had to bend at the waist as he and Thompson headed for the tree line.

"Just a few more steps," Paxton assured as they made it to the forest. He looked over his shoulder. Damned Serbs could show up any time.

The two men pushed their way between two pine trees, and Paxton lowered Thompson to the ground until he was in a sitting position. He placed his hand on Thompson's shoulder. "Wait here, sir. I'll be right back to administer what aid I can."

Thompson nodded. Paxton ran to the pilot's landing site and located the lines from the parachute. The fire offered enough light to work by. He gatheredup the lines in his hands and yanked the parachute off the tree. After wadding it at the base of the tree, he turned around and inspected the area.

He could clearly see the man-shaped impression Thompson's impact had left in the grass and dirt—more evidence that had to be erased.

He dashed to the tree line and broke off a lower branch from a fir tree and brushed the dirt in a random pattern. Sweating profusely, he kicked rocks into the swirled dirt, hoping it would fool Serbian soldiers.

What the hell is that? Paxton spun around, ready to use the branch as a weapon. The fire illuminated Weil walking toward him. The man carried his parachute under his right arm while steadying it with his left. The knees of his flight suit were torn and dark blood stained his exposed skin.

"Is Major Thompson all right?"

"Mostly. Broken tibia and fibula. Probably a concussion." Paxton looked at Weil's condition. "What happened to you?"

"I got scraped up on the road."

"What road?"

"Over there." Weil turned slightly and jerked his head to the right. "I landed hard and was dragged forward by my chute. Got a helluva road rash."

Shit, shit, *shit*. A road meant that the Serbs could reach the crash site quickly. "We've got to get out of here. Do you have any survival gear?"

Weil shook his head. "No. I only had time to get the parachute on Thompson."

"No radio? No medical kit? No gun?"

"Nope. Where's Major Thompson?"

"Behind those trees." Paxton pointed in the direction marked by the prints of three boots—Paxton's and Thompson's one good leg. "How did you find us?"

Weil smiled grimly. "I heard a scream."

"Give me your parachute." Paxton tossed his branch into the trees. Paxton knew that the co-pilot was capable of disposing of his own parachute, but when it came to matters of life and death, he preferred to handle matters himself. Besides, Thompson's injuries didn't appear to be life-threatening. Aid could wait. Weil handed him the parachute. Paxton grabbed it in his hands and then picked up Thompson's as well. "Check on Thompson. I'll get rid of these."

Paxton returned to his landing spot and covered the impression he had left. Satisfied that he had done the best he could, he dropped the two parachutes and hurried into the woods. The log was farther back than he remembered, but he found it. He untucked the buried 'chute and carried it out to the clearing.

He tossed his parachute on top of the other two, then he bent down, gathered all three parachutes in his arms, and stood up. Nylon spilled out from his arms and the lines dragged on the ground as he humped toward the burning wreckage. The noxious stench strengthened the closer he got to the crash site.

Jet fuel burned very hot—so hot it could melt steel. Paxton felt the heat on his face as he approached the edge of the flames. The huge fire had assaulted numerous trees, adding their fuel of wood and sap. Nothing resembled an aircraft—nothing resembled *anything*, except maybe the cauldron of Hell.

Paxton got as close to the fire as possible and heaved the parachutes with all his might. They flew apart and spread out. The wind resistance caused them to buckle and stop their forward momentum. They whirled around in the fire wind and settled down at the edge of the flames. Nothing happened for a moment. Then a flame or two popped through the nylon and the material was consumed in a smoky toxic blackness. Satisfied, Paxton turned around and ran.

Paxton stayed in the clearing, but he remained close to the tree line in case he had to duck in for cover. He was about halfway back when he heard something. He dropped into a crouch and listened intently. The sounds were unmistakable: footsteps. And they were coming from the direction of the road. *More than one person.* Metal clanged … equipment? Or weapons?

Paxton ducked left into the woods. Adrenaline kicked his heart into overdrive. He sure as hell hoped Thompson and Weil heard them too. He hoped they were staying silent and out of sight. He still had a good fifty yards to get back to where they were hiding.

The sounds got louder. The men were getting closer, but Paxton still could not see them. He looked around for something, anything, that he could use as a weapon. He settled on a rock. He dug it out and lifted it from the ground. It was fairly hefty, slightly larger than his right hand, and it sloped down to a relatively sharp edge on one side. It wouldn't cut paper but thrown with sufficient force, it would leave a nasty gash. It was white, contrasting with the darkness that surrounded him. A rock. *How pathetic.*

He looked across the clearing again in the direction of the road. And he waited. He wished he was with the pilots, but he couldn't risk moving now. Even if he stayed in the trees, someone would surely see the branches move or hear the crack of twigs if he moved.

Paxton's thoughts turned to his family. He dreamt of taking his son camping. They would build a campfire together and pitch a tent. He wanted to teach his son to fish. *Why haven't I taken him fishing yet?* Even though John, Jr. was only four, he could hold a Snoopy fishing rod.

The job always interfered.

He thought becoming an instructor instead of an active PJ would allow him to spend more time with his family. But it hadn't given him enough. *I should have gotten out a long time ago. If I survive this clusterfuck, I'm taking my son fishing and my wife dancing. Screw Reed and the Air Force. I'm done.*

Movement near the edge of the clearing caught his eye. Illuminated by the fire were several figures clad in camouflage. They walked into the clearing. Several of the men were carrying rifles. Paxton gripped his rock so hard that it was starting to cut into his palms.

Doubts tumbled in his mind. Had he done a good enough job concealing the landing sites? Had he picked up all the evidence? Were those damn parachutes burned up yet? Maybe he should have toughed out the heat and kicked the parachutes all the way into the fire. Had Weil left any signs of his landing?

The men were getting too close to Thompson and Weil's hiding place. *What can I do?* He looked at his rock and reality set in. Throwing one measly rock wouldn't injure the enemy or save his ass. Still, he was reluctant to give up his one viable weapon. Sweat dripped into his eyes, so he wiped the moisture off with his sleeve. He froze staring at the green material. *That's right,* Paxton thought, *I'm wearing a mercenary uniform.*

If he saw the men head toward where the pilots were hiding, he would jump out from the brush and try to convince the Serbs, somehow, that he was a mercenary on their side. He'd feed 'em some story about finding members of the aircrew alive and get them to follow him—in the opposite direction. Maybe his story would cause enough confusion that his compatriots could get away. The plan was suicidal in nature, but it was the only one he had. Even so, Paxton prayed the men would pass by and not turn toward the woods. He hunkered down and waited.

He felt chilled. It hadn't noticed the cold before now. It was hard to sit still. He tightened all his muscles. *What are they doing?* The anticipation was agony. He leaned forward, separating some low branches to see what was going on in the clearing.

It was empty.

He leaned out farther and spotted them walking along the tree line about thirty yards from the spot where Thompson and Weil were holed up. Then Paxton saw a glint of firelight reflect off glass goggles covering the leader's face. Paxton recoiled, his heart thundering.

Shit! Night vision!

With NVGs the Serbs would be able to look into the dark woods and easily distinguish the shapes of men hiding. He should have taken Thompson deeper into the woods even though he knew it would have been difficult for the man to traverse that dense vegetation with a broken leg. The fractured bones would have scraped nerve endings every time his foot hit a shrub. Without morphine, Paxton doubted Thompson could have made it much farther without howling in pain. No man could. Or was he rationalizing his mistake? There was nothing he could do about it now.

The men were not talking. No doubt they were communicating with hand signals. But the sound of their footsteps and the chink, chink of their equipment was unmistakable. *Surely Thompson and Weil hear them.*

Paxton fought the urge to bolt deeper into the woods; the men would hear him. Once they knew there was a survivor, the search would be relentless. They would find him, and eventually they would find the pilots, too. A prone position would make him more difficult to discover, but any movement now would surely be noticed. So Paxton remained crouched, muscles straining, breath harsh, shivering in the early morning air.

After a few moments, he carefully leaned out once more and peeked through the branches. *How many men are there?* He couldn't see them all. The leader was very near the pilots' location, scanning the woods with his NVGs. He suddenly stopped, raising his hand for the others to halt. He was focusing on a particular spot in the woods.

Shit!

The other men gathered around their leader, all facing the direction he was looking.

Paxton had to create a distraction. Maybe the pilots could slip away if he caused enough chaos.

Might as well get it over with. Paxton took a deep breath, crossed himself, and bolted up and out. The branches slapped his face and body as he leapt out into the clearing. Free of the plants, Paxton turned and faced the soldiers, waved his arms over his head and shouted, "Hey, guys! Over here!"

• • •

General Reed was sound asleep, reclined in his soft leather seat high over the Atlantic. Across the aisle slept Marshall, similarly reclined. Empty drink tumblers sat on the trays in front of the men. The cockpit door popped open and the co-pilot of the C-37A stepped into the cabin. He hesitated, looking at both sleeping men. He made his decision and crossed to Marshall. He touched Marshall's right shoulder. "Sir, wake up."

Marshall's head rolled around on the seatback, he moaned and then opened his eyes. "Whaaa?"

"Sir, we received a communication from Aviano."

Marshall blinked and sat up. "Aviano! What did they say?"

As the co-pilot told Marshall the news, he put his head in his hand and screwed his eyes shut. He did not want to have to give the general the message.

The co-pilot nodded goodbye, then turned and opened

the cockpit door. He stepped inside and pulled the door shut behind him.

Marshall sat there for a long moment, his hand clutching his forehead. Then he bolstered himself mentally and pushed to his feet. He debated fixing drinks first, but decided against it.

He reached across the aisle and gently shook the general's arm. "Sir."

Reed blinked until he was fully awake. "What's going on, Marshall?"

"Sir, Aviano called." He paused. "Our Globemaster's down."

"What? Down? No!"

"Yes sir. AWACS aircraft lost contact with it right after it sensed a missile launch," Marshall explained.

"Shit. Any sign of survivors?"

"No. They haven't received signals from recovery beacons or radios. Anything's possible, sir, but the plane was over 40,000 feet when it broke up. Should we launch a rescue mission, just in case?"

"We are not in the rescue business."

"Yes sir. I understand. Our presumption then is that all aboard perished."

Reed sighed deeply and nodded.

"What now, sir?"

Reed stared at Marshall. "Plan A has failed. We move on to Plan B."

"Plan B it is, sir."

• • •

Jill Paxton was sound asleep in the sleigh bed. The thick comforter was pulled up to her ears for warmth and security. Next to her, under the covers, were her two small children. She didn't like to sleep alone, and when John was gone, she allowed them to sleep with her.

Jill dreamed about her husband. Somehow he had gotten separated from the rest of the family. She searched frantically for him, but no one knew his location. And no one would help her find him. She pounded on door after door, but muffled voices offered vague apologies.

Then she was running. She carried her daughter and dragged her son as fast as his little legs could go. Her children wailed. She was afraid she was going to lose them too. It was visceral. It was real. Her body was reacting to the situation her mind had created. Until it became too much and she bolted upright in bed, wide awake and sweating.

She looked at the digital clock. It was still the middle of the night. She flipped on the bedside light. She was in her own bed, in her own home, on the outskirts of San Antonio, Texas. Her children were safely sleeping beside her. But her husband really was gone—separated from the rest of the family. And no one knew where he was; or, more accurately, those who knew where he was refused to tell her. No one would help her find him. No one would help her contact him. That part of the nightmare was all too real.

She looked at the telephone, which was next to the digital

clock and lamp on the bedside table. She lifted the receiver and heard the buzz of the dial tone. Then she punched in the numbers to Paxton's cell phone. It immediately went to voice mail without even ringing once, just as it had done the last dozen or so times she'd called. His voice invited her to leave a message. She had already left many. *He will call me.*

She hung up the phone and stared at it. She knew that he *would* call her.

If he could....

CHAPTER 14

AMANDA LAY ON THE HOTEL BED, DELEVIC BEHIND HER, spooning her naked body. His hand cupped her right breast as he slept. Shivering, she awoke. Even the heat of Delevic's body did not overcome the arctic blast from the air conditioner. She pulled the wool blanket over her head and tried to go back to sleep.

She heard the buzz of Delevic's snoring over the hum of the air conditioner. The room was dark except for the light from the parking lot that filtered through the curtains. It was an ordinary hotel room, like thousands of others. It had a sink in a small partitioned area at one end of the room. There was a chrome pipe intended for hanging up one's clothes. No closet door. The only door besides the entrance was the door to the bathroom, next to the sink. The main room had a dresser with a television set on top, a small round table, two vinyl-covered chairs and two full-sized beds. The "hotel smell" permeated the room.

She curled up, her hands together under her cheek. She wanted to get up to adjust the air conditioner, but she was too cold to get out from under the blanket. Maybe she should nudge Delevic awake and ask him to get up and turn off the blizzard. He would do it for her she was sure. But once he was awake, no doubt he would want to go for another round. No. He was too rough; too intense.

Hell, the blanket wasn't helping anyway. She might as well get up and turn off the air conditioning unit. Maybe she would even turn on the heat for a few minutes.

What she really wanted was to go home and be in her own bed. Regret crawled through her. *What am I doing here? Why did I sleep with him?*

He was charming. He had those European eyes. The drinks had gone straight to her head. Now her tongue was thick in her mouth and she felt a dull ache in her temples. She was ready to go home. But she'd left her car in the bar's parking lot. Crap. She hoped no one noticed her car; she didn't want to explain she'd gone off with a customer. Probably no one had noticed. She'd have to wake Delevic for a ride—and again, she thought about his rough lovemaking. No. Let him sleep.

She braced herself for her trek to the thermostat. Where was the temperature control? She tried to envision the room. She couldn't remember seeing the control. Shit. She'd flip on the lights until she could find the thermostat. She hoped Delevic wouldn't wake up.

The light switch was by the front door. Amanda threw off the blanket and dashed to the light switch. The blast of icy air seized her naked skin. Her hand pawed the wall until she found switches. She flipped the first one and nothing happened. She flipped the second one and the lights over the television set popped on. She scanned the room for the thermostat. She saw it, on the other side of the dresser, on the wall over Delevic's suitcase, which sat on a folding stand.

She tiptoed quickly in her bare feet between the dresser and the sleeping Delevic. The light didn't seem to disturb him. She was covered in goose bumps, her arms folded in front of her breasts, rubbing her shoulders for warmth.

Unsteadily, she plowed into the suitcase and knocked it and the folding stand over with a crash. The suitcase sprung open and its contents spilled onto the carpet.

Some guns were beautiful works of art, hand crafted by skilled artisan hands. Not the MAC-10. Purely utilitarian, it's black and boxy, with a wiry trigger guard and a knob to operate the bolt. The magazine extended well below the end of the grip, as if it were an add-on. Designed to be held in one hand and fired like a pistol, its firing rate was 1,100 rounds per minute. It had a sound suppressor screwed onto its stubby barrel that looked like a thick black paper-towel tube. Ugly, but effective, it could be used to silently kill everyone in one room without disturbing anyone in the next.

Amanda gasped and stood there, frozen, staring at the big, ugly weapon on the carpet at her feet.

Oh my God!

Delevic jolted awake. He sat up, his gaze on Amanda.

She wasn't looking at him. She didn't feel cold anymore. She didn't feel anything. Her eyes didn't leave the machine gun.

Delevic scooted off the bed and moved toward her.

"Who are you?" she asked weakly.

"I already told you who I am."

She shook her head, tears in her eyes. She dodged him and grabbed the blanket off the bed. "What is that for?" she asked, gesturing toward the gun.

Delevic looked down. "That is one of my products."

Amanda continued her retreat until her back touched the wall. "You said you sold construction equipment."

Delevic smiled. "I work for a defense contractor and that is a non-working model of one of our products."

"Liar!"

"Here, let me show you." He bent down to retrieve the MAC-10.

Amanda shrieked.

Delevic left the gun on the floor, stood up and held his hands out for her to quiet down. He shushed her.

She collapsed down to the floor and sobbed uncontrollably. "I want to go home."

"Yes, yes, home, of course." He held out his palms in supplication. "Let me get dressed. I'll drive you home."

"No! I'll call a cab, thank you." She wiped her face on the blanket. "Where are my clothes?"

Delevic looked around the room. He saw various pieces of both their wardrobes scattered about the room. "I'll get them for you."

Amanda didn't say anything. She sat on the floor, back to the wall, wrapped in her blanket, watching every move Delevic made.

Delevic collected her bra, panties, jeans, purse and tee shirt. He left the machine gun on the floor untouched. He held her garments out to her. She snatched them from his hand.

"Turn around!" she ordered.

Delevic smiled and complied. He turned as he heard the door open and watched Amanda hurry out. The door slammed.

Sighing, Delevic walked to the mess of clothes and the firearm on the floor. He setup the folding stand and placed the suitcase on it. He picked everything off the floor and packed it back in the case.

When he was finished, he walked to the bedside table and picked up his cell phone. He dialed Labus's number.

Labus answered on the third ring.

"It's me," Delevic said. "Did you get that rental car like I asked you to?"

"Yes. Why?"

"We have a problem," Delevic replied. "And I need you to take care of it."

• • •

The phone next to Colonel Ward's bed rang. His snoring skipped a beat. Then Ward awoke, rolled over, and grabbed the receiver.

"Ward here," he mumbled.

"Colonel Ward, this is Airman First Class Leigh. Sorry to bother you so late, sir."

Ward grunted into the phone.

"I'm at MPC, at the Casualty Command Post."

"Yes?" Ward asked, confused and sleepy. Why was the Military Personnel Center calling him?

"Do you have a Senior Master Sergeant John Paxton in your command?"

Ward was suddenly wide-awake. "Yes, I do."

"Sir, I'm sorry to report that Sergeant Paxton's plane went down."

Ward sat straight up. "What happened?"

"I don't have that information, sir."

The bile rose in his esophagus. "Where did the plane go down?"

"The location is classified."

"Goddamn it. Has Combat Search and Rescue been notified?"

"They've been recalled. They were given RTB orders."

"Who the hell gave Return To Base orders?"

"Major General Reed, sir."

Fury roared through him. "That son of a—Airman, is there a contact number for Reed?"

"No sir."

"Fax that report to me *immediately.*" Ward gave the airman his office fax number. "Has Paxton's spouse been notified?"

"No sir."

"Do *not* send anyone to her house. I will notify her." Ward hung up the phone.

"What's the matter?" his wife asked sleepily.

"Paxton's plane went down." Ward climbed out of bed and headed over to his closet. "I have to go to the office."

"Oh God. Is he dead?" she asked. "He's got those young children. This is terrible!"

"Yes, it is." Ward pulled on his BDU pants then buttoned up his BDU blouse. He picked up the phone and dialed.

"PJ Duty Desk, Sergeant Machette speaking."

"Sergeant Machette, this is Col. Ward. Find out how to contact Major General Reed. He's from the Pentagon."

"Pentagon. Got it, sir," Machette replied.

"This is an emergency, Sergeant. I'm on my way to the office. Have that contact information for me when I get there."

"Will do, sir."

"Thank you," Ward said and hung up. Ward sat on the edge of the bed and pulled on his boots.

"Honey, what can I do?"

The worry in his wife's voice stalled him. Ward stopped dressing and turned to face her. "There's only one thing to do, dear." He kissed her gently. "Pray."

• • •

Amanda was still shaking as she burst through the doors of the hotel office. The night clerk, paperback in hand, turned to look at her.

"Call me a taxi, please," she blurted.

The clerk stood and leaned on the desk. "Is everything okay, ma'am?" His accent was foreign.

"Just call the taxi!"

"Yes, ma'am." The clerk picked up the phone on the desk, punched in the familiar numbers, and spoke softly into the mouthpiece. Then he hung up. "Taxi coming."

"Thank you." Amanda opened the front glass doors and stepped outside. It was dark and she was alone. *Screw this.* She walked back inside the office. She felt safer with some-one else nearby.

"Can I do anything else for you, ma'am?"

Amanda shook her head. She tried to busy herself by browsing the pamphlets for tourist attractions neatly stacked in a stand by the wall. The clerk stood there behind the desk, looking at her as if he were not sure if he should remain standing or sit back down.

She combed her fingers through her hair in an attempt to put herself back together. She took a wadded tissue out of her purse and rubbed her nose. She turned and saw the clerk star-ing at her. Shrugging, the clerk turned, sat down and returned to reading his novel.

How could I have been so stupid? The more she thought about Boris, the angrier she got. He had played her. How many oth-er women had he wooed with food and drink? Jerk! Hmm. Should she tell someone about Boris and his nasty gun? No, she didn't want to get involved. *I'm going to go get my car and pretend nothing happened.*

She walked to the cloth couch next to the pamphlet display and plopped onto it. She held her purse between her forearm and her thigh. She sat half-turned toward the front door waiting for her ride. She wanted a cigarette and she didn't smoke anymore.

What's taking this damn taxi so long?

"You sure it's coming?" she demanded of the clerk.

"Yes, ma'am."

"Well, they suck."

"Yes, ma'am." He returned to his book.

By the time the lights of the cab swept the office through the glass doors, Amanda was really pissed. She stormed out past the clerk.

"Good night, ma'am."

"Screw you." She hurried out the door and stormed toward the taxi idling under the overhang. She jerked open the door and climbed in the backseat. "Take me to *The Dugout*."

The driver looked at her in his rearview mirror. "It's closed at this hour."

"I know that! I work there. See my shirt? Just take me there."

"Okay," the driver said, still looking at her in his mirror, paying closer attention to what was *in* the shirt than what was *on* it.

"What are you waiting for?" Amanda snapped, annoyed with all men on the planet.

The driver shifted the taxi into drive and sped off.

• • •

Colonel Ward lived in officer's housing on Lackland, so it didn't take long to drive to his office at the pararescue school. He parked his sedan and shut off the lights. A warning chimed as he opened his door with the keys still in the ignition. He tugged the keys, climbed out and shut the door, not taking the time to lock it. He fingered through his keys, searching for the right one, as he walked to the front door. He inserted the key, turned it and opened the door.

It was bright inside. Something was always going on in the world of pararescue. The fact that this was merely the training ground for PJs didn't alter that fact one bit.

Ward smelled coffee. Instead of giving in to the temptation of pouring a cup, he located Sgt. Machette. "You got a fax for me?"

"Yes, sir." Machette handed him the slick papers.

"Thank you. And the number for Reed?"

"I called his office number at the Pentagon, sir, and the duty airman said Gen. Reed is en route to Italy."

"I need to talk to him right now."

"I arranged for you to call his plane … whenever you're ready, sir."

"Thank you, Machette."

"Sir?"

"Yes?"

"I read the fax. I'm sick about it." Machette's expression flattened. "We need to get Pax back, sir."

"Damned right we do."

• • •

Thompson and Weil heard the men coming. They lay down, flat in the brush next to each other. Thompson winced with the pain, but he bit his lip to avoid crying out. They remained quiet and motionless, except for their breathing. The sound of the men approaching got louder. They both wondered about Paxton. They both independently prayed that he would stay out of sight and silent.

The men were almost on top of them. They held their breath and tried to become one with the ground.

The men stopped.

Both men had closed their eyes, partly to focus on their auditory sense and partly because it made them feel less visible. They didn't move. They didn't make a sound.

Then, in the distance, branches snapped and Paxton yelled, "Hey, guys! Over here!"

Thompson squeezed his eyes closed. *What an idiot!*

• • •

The C-37A co-pilot popped open the cockpit door and stepped into the cabin again. The flight was on the last leg of its trip to Italy. This time Reed and Marshall were wide awake, huddled over documents and binders. They both looked up.

"General Reed, you have a phone call," the co-pilot said. "A Colonel Ward from Lackland. I can put the call through to your handset."

"Fine."

Reed turned and scowled at Marshall, as if it was his fault for the interruption. Marshall looked back helplessly. The phone built into the armrest of Reed's chair buzzed. Reed pushed the button to unclip the receiver and raised it up to his ear. "I'm very busy, Colonel. What do you need?"

"Sir, I just got word that Sergeant Paxton's plane went down. It's my understanding you called off search and rescue efforts. Is that so?"

"Yes. It's a terrible tragedy." Reed's voice was emotionless. "The plane was shot down by a missile over Yugoslavia. It disintegrated at an altitude of 40,000 feet. There is no one to rescue."

"With all due respect, we work from the presumption there are survivors until we find evidence there aren't."

"I don't care about your fairy tale presumptions."

"Sir—"

"My decision is final. It's too dangerous for rescue teams. We're leveling that whole area. If you'll excuse me, Colonel, I have to get back to work."

"No sir, I will not excuse you. We *will* search for survivors."

"I don't like your tone, Colonel."

"I don't give a damn what you like," Ward snapped. "You are acting in an unlawful manner, *General*. I will go to the I.G."

"The Inspector General?" Reed laughed menacingly. "Need I remind you I'm a two-star general? I eat bird colonels for lunch. When I get through with you, you'll be breaking rocks at Leavenworth at the rank of airman basic. So cut the bullshit."

"No bullshit, sir. I won't give up on Pax or the PJs."

Reed realized the Colonel wasn't bluffing. He scowled. The last thing in the world he needed was the Inspector General's office staff poking around. Once he had results, he wouldn't care—but not at this stage of the game.

"You're not going to find anyone alive, but search if you must. You have thirty-six hours."

"Sir, give us at least forty-eight."

"No, and use your time wisely. After thirty-six hours, I wouldn't bet a plug nickel on the life of anyone on the ground." Reed hung up then turned to Marshall. "Hold off on executing Plan B. Let Ward make an ass of himself while we finish preparations."

• • •

Ward slammed down the phone. "Machette, get in here!"

Machette popped into Ward's office, a cup of coffee in his hand. "Yes, sir?"

"Get me Brindisi Airbase on the phone. The 255th Rescue Squadron." He grinned. "The rescue is on."

"Hoo-yah, Colonel!"

"Don't get too excited, Sergeant. We only have thirty-six hours." Ward looked longingly at the Sergeant's coffee. "I need you to go with me to see Jill Paxton."

"Yes, sir. Should I change?"

"No. If we show up in Class A's, she'll think the worst."

CHAPTER 15

THE TAXICAB ROLLED UP BESIDE THE OLDER MODEL Toyota in *The Dugout's* parking lot. The lot was relatively well lit, but all the stores in the plaza were closed. Not a soul was in sight except for Amanda and the cab driver.

"Twelve dollars, Miss."

Amanda dug into her purse. "What a rip-off."

"Walking's cheaper."

"Great. A comedian." She sorted through her tips and pulled out two tens. She tossed the bills at the driver. The driver turned on the overhead light and fished out a five and three ones as change, offering them to Amanda. She grabbed the five, opened the door and climbed out. The taxi tires chirped as the driver drove off.

Amanda dug into her purse again and pulled out her keys. She unlocked the door and got in, jabbing the key at the ignition a couple times. Damned dome light must have burned out. Finally, she got the key inserted and turned it.

Click.

Her heart sunk. She turned it back and forward again.

Click.

Nothing.

Click. Click.

What the hell? Was the battery dead?

Click. Click. Click.

How was she supposed to get home? The taxi had already left the parking lot. *What a night!* She put her head on the steering wheel.

A shadow passed over her. She turned her head without lifting it off the wheel and looked out her side window. All she saw was a big belly. She gasped in astonishment.

Her door opened and a big face leaned down. She recognized the man immediately. *Milo!*

"You having a problem, Amanda?" Labus asked, smiling. He already knew the answer. After all, he had caused the problem.

"Leave me alone!" she shouted.

Labus's smile widened. He maneuvered his body between the door and the jam making it impossible to close. She lunged to her right, trying desperately to reach the passenger door. He reached out one massive hand and pulled her back into the seat.

She screamed.

"Stop that!" Labus ordered.

She continued to scream—until he pointed the .40-caliber Beretta automatic at her face. She didn't know much about guns, but from television and movies, she recognized the tube screwed onto the end of the barrel as a silencer. Helplessness washed over her as she realized no one would even hear if he shot her. Her whole body quivered, her eyes locked on the end of the silencer.

Labus looked at her, all small and teary. She wasn't so confident now, was she? She blew him off earlier that night, but she would pay attention to him now. He flexed his fingers and re-gripped the pistol. Amanda jumped at the sight of his fingers moving so near the trigger.

"Listen to me and you won't get hurt," he lied. Why did Delevic get all the fun? *I always have to clean up his messes. He plays and I do the dirty work.* She was very cute. *Bet Delevic had lots of fun with her.*

Labus looked at her red eyes, tears blackened with mascara streamed down her cheeks. She looked up at him, pleading without saying a word.

Kill her! Dispose of the body! Do this! Do that!

Delevic always ordered him around. *Why doesn't he kill her himself?*

"What are you going to do to me?" she asked suddenly, snapping him out of his thoughts. "I don't want to die," she sobbed.

He brushed her auburn hair off her face with his free hand. "Tell me, Amanda, what did you see?"

"No-no-nothing."

"Don't lie. I already talked to your boyfriend. I heard about everything you did tonight."

Ludicrously, shame welled up to join the fear that gripped her. "Please, Milo, please don't hurt me."

He liked hearing her say his name in her Southern drawl. He especially liked hearing her use his name while she begged for her life.

"Tell me, Amanda, why did you go with Delevic and ignore me? Why did you do things with him that girlfriends only do for boyfriends?"

Amanda was blinking, not knowing what to say. Not knowing how to save her life.

"I don't have a girlfriend."

"I'm sure there are plenty of nice girls that would love to be your girlfriend." She was scrambling for hope, desperately trying to build rapport.

"I don't want a nice girl. I want a girl like you." His expression was angry. "If I ask, will you be my girlfriend?"

"I…"

"You're gonna say no just like the rest, aren't you?" He looked at her and licked his lips. "Do with me what you did with Delevic."

"Milo!"

Labus shoved her down across the two front bucket seats. She screamed.

"Hush!" He jammed the end of the silencer into her cheek. She swallowed the rest of the scream.

She wept as he climbed in on top of her. Her right hand was still on the steering wheel. She reached and punched the horn button with the side of her fist with all her might, but the horn remained silent. She grabbed the right side of the steering wheel again. His leg was on top of her left leg and his weight seemed as if it would snap her femur.

"Oh my God! Please don't! Milo, please don't!!"

"I knew you would say no. You're just like all the rest," Labus growled through gritted teeth. "Well, I'm gonna teach you what I taught the others … Milo Labus doesn't take no for an answer."

Amanda gripped the steering wheel with all her might, her knuckles turning white with strain.

• • •

Delevic pushed his plate toward the middle of the table, the omelet only half eaten. The waitress in the all-night diner walked up, coffee pot in hand. "Not very hungry?" she asked.

"No. How do you Americans say it? My eyeballs were bigger than my stomach."

The waitress chuckled as she refilled his coffee cup. "Can I get you anything else?"

He looked up at her, smiling charmingly. "No, thank you, my darling. Just the check."

The waitress smiled back. "No problem, hon." She turned and walked off. Delevic watched, admiring her calves. He would sit there, drinking coffee until he got the all-clear call on his cell phone from Labus. That thought made him look at his watch. *What's taking him so long?*

Once he got the call, he would pay his bill with a credit card. If anyone saw him tonight with Amanda, he wanted to have an ironclad alibi for the time of her death. He was quite sure the waitress would remember the dark-haired man with the funny accent who sat and drank coffee at her table. To make sure she remembered, he would tip her generously. And he would have the credit card receipt as proof of his innocence.

Not that he worried much about the police. The police were but a minor irritation. He wanted to avoid any hassles that might delay him in his work. He always had to be ready. The general might call at any time.

• • •

Labus pulled the handle and popped the hood on Amanda's car. He walked around, reached in, squeezed the lever and lifted the hood. He replaced the battery cable onto the terminal, undoing the impairment. He dropped the hood back into place. Her car was fixed. He walked to the driver's side door, which stood open. He paused and admired his girlfriend in the glow of the dome light. She sure was cute. He would have loved to show her off to his friends back home. *Look what I got!* He was grinning, satisfied.

He stepped closer to the driver's side and bent down. He reached in and pulled her body to the sitting position in the driver's seat. Rigor mortis had not yet set in. But her hand was still clamped on the steering wheel. *Good.* He had replaced her clothes and fixed her hair. She looked beautiful.

After she did the things for him that girlfriends do for boy-friends, he squeezed off the blood flow to her brain at her neck until she was dead. No bullet holes. No knife scratches on any bones. Of course, the cause of death would be obvious to the coroner, particularly with the bruising and swelling around her neck—*if* he left her like that. But he was no dummy. He wasn't done with her.

He reached into his pocket and produced a pack of ciga-rettes and a lighter. He took the pack and removed a cigarette. He put it in his mouth and lit it. He puffed until it was going good. He then took the cigarette and laid it on the cloth driv-er's seat of her car. It smoldered right next to her leg. He then took another one out of the pack and lit it. This one was for his own enjoyment. He then tossed the pack onto the dash of her car. The cloth glowed orange then turned black. He bent down and blew on it. The foam insulation of the seat was now exposed and began to smolder. He coughed from the smoke in his face. He blew some more and the orange embers flashed into a small flame. Bingo. The black smoke billowed up out of the driver's side door. He cranked the window down to allow sufficient oxygen to enter the car and slammed the door shut. Flames started consuming part of Amanda's leg.

Bartender falls asleep smoking in her car, dies in fire. It wasn't perfect. If the police looked close enough, and he knew they would, they would discover that it was a homicide. By the time they put the pieces together, he and Delevic would be long gone. All he was interested in was buying time.

Labus puffed his cigarette as he walked around to the back of the building to retrieve his rental car. He felt like a million dollars. He felt like a man.

Amanda's car was fully ablaze when he pulled out of the parking lot onto the main road. He took a deep breath. Then he pulled out his cell phone and dialed Delevic's number.

• • •

The second time the doorbell rang, Jill Paxton jolted up in bed. Her babies stirred with her sudden movement, but they didn't wake up. Her bedroom was dark except for the light that washed in from the master bath. She left the light on in the bathroom, with the door partially open in case her son got up in the middle of the night to go potty. It was still dark outside—the middle of the night. Who would ring the doorbell at this hour?

Oh my God! She felt sick. *John!*

She jumped out of bed and grabbed her robe. She was halfway down the stairs before she had her robe all the way on. She was still tying it as she peered through the peephole of the front door. She saw the distorted fun-house image of Colonel Ward illuminated by her porch light. She turned the lock and yanked open the front door.

"Tell me what happened to my husband!"

Ward held his hands up, open palms toward her, "Calm down, Jill."

"I *won't* calm down!" She ran a hand through her disheveled blonde hair. "Is John dead?"

"No. It's not what you think. May we come in?"

"Thank God! Yes, please, Colonel. You, too, Sergeant Machette. I'm sorry."

He and Machette followed her into her foyer. Ward held his hat in both hands in front of him. "John's plane has been shot down."

"Ohhhh!" Jill sobbed, her knees giving out. She lost her balance. Ward caught her and took her in his arms. Machette rubbed her silk robe-covered arm, feeling inadequate. Jill cried on Ward's shoulder while he held her. "We are doing everything humanly possible to rescue John."

Ward looked at Machette, who was obviously uncomfortable. Like most PJs, he preferred facing the danger of enemy fire to rescue someone in need than giving bad news to the spouse of a fellow airman.

Finally, Jill regained some of her composure. She pulled back from Ward. "What happened?"

"Did you hear about the Stealth fighter that was shot down over Yugoslavia?"

Jill looked at Ward, her eyes filled with disbelief. "Yeah, I heard about it. What's that got to do with John?"

Ward looked at Machette. He knew he was about to say more than he should. "John was called upon to assist in the rescue of the pilot."

"You mean he's over *there*? Why?" she sobbed. "He doesn't do *that* anymore. He promised me…." Her words trailed off.

"I'm sorry, Jill. It was a special circumstance," Ward said, realizing how inadequate his words sounded.

Machette felt helpless. He looked at the family pictures on the wall of the foyer. Happy. Carefree. Frozen in a time when they were all together. And all safe.

"Why did you send John? He's an *instructor*."

"It wasn't up to me."

"That's bull. You're his commander."

"I'm sick about what's happened. I assure you that the PJs will bring him out if he is—"

"You don't ... oh my God! You don't know if he's alive!"

Machette turned away and looked at the floor. Ward's chin dropped to his chest and he closed his eyes. He couldn't bear to look at her. "No, we don't know."

She lost her composure. This time, she turned her back to the airmen as she cried. Ward looked at Jill, her world in limbo. The fate of her family danced on a tightrope between heaven and hell. And there wasn't a damn thing any of them could do to change the situation.

"What do I tell my children?"

"You probably shouldn't say anything until we know more."

Jill nodded, snuffling back tears.

Ward and Machette stood there in silence; Ward's hand rested on Jill's shoulder. He asked, "Can we take you anywhere? Would you like to stay with someone?"

Jill shook her head and turned toward the men. Her eyes were red. "No, I want to stay here, in my home. The kids are comfortable here. I don't want their routine disrupted. I don't want them to know anything is wrong."

Ward nodded.

"If there is anything we can do, please let us know," Machette said.

Jill nodded. "Thank you."

"We're gonna bring him home safe," Ward added.

"You can't promise me that," she said softly. "I want to show you something. Wait here."

Jill left the foyer. Quick movement near the top of the stairway caught his eye. There was just enough light to see a small boy, dressed in pajamas, stand and dash back up the stairs. Ward wondered how much he had heard.

Jill returned with a piece of paper in her hand. "Colonel, take a look at this."

Ward read the letter silently while Machette read it over his shoulder. Ward looked at Jill, his heart clenching. "Congratulations."

• • •

After Ward and Machette left, Jill returned to her bedroom. She found her son, John, Jr., lying in her bed crying. Her daughter was still asleep.

"What's the matter, baby?" she whispered, scooting next to him and patting his back.

"Somethin's wrong with Daddy."

"Don't worry. Daddy is fine."

The little boy sat up and stared at his mother. "Then why were you crying, Mommy?"

She wrapped her son in her arms and squeezed. "I miss Daddy."

"Me, too."

Together, mother and son wept.

• • •

A passing motorist summoned the fire department. The firemen arrived and sprayed the burning hulk of metal that everyone had assumed was an abandoned vehicle parked outside a neighborhood bar. The police officer on the scene had checked out the vehicle on routine patrol earlier and found it empty.

After the last of the gasoline-fueled flames were extinguished and the charred metal frame was closely inspected for glowing embers, the firefighters discovered a smoldering human skeleton seated on the springs that once supported the driver's seat.

The bones of the skeleton's right hand were wrapped around the metal core of the steering wheel.

CHAPTER 16

No less than eight men turned to face Paxton, some of whom brought their automatic weapons to bear upon his person. All of the men had turned toward him almost simultaneously, but only four seemed to be visibly armed.

A fusillade of bullets should have torn through him. They *should* have killed Paxton, then turned their attention to the two other men they had located hiding in the woods—men discovered with the help of night vision equipment.

How else would they be expected to conduct themselves in the midst of combat when a man springs unexpectedly from cover?

These were no ordinary men. They were highly trained. They had the discipline and experience to determine at whom they are shooting before they pull the trigger. In fact, much of their training and discipline had been instilled in them by Paxton himself.

"Sergeant Paxton?" The airman with the NVGs examined him carefully from a distance. "Goddamn! That is you! Pax, what the hell are you doing?"

Paxton's mind reeled. "Smith?"

"Yes sir."

"I thought you were dead," Paxton said.

"Yeah, well, the feeling's mutual."

Paxton walked toward the group. "What happened?"

"We got out … all of us. Including the loadmaster. Are the pilots over there?" Smith asked, pointing at the woods

"Yeah. They're okay for the most part." He reached the group, many who were still on alert, studying the terrain. Relief cascaded through him. Son-of-a-bitch. His men got out of that clusterfuck alive. "This place will swarm with Serbs any second. There's a road over there. They'll be able to drive in truckloads of troops. We've got to move and fast."

"We crossed the road when we came looking for you," Smith replied.

"So you thought the pilots and I were probably dead, but you came looking for us anyway?"

"Yes."

"Good call." Paxton looked at Smith and grinned, "Good job."

"Just doing my job."

"Thompson's hurt pretty bad; broken leg and probably concussion. Weil is scraped up pretty bad."

"We're on it. Petersen! Dobbins!"

"Yes, Sergeant Smith," the two PJ's replied.

"Get the pilots stabilized and ready to ambulate. We're getting the heck out of Dodge."

"Yes, sergeant." They ran toward the injured crewmen. One of them carried a medical bag.

Smith and Paxton walked side-by-side now, creating distance between themselves and the others. Four of the other men stood at the ready, scanning the surroundings through the optical sights of their rifles. The loadmaster stood there as well with nothing to do but look around nervously.

"We don't have much. We scrounged four M-4's, one medical kit, some rations—maybe enough to feed an anorexic Hollywood starlet for a day—some flashlights, signal flares and miscellaneous tools."

"How 'bout a radio?" Paxton asked.

Smith shook his head.

"Damn."

"What about the pilots? Don't they have their survival radios?"

"The pilots were lucky to get out with their lives. What about ammo?"

"Each M-4 had a 30 round magazine in it. We have maybe three or four more magazines and that's it. We can't hold off the Serbian army."

"No shit. I don't even have a knife."

"I got one," Smith said as he reached for his boot knife. "You want it?"

"Keep it."

"I was lucky to have the NVGs. Just happened to have 'em

on when the plane cracked up." He looked at Paxton and frowned. "If you thought we were dead ... why the hell did you jump out of the brush and yell at us?"

"Thought you were Serbs. I saw you discover the pilots. I figured that if I jumped out and made enough noise, I'd distract you and they could slip away."

Smith shook his head; a knowing smile on his face. "Pax, you're crazy."

Paxton grunted an agreement. "Just doing my job."

• • •

Detective Margolis of the Lake Mary, Florida Police Department rubbed the stubble on his chin and asked the patrol officer, "You're absolutely sure the car was empty when you checked it earlier?" He and the officer stood in the plaza parking lot near the charred hulk of the Toyota. Crime scene tape surrounded the vehicle and crime scene investigators from the Seminole County Sheriff's Office picked through the remnants. A sheet covered the charred skeleton.

"Yes. No one was in that car. I figured someone got too drunk to drive home and called a cab," the officer said. "I ran the tag. The car is registered to Amanda Cole of Lake Mary."

Margolis made some notes. "So that might be Amanda's body?"

An investigator joined Margolis; he carried a clear evidence bag with a piece of burnt foil inside it. "Detective, I'd thought you should see this." He held up the bag. "Foil from a pack of cigarettes. We found it on the dash. Maybe we have an accidental fire. Another smoking related death."

Margolis shook his head. "Car was empty. Then a few hours later, it suddenly burns up with a body in it? I'm not buying it."

• • •

Dawn arrived by the time the PJs finished splinting Thompson's leg and treating Weil's wounds. Paxton, Smith and the others had moved into the woods to avoid detection. The PJs with rifles continued their vigilant watch of the surroundings. Incredibly, there was no sign of Serbs. The Globemaster wreckage and the surrounding woods still burned; thick black smoke billowed into the sky.

"Any idea where we are?" Paxton asked.

"None," Smith replied.

Paxton sat on the ground thinking. Damn, he was tired. How many hours had he gone without sleep? "Thompson can't move very quickly or very far. Our best bet is to position ourselves near the road. We commandeer the first car or truck that comes along and pile everyone in. We drive it as fast as we can to the border and go home."

"What about Cue Ball?"

"Don't worry about Cue Ball. We've got to get our own aircrew to safety. Are the pilots ready to move?"

"Yes, sir."

"Good. Pass the word."

"You sure we shouldn't at least try to look for Cue Ball?"

"No, and that's an order. Our mission is now limited to one thing: getting all of us to safety. That is all we can do at this point. Our hands are full enough as it is. We'll be lucky if we get out alive. Getting to NATO troops stationed in Bosnia without getting stopped is going to be a good trick. So forget about Cue Ball," Paxton commanded.

"You're the boss," Smith replied.

One of the PJs assigned to perimeter security whispered. "Somebody's coming." Everyone became alert and still. Paxton regretted not moving deeper into the woods. The PJs with the rifles were lying prone, utilizing the 4x scopes mounted on the tops of their M-4 assault rifles to assess the approaching threat. Fingers hovered outside the trigger guards, ready to insert and pull at the appropriate moment. Ammunition was limited. Firepower was limited. Resources were limited. Manpower was limited. As Smith had so aptly put it, they would not be able to hold off the Serbian army. With their first shot, they would make their position known and would draw unrelenting fire from the Serbs. To pull the trigger was a sure death sentence to them all. But failing to pull the trigger would also be a death sentence.

All four M-4s aimed at the opening of the clearing. From the direction of the road appeared an armed figure clad in dark green.

He strode toward their position.

Four fingers moved into four trigger guards, the pads of those rock-steady fingers resting on the triggers.

• • •

Detective Margolis had pounded on the door to Amanda's apartment until her roommate, still half asleep, answered. He showed his badge and peppered the girl with questions. *No, Amanda didn't come home last night. No, I don't know where she is. Yes, she usually comes home after work.*

"Where does she work?" Margolis asked the woman clad only in a large T-shirt.

"The Dugout."

"What kind of vehicle does she drive?"

"An old Toyota. Is Amanda okay?"

"That's what I'm trying to determine. Do you know anyone who would want to hurt her?"

"No way. She's a sweet girl." The roommate gazed at him with worried eyes. "What happened?"

"Where have you been all night?"

"I was here by myself."

"Is she seeing anyone right now?"

"No. Her boyfriend ended their relationship and left for the service. Amanda was heartbroken."

Margolis made notes in his notebook. "Did she owe anyone any money?"

"Yeah, the same bastards we all owe—Visa and Mastercard."

"Did she have a life insurance policy?"

"She's a bartender! She could barely pay the rent. She couldn't afford health insurance, let alone life insurance." She looked at Margolis, frowning. "You're scaring the shit out of me. Where is Amanda?"

"I don't know." Margolis offered his card to the girl. "Please call me if you hear from her or if you think of anything else."

As the woman closed the door, Margolis flattened his palm on the flimsy wood and stopped its movement. "One more question," he said. "Did Amanda smoke?"

"Of course not! She quit after her mother died of lung cancer. She wouldn't touch a cigarette."

· · ·

"Hold your fire," Senior Airman Maxwell said, the highest-ranking PJ with a rifle. The others obeyed without question. Through their scopes, they saw what Maxwell saw. The brightening daylight and the 4x magnifications of their scopes made it impossible to misidentify. The armed man in dark green camouflage walking into the clearing was no Serbian.

"It's McMurphy," Maxwell said.

"Go ahead and shoot," Paxton said.

"Sir?"

He sighed. "Better not. Anyone with him?"

"Not that I can see."

"Okay. Stay right here. Don't take your sights off him." Paxton got up and walked out of the woods into the clearing.

McMurphy reacted when he saw Paxton, raising his AK-74, but then he obviously recognized the sergeant and relaxed.

"What the hell are you doing here?" Paxton yelled.

"More important, what the hell are you *still* doing here?"

McMurphy shouted as he walked toward Paxton.

"Waiting for you. What else?"

"Idiot! If I can find you, don't you think the Serbs can, too? Never thought the great Paxton would be hanging around the wreckage of his plane. Fucking stupid. Reed's confidence in you is severely misplaced."

Paxton ignored the jibe. "You're lucky you're not dead. We had you in our sights."

"Your men wouldn't shoot me." McMurphy stopped a couple feet from Paxton.

"Maybe they will if you don't start being a team player."

"Just remember, asshole, I don't work for you."

"Who do you work for? The Serbs?"

"Don't make me laugh," McMurphy replied.

"Where's your green backpack?" he asked.

"Left it in the car. I parked it on the other side of those trees." McMurphy waved behind him.

Where the hell had McMurphy gotten a car? "You have a radio?" Paxton asked.

"Nope. Don't you have one?"

"No."

"Sucks, don't it?"

"Yeah, can't find out how the Cubs are doing in Spring Training."

"So no one knows you're here?" McMurphy laughed softly. "Who will rescue the rescuers?"

"We'll rescue ourselves."

"This place will be crawling with Serbs any minute."

McMurphy said. "Better get your slow ass moving, Paxton. C'mon, I need your help."

"Screw you. You're on your own. We're getting the hell out of here."

"Good luck." McMurphy shrugged. "You're stuck out here and no one knows you're alive. Oh, and don't get any bright ideas about stealing a vehicle and going to Bosnia. You won't get ten kilometers without hitting a checkpoint." He grinned, his eyes cold and mean. "Too bad you don't know how to contact Jashari."

Shit. Jashari was McMurphy's trump card. Only McMurphy knew how to contact Jashari, who was their way out if the Globemaster couldn't extract them. Obviously the Globemaster was never going to extract anyone ever again. Paxton had to get his team home safely. Jill and the kids were in San Antonio with no idea where he was or what he was doing. God knew what they'd been told. Maybe she already thought he was dead. *They need me. I need them.* He didn't even get the chance to say goodbye. Fucking McMurphy was the linchpin. *Jashari.*

Paxton knew what he had to do ... so that others may live. "Okay, McMurphy, what is it that you want me to do?"

McMurphy smiled.

CHAPTER 17

By THE TIME DETECTIVE MARGOLIS RETURNED TO THE parking lot outside *The Dugout*, all of the investigative photographs and measurements had been taken and the body had been removed from the vehicle by the medical examiner's staff.

Having determined Amanda worked at the bar as a bartender and she had not returned home after work, Margolis suspected that the body was hers. He chatted with the medical examiner's people as they loaded the body bag into the back of a white, unmarked windowless van. They had conducted a cursory examination of the body, including a rough measurement. The skeleton was female, based upon the shape of the pelvis, and the estimated height was between 5' 5" and 5' 7". Margolis jotted more notes in his book. They could not confirm cause of death until further examination at their facilities. Positive identification would likely be obtained through dental records.

A flatbed tow truck sat in the lot idling with only its parking lights on, the driver waiting for the investigators to finish their work. Once the medical examiner's van drove off, the CSI leader waved the truck over. The driver turned on its headlights, revved its diesel engine and maneuvered into position, lining up with the charred skeleton of a car. While the tow truck operator worked, Margolis got into his car and fired up his laptop. He logged in and connected to the department's computers via a wireless connection. He called up the Department of Motor Vehicle records on Amanda and read the information from her driver's license file.

While he waited for official identification, in Margolis's mind, he was already investigating the death of Amanda Cole. The next challenge would be to determine if she met her demise through natural causes, accident, or foul play. He had more than ten years experience as a detective and he had learned to trust his instincts. And this so-called accident had crime written all over it.

He lit a cigarette as he sat there in the sedan, driver's side door open. He looked at his watch. It had been 45 minutes since he called the owner of *The Dugout* and asked him to come out.

Amanda's car had been loaded onto the tow truck by the time the bar owner drove up and parked along the sidewalk outside *The Dugout's* entrance. Margolis got out of the car, slammed the door shut and tossed the glowing butt of his cigarette onto the asphalt. Their eyes met and Margolis gave him a slight nod, waiting for the man to join him. He showed his badge and they shook hands.

The owner introduced himself as Tom McKinnon. "What's

going on?" McKinnon asked.

"I'd like to take a look around inside," Margolis replied.

The men crossed the parking lot and the detective stood behind McKinnon as he unlocked the front door. He switched on the lights and both men stepped inside.

Margolis looked around and asked, "Does everything appear to be in order?"

"Looks okay."

"Were you here tonight?"

"I took today off."

"Who was in charge?"

"I have two managers. They work alternating shifts."

"I'll need to get their names and numbers. You employ a woman by the name of Amanda Cole."

"She's new. Nice girl. Does this have something to do with Amanda?"

"I don't know yet. Did your manager report any trouble last night?"

"No. Why?"

Margolis didn't answer as examined the room. He pointed to two smoked glass hemispheres on the ceiling. "Those work?"

"Sure do," the owner said proudly. "State-of-the-art system. It records twenty-four, seven."

"You have the tape for tonight?"

"Better. The cameras feed digital signals straight onto a computer and get stored on the hard drive." The owner waved the detective forward. "Come back to my office. I'll show you."

• • •

Nikolic looked weary as he stood in front of Rugova's desk. The morning sun shone through the lone window and splashed warmly all over Nikolic, the top of the desk and the floor. Rugova sat behind the desk, his face still in shadow. Nikolic couldn't see the expression of his superior's face, but from the tone of his booming voice, he knew he was in trouble.

"Yesterday you told me you had things under control!"

"Yes, sir," Nikolic said.

"More than twenty-four hours have passed and you don't have what I want."

"I need more time, sir."

"I *need* results!"

"Yes, sir." Nikolic shifted his weight from foot to foot, like a small boy being scolded. "We shot down a cargo plane last night."

"I'm not interested in cargo planes," Rugova screamed as he slammed his fist on his desk, rattling everything on it. "Where is the device?"

Startled at Rugova's vitriol, Nikolic barely controlled his flinch. "It's a very technical piece of equipment—"

"I *know* that."

"Special expertise is required," explained Nikolic, visibly sweating. "You wouldn't want it damaged, would you?"

"Don't be stupid." Rugova leaned forward and stared hard at Nikolic. "Where is the Stealth pilot?"

"We are looking for him and for any survivors from the cargo plane."

"I don't care about any cargo plane!" Rugova's fist struck the top of the desk again. "Pull all your men from the cargo plane search and put them onto the search for the Stealth pilot. He is the one I want."

"Yes, sir. I understand, sir." Nikolic saluted. He turned and left.

Once Nikolic was outside the front doors of the 6th Army's headquarters, he got on his radio and issued orders—that didn't entirely follow Rugova's stern command.

Nikolic understood the significance of shooting down the cargo plane in ways Rugova couldn't. He wasn't stupid, but he didn't have all the information. And Nikolic planned to keep it that way—having information that Rugova didn't was his best way of staying alive.

Nikolic pulled all the teams off the cargo plane search except for one—his most trusted team. To them, he gave explicit orders: Search for survivors from the cargo plane and report only to him what they discovered.

Rugova demanded results.

Nikolic intended to deliver results.

• • •

Paxton and McMurphy walked to the pilot who sat on the ground concealed in thick brush. Paxton wanted to update Thompson on the new plans, which were based upon McMurphy's unwavering requirements. Thompson's leg was splinted and carefully wrapped with gauze. McMurphy had his rifle slung in front of him, barrel pointed down. Weil was seated on the ground behind Thompson and the loadmaster leaned against a nearby tree. The rest of the team was several yards away, preparing to move out. Thompson evidently felt better because he was pissed.

"You two!" Thompson glared at Paxton and McMurphy as if he just recognized who they were. "You're the reason we crashed. I remember it all now. You two were fighting and shot the tie-downs for the bulldozer. That's why it shifted and tore the Globemaster apart."

McMurphy shrugged. Thompson looked like he wanted to strangle the man.

"We wanted to tell you the plan," Paxton said.

"Plan? No, *you* don't get to *plan*. You're the reason we're all in this mess," Thompson shot back.

"I'm also the reason you're alive," Paxton said. "I dragged your sorry ass out of the cockpit and got you off the plane. And I'm the one who helped you get to cover after you landed."

"You want kudos for doing your *job*?" Thompson turned to the loadmaster. "Airman, take Sergeant Paxton and McMurphy into custody."

"Sir?" the loadmaster asked incredulously.

"I'm the pilot, damn it. Do what I said."

He must've hit his head harder than I thought. "This is ridiculous," Paxton said.

"In case you haven't noticed, Major Thompson, your plane is gone," McMurphy said. "You ain't pilot of shit."

"I'm still the ranking officer. You're under arrest."

Sighing, the loadmaster pushed off the tree and walked toward Paxton and McMurphy. "Sir," he said to McMurphy. "Please put your hands behind your back."

McMurphy looked at the loadmaster as he slowly raised his hands up to chest level, as if in surrender. Then he suddenly shoved the loadmaster with both arms. The loadmaster toppled backwards and landed in a sitting position next to Thompson. Weil started to stand, and McMurphy grabbed the AK-74.

Paxton restrained McMurphy. "Let's not do it this way."

The loadmaster stayed on the ground and Weil sat back down. McMurphy relaxed and Paxton let go of McMurphy's rifle.

"So you're going to resist arrest?" Thompson asked.

Paxton turned back toward the seated pilot. "Sir, do you know where we are?" he asked.

"Don't insult me! I know exactly where we are and you put us all here." He turned toward the PJs who were several yards away. They had stopped packing and were watching the confrontation. "Sergeant Smith!"

Paxton and McMurphy looked at each other again. They were both a mess in their rumpled mercenary uniforms. McMurphy's nose was obviously broken, dried blood caked around the nostrils and Paxton had visible burns on his face. Smith hurried forward and he had a M-4 carbine with him. "Yes, sir?"

"Arrest these men."

"Sir?"

"They are being charged with attempted murder, insubordination, assault, and resisting arrest." Thompson nodded toward Paxton and McMurphy. "That's a direct order, Sergeant."

"Don't do it, Smith," Paxton ordered.

"Don't listen to him. I'm the ranking officer here. You'll do as I say," Thompson demanded.

Smith looked back down at Thompson. He was stuck in the middle.

"This is a rescue mission. I'm in charge of the rescue mission. You'll do as I say, Sergeant Smith."

Smith looked at Paxton, torn between two superiors. He looked at his team leader. "Pax, he's a *Major.*"

"As the ranking *medical officer, I've determined that Major Thompson is not medically fit for command.*"

"What?" Thompson yelled. He shifted around as if he were going to try to stand up, despite his broken leg.

"This is stupid," McMurphy said to no one in particular, "You military-types fight this out; I've got a job to do." He turned and walked away.

Smith shouted, "Gun!"

Thompson had reached into his survival belt, which was still strapped around his waist, and produced a nine-millimeter automatic pistol. He pointed it, with shaky hands, at McMurphy's back, his finger on the trigger.

McMurphy was a statue.

Everyone froze, holding their breaths.

"You are under arrest!" Thompson shouted. "One more move and I'll shoot."

No one doubted his sincerity.

"Sir, please put that away," Smith said. "The Serbs are looking for us. We need to get to safety ... then we handle the problems with Paxton and McMurphy."

"We go when I say we go." He looked at Paxton, his eyes glazed. Paxton wondered if the pilot really had taken a hit to the skull or if he had a fever brought on by an infection. "We need to make sure these two don't cause any more trouble."

We don't have time for this shit, thought Paxton. "Major Thompson, if we don't get out of here now, you're going to have all the trouble you can stand."

"Shut up!" Thompson demanded, waving his gun between McMurphy and Paxton. Paxton stood motionless with his hands slightly up, palms out, looking as harmless as a muscular 6' 2" tall muddy pararescueman, his pant leg torn and dark with dried blood, could manage. McMurphy stood next to Paxton, his back to Thompson. Thompson looked up at Smith. "Tie those two up. We have a pilot to rescue."

"We're not rescuing the pilot," Paxton said. "We're getting the hell out of here."

"Shut up! We lost our plane and almost got killed to rescue Cue Ball. And that's what we're going to do."

"Sir, you don't have all the facts—"

"I said shut up!" Thompson raised the pistol until it was aimed at the center of Paxton's face.

Paxton shut up.

McMurphy shook his head. "You're making a huge mistake."

"You shut up, too!" Thompson shouted. "Tie them up," he ordered Smith.

Smith hesitated. If he followed Thompson's orders, as unpleasant as that might be, they would get the chance to rescue the Stealth pilot. It was what they trained to do—it was what *Paxton* trained them to do. If they saved the Stealth pilot, then they could *all* go home. Following Paxton's lead meant abandoning Cue Ball. Then again, Cue Ball might already be dead. *Damn it.* If he disobeyed Thompson, he would violate a direct order of a superior officer and he would be court-martialed right along with Paxton.

Of course, no matter which decision he made, tying up Paxton and McMurphy made no sense. He didn't know why the Serbs hadn't arrived yet, but they would be drawn to the burning wreckage of the Globemaster.

Everyone was staring at Smith: Thompson, Weil, the loadmaster, and Paxton. Jennings stood there, M-4 in hand, waiting for further instructions from Smith, who was his immediate superior. Even McMurphy had turned his head slightly to see what Smith was going to do. Thompson stared at him, but his pistol was still pointed at Paxton's face. "Sergeant?" he prompted.

Smith knew both men were trying to take what they felt was the right action, but *he* couldn't serve two masters. If he disobeyed Paxton, his career as a PJ was likely over. If he disobeyed Thompson, his career in the Air Force was over, period. At this moment he'd rather have been in the tortuous pool at Superman school trying to catch his breath than standing here between Paxton and Thompson.

Even so, he made his decision.

He snapped out his right leg and kicked the pistol out of Thompson's hand. It was a beautiful punt, perfectly executed. The pistol flew up and out, arced through the air, and disappeared into the woods. Everyone watched the flight of the pistol. They were motionless, stunned.

"What the hell!" Thompson cradled his hand, his angry gaze on Smith. "You broke my hand!"

The co-pilot and the loadmaster jumped to their feet and barreled at Smith. Paxton and Jennings stepped forward and stopped them.

"Everyone calm down," Paxton commanded. Weil and loadmaster backed down, mostly because Jennings was armed.

"I'm sorry, Major Thompson," Smith said. "But we follow Sergeant Paxton's orders. He says it's time to go home, so we go home."

"There's a problem," Paxton said.

"*Sir?*" Smith turned to him, incredulous.

Paxton didn't know how to give Smith the bad news. He looked his former student in the eye, regretting that he had forced Smith to make a difficult decision. He just hoped the man wouldn't be punished for his loyalty. Moments before, Paxton had made a deal with the devil. He agreed to help McMurphy in exchange for contact with Jashari who was their only way to get out of the country safely. "We will all go home," Paxton said, "but *first* McMurphy and I have a mission to complete."

• • •

Margolis and the bar owner sat side by side in the small office in the back of *The Dugout*. In front of them on the cluttered desk was a computer monitor displaying a split screen. One side of the screen showed the left side of the bar and the other side of the screen showed the right. The image was black and white. A time-clock counter was in the corner of each image and indicated that they were synchronized. The owner had been using the mouse to fast forward through the previous day's activities. Both men stared intently at the screen. Patrons came and went, and Amanda tended to them from behind the bar at comical speed.

"Do you recognize the customers?" Margolis asked.

The owner studied the flitting images. "Hmmm, most are regulars."

"Any troublemakers?"

"A few, but nothing serious. Shit! I can't believe it!" the owner exclaimed.

"What?"

"She's *drinking* on the job."

Margolis watched as Amanda stood across the bar from a dark-haired patron wearing a jacket. She sipping from a glass obviously filled with alcohol. "That's against the rules, I take it?"

"It sure is. I'm going to have to fire her."

Margolis said nothing.

"Who's that she's drinking with?"

"I don't know. Never seen him before."

"Rewind it. Start from when he comes in."

"Okay." The owner clicked the appropriate buttons.

The two men watched again as the dark-haired man walked in with a larger man. They both sat down at the bar. The dark-haired man and Amanda were talking. "Where's the sound?"

"My lawyer says I can film people all I want, but in Florida it's illegal to record their conversations."

"You have a very wise lawyer," Margolis replied, his eyes never leaving the screen.

"I have a very expensive lawyer."

"Is there any other kind?"

On the screen, the dark-haired man gave the bigger man something and then the bigger man clapped him on the shoulder and left. The dark-haired man and Amanda continued to talk.

"It seems the stranger has taken an interest in Amanda," Margolis said. "She seems to like him, too."

The owner slowed the tape down to almost normal speed. "See that? He must have struck out. He's leaving."

"Any chance of them hooking up later?" Margolis asked.

"Doubt it."

"Why?"

"She's not into temporary hook-ups."

"You sound like you have personal knowledge."

The owner said nothing. He fast-forwarded through the rest of the evening until the manager closed up.

"Can I get a copy?" Margolis asked.

"I'll burn it to a disk for you."

"Thank you. When's Amanda scheduled to work again?"

"Tomorrow—I mean today," the owner said, eyeing his watch. "Her shift starts at 11 a.m. But it'll be the shortest shift on record. I'm firing her."

Margolis resisted rolling his eyes. The owner had no idea Amanda probably had already been fired—literally. "When you see her, give me a call," Margolis said, handing the owner his card. "I really need to speak with her."

• • •

The two pilots and the loadmaster were seated on the ground side by side under the watchful eye of Jennings. They were still in the brush near the edge of the clearing. It was already mid-morning and the sunlight streamed through the branches. Paxton had ordered the search of the aircrew, but no other weapons were located. The aircrew was not restrained because doing so would slow their movements and endanger their lives. While Weil and the loadmaster had vocally sided with Thompson, they were both well aware that Paxton and Smith had saved all their lives. They were secretly relieved that the pilot had been subdued, even if it meant they had been subdued with him.

Everyone was ready to move out, and Paxton had everyone under control.

"Sergeant Paxton, it's time for you and me to go," McMurphy demanded.

Well, almost everyone under control, thought Paxton. "I'll be ready in a moment."

McMurphy looked at his watch. "We need to hurry."

"No shit." The plan called for Paxton to go with McMurphy to assist him with his special mission, and for Smith to lead the others to a sheltered position away from the Globemaster wreckage. Smith and the others were to wait until Paxton and McMurphy return with Jashari. Then the KLA leader would lead them to safety.

"If only we had a map…" Paxton mused.

"You were given one, along with a GPS receiver, in your pack."

"My stuff went down with the plane—after you decided to pull that crap with my gun."

"Next time don't wrap a damn rope around my throat!"

Paxton stepped up to McMurphy. Both men were chest to chest.

"Okay, okay," Smith said, forcing his body between the two taller men. "We need to cut the bullshit and get out of here. I can't believe the Serbs haven't arrived already."

"Do you want a map or not?" McMurphy asked. "I have one."

Paxton calmed himself, then he replied, "We'll take it."

McMurphy pulled the map out of his small pack. It was enclosed in a clear waterproof plastic bag. "Do you want my GPS too?"

"Yes," Smith said. He took the map and the handheld GPS unit.

Smith and Paxton turned their backs to McMurphy and

examined the map. McMurphy watched them then looked at his watch again. He stepped beside them, "Here, let me help you."

McMurphy pointed out their position on the map then the road. He recommended where the PJs and aircrew should make camp. He assured them that the location was secluded and densely wooded and that they could remain there unmolested.

"How do you know so much about this country?" Paxton asked.

"I've been here before," McMurphy answered.

Paxton eyed him then returned his attention to the map. "That spot is several clicks away—a long way to go with a man with a broken leg." Paxton paused and looked at McMurphy. "You think we could use your car to move Thompson?"

"Sorry. No time." McMurphy stalked away.

Paxton sighed. "Looks like you're going to have to carry him, Smith."

"We'll get him there, sir. I'll get them all there."

Paxton smiled. He liked Smith's attitude.

"Have someone retrieve Major Thompson's pistol. You'll need all the firepower you can carry."

"Okay, Pax."

Paxton indicated on the map the location McMurphy had suggested. "Stay put and out of sight. If McMurphy and I don't return in twenty-four hours, presume we are not returning. Do not—I repeat—*do not* come looking for us. Just get yourselves the hell out of the country. I don't care how you do it. You'll have the map and the GPS."

Smith opened his mouth and Paxton waved away the man's protest. "I'm leaving you in charge. If I don't return, it's your responsibility to see to it that everyone makes it home safely."

"Pax, what about Cue Ball? After I get the aircrew to the hideout, I want take some men and go look for him."

"I'm ordering you to stay put."

"Goddamn it! I just kicked a firearm out of an officer's hand. I probably just punted my career. I'll probably go to jail. I did it because I thought we would be getting everyone out of here. I did it because I believe in you. This isn't right. And it's not what you taught us."

Paxton studied Smith's determined expression. The man might try to rescue Cue Ball no matter what Paxton said. He arrived at a decision. "We need to talk."

CHAPTER 18

THE NEXT DAY AROUND NOON, DETECTIVE MARGOLIS went to the police station. A stack of messages awaited him. Amanda's roommate had called numerous times, worried sick because Amanda never returned home and never called. Another message was from the owner of *The Dugout*. Amanda had not shown up for her shift. There was a call from Amanda's sister who lived in California. Evidently the roommate had contacted her and now she was worried about her little sis.

Margolis called the Medical Examiner's office to find out if the body had been identified. He was told to check back later that afternoon.

He flipped through the messages and noted a second one from McKinnon. He had some information that might be helpful and urged him to come down to the bar as soon as possible.

Margolis didn't call the roommate or the sister. He didn't

have anything to tell them. He left his desk, went outside and hopped into his sedan. It was only a six-minute drive to *The Dugout.* He parked out front. Amazingly, the spot where Amanda's car had burned was already cleaned up and a SUV was parked in its place. He locked his car and crossed to the doorway.

He stepped inside the dark, cool room and spotted McKinnon behind the bar. He was speaking with an elderly gentleman. He saw Margolis and signaled for him to come over.

The detective obliged. Margolis recognized the old man from the security tape. The bar owner introduced the two men and explained that the elderly man, whose name was Strickland, had some information that Margolis might find useful. Margolis pulled out his notepad.

"I came here for a drink or two like I always do," the elderly man began, "and I asked about Amanda. She usually serves me. Pretty girl. Ol' Tom here," the old man said, jerking a thumb at the owner, "he said you come 'round here in the middle of the night askin' questions about her and all. So's I'ze a little worried. Tom sayz she didn't show up to work today. Didn't call or nuthin'."

"Tom says you have some information that may help me."

"I'm gettin' to that. Anyway, Tom sayz no one knows where Amanda is."

"Do you know where she is?"

"No, but I know who she left *with* last night." The old man sipped his drink. "That foreigner with the dark hair and fancy jacket. He was sweet talkin' her."

"Are you sure?"

"Sure, I'm sure. I looked through the window and saw her get into his car."

"Thank you." Margolis turned to the owner. "Do you have a name for the man in the jacket? Did he pay by credit card?"

McKinnon shook his head. "Already checked. He used cash."

The old man described the foreigner's car, but didn't get a license plate number. He said that the man introduced himself with some foreign name, Igor, Boris or something like that. He couldn't remember exactly. He didn't think it was important at the time.

"Could you hear the conversation between the man and his companion?" Margolis asked.

"They weren't speakin' American. Sure as hell wasn't Spanish. I hear Spanish all the time, and it weren't that."

"So you couldn't give me a guess? Arabic? French? Swahili?"

"Sounded like gobbledygook to me, detective."

"Okay. Thank you." Margolis closed his notebook. The old man was out of useful information, but now Margolis knew what his prime suspect looked like. And he knew which step to take next.

• • •

At Brindisi Airbase in Italy, the rotor blades on two Pave Hawk helicopters whirled as they prepared to leave for the second time that day. They had gotten word that the stand down order had been rescinded, and the search and rescue of the possible survivors of the downed C-17 Globemaster III was reinstated. The PJs on board checked their equipment and braced themselves for takeoff.

The helicopters lifted off and headed east toward Serbia. They were on their way to the last known position of the plane carrying Paxton and his team. They knew they had less than thirty-six hours to locate and extract any survivors. Many of them knew Paxton. They were determined to rescue their own—or die trying.

● ● ●

Margolis knocked on the apartment door. Amanda's room-mate answered almost immediately. "Here," she said, handing Margolis an envelope.

Margolis opened the envelope and peered inside. It contained several 4x6 photographs of Amanda. He peered at her smiling face, captured in various situations—fun with friends. "These will do nicely. Thank you."

"Will I get them back? I took 'em out of her drawer."

"Yes, of course."

"Have you found out anything else?"

"No," Margolis lied.

"You will call me as soon as you learn anything?"

"Yes, I will. Thank you again."

• • •

Paxton and Smith walked out of earshot of the others. They stayed out of the clearing so their camouflage, Smith's Air Force BDUs and Paxton's mercenary uniform, gave them some measure of concealment. The other airmen and Mc-Murphy were grouped by the injured pilot and were getting antsy to leave.

"A two-star general named Reed ordered me to send you and the rest of the team out to search for Cue Ball," Paxton said. "I'm disobeying that direct order, Smith. And I'm going to disobey another one."

"Oh, Christ."

"Reed doesn't care if we rescue Cue Ball or not. Our efforts are only a distraction."

"From what?"

"Reed's true goal." Paxton explained. "I don't know what that is, either. But he's an asshole, so I don't think his intentions are good."

"You're making no damn sense. You sure you didn't hit *your* head?" Smith studied his leader. "What the hell are you not telling me?"

"Here's where I disobey the second order by telling you this: We were supposed to use the bulldozer and the dump truck to recover the Stealth fighter wreckage. Then we were supposed to drive the dump truck onto the Globemaster and bring it to the States."

"Why would he want us to bring back wreckage?"

"A less suspicious man would say Reed doesn't want the bird to get into the wrong hands. Both the Russians and the Chinese would love to get a close look at a real Stealth fighter."

"Why not just bomb the hell out of it?"

Pax shrugged.

"'So others may live' *doesn't* include hunks of metal," Smith said. "And even if it did, we can't recover the plane without the bulldozer. Maybe we should search for Cue Ball. We can't get the wreckage."

"I think Cue Ball is safe and sound," Paxton explained. "We're the B Team, my man. My guess is that the A Team already rescued Cue Ball."

"That's bullshit, Pax."

"Think about it. There's no way a team launched from the States would get here in time to be of significant value in a rescue. Teams would have been launched from within the theater. Either from Italy or from a Navy ship in the Adriatic."

"I thought the rescue crews were overwhelmed."

"No. Rescues worldwide are coordinated out of Scott AFB in Illinois, and I'll bet my next paycheck that the only two planes to go down are the Stealth and ours." Pax scanned the forest around them. Everyone was within viewing distance. He knew he had to wrap this up before McMurphy tracked him down. "It gets worse, Smith. Our flight was not logged into any official records anywhere. If we're caught or killed, we're on our own. Reed told me that we don't exist."

Smith's eyes widened. "Son of a bitch!"

"If we're getting out of here, we have to do it without any

help from the U.S. military. We need the assistance of a local Muslim named Jashari who's part of the KLA. He's our ticket out of here ... and only McMurphy knows how to contact him."

"That's why you're doing a mission with him, isn't it? He won't give you the information unless you do whatever the hell it is he wants." Smith shook his head. "And if you don't show up in twenty-four hours, we're on our own. This is one helluva stupid plan, Pax."

"You have a better one?"

"Let's beat the shit out of McMurphy and make him tell us how to contact Jashari," Smith offered.

"I already tried that. McMurphy won't talk."

"So that's why you scuffled with him on the plane?"

"Yeah."

"What does McMurphy want from you?"

"To watch his back."

"Right." Smith kicked the hard ground. "This is such a clusterfuck. Why did Reed launch this mission from the States? If it was so important to recover the plane, why waste the flight time? Don't they have bulldozers in Italy?"

"Maybe the mission isn't about recovering the plane or the pilot." Paxton's gaze landed on McMurphy, who was looking pissed and impatient. "The whole purpose was to insert McMurphy so he could execute Reed's plans."

"They didn't need all of us to do that!" Smith exclaimed. "Can I tell the others about this?"

"Hell, no."

"No offense, Pax, but why did they pick you? They didn't need to fly you from Texas to create a distraction. We could have done that without you—you're an old man."

"Screw you," he said, grinning. "Reed told me I was qualified."

Smith grinned back, but he knew that chances were slim any of them would leave Yugoslavia. "This is fucked up."

"Yeah," Paxton said. "Let's get out of here."

• • •

Margolis sat across the desk from the news editor of the local television station. The Lake Mary station served the Orlando area and was affiliated with a national cable news network. Margolis had called upon the station for their assistance in the past. He pushed the photographs that Amanda's roommate had given him across the desk along with the CD that the bar owner had given him.

"I'd really appreciate any exposure you could give us on this," Margolis said.

"Too late to get on the early evening news, but we can do something on the ten o'clock news. So this is a missing person's case?"

"Yes. I'm hoping maybe one of your viewers might have seen either the young woman or the man with the jacket," Margolis said, tapping the CD.

The newsman loaded the CD into his computer. Within seconds, the bar's surveillance tape began to play on the screen.

"That's him," Margolis said as the dark-haired man walked inside with his large companion. "See if you can capture a good frontal shot of him and his friend and show those on tonight's news along with a picture of the woman. Ask anyone who recognizes them or who has seen them recently to call the department and ask for me."

"No problem," the newsman said.

CHAPTER 19

PAXTON AND SMITH JOINED THE OTHERS IN THE WOODS AT the edge of the clearing. Thompson was seated on the ground, his broken leg roughly splinted and bandaged. Next to him sat the co-pilot and the loadmaster. Three of the PJs and the Combat Controller watched the clearing through the scopes of their rifles, expecting trouble to arrive at any moment. The remaining PJs were removing evidence of the group's existence. McMurphy stood there, leaning with his outstretched right arm on a tree, impatiently looking at his watch.

"You all are the sorriest rescue team I've ever seen in my life," Thompson said. "You've given Cue Ball a death sentence."

"Let's go, Paxton," McMurphy demanded. "And take a weapon."

"No, my team keeps the weapons. They've injured men to protect," Paxton replied.

"You can't watch my back if you don't have a goddamned gun."

"Guess you better hope I'm good at hand-to-hand," Paxton replied.

"Take Major Thompson's pistol," Smith said.

"No."

"We're late," McMurphy snapped. He spun on his heel and walked toward the clearing.

Paxton looked at Smith. "Good luck, Sergeant."

"Pax ... don't get yourself killed."

"Wouldn't dream of it." Paxton followed McMurphy. It only took a moment for him to catch up. "So where we going?" Paxton asked.

"Belgrade."

"Aren't we bombing that city?"

"U.S. forces are conducting bombing sorties."

"What's your plan to avoid getting blown up?"

"Simple. I won't stand under any bombs," McMurphy answered. "I highly recommend you do the same."

The two men continued walking in silence. They reached the tree line on the other side of the clearing and pushed their way into the dense forest. The air was chilly. The heavy scent of pine trees blotted out the lingering smell from the burning wreckage of the Globemaster.

"So why do you *really* need me?" Paxton asked as he and Mc-Murphy made their way under branches and around trunks.

"Like I said, to watch my back."

"Dammit McMurphy, you're impossible. Give me some answers."

"No can do. Sorry." Again McMurphy's tone was not apologetic.

"Who am I watching out for?"

"The bad guys." McMurphy looked at Paxton over his shoulder. "Anyone who wants to harm me is a bad guy."

"Shit, McMurphy, that makes me a bad guy."

Paxton thought he heard McMurphy chuckle, but wasn't sure. *Nah. He doesn't have a sense of humor.* Paxton followed him to where the forest thinned out and revealed a paved road. He spotted the subcompact car and followed McMurphy to the old Yugo Koral.

"You've got to be kidding me," Paxton said as he looked at the dented fenders and rusted red paint. "A Yugo?"

"They make them over at the Zastava Yugo plant in Kragujevac. It's a nice university town not all that far from here," McMurphysaid as he opened the driver's side door. "It's better than walking."

Paxton looked at the balding tires caked with mud. "Don't count on it."

"Get in," McMurphy commanded.

Paxton reluctantly opened the passenger door. It creaked and popped as he swung it wide. A dank smell wafted out from the torn vinyl interior. Blech. The seat squashed down to its wiry frame under Paxton's weight and emitted a musty puff of air. His knees wedged against the cracked dashboard. Reaching down, he depressed the lever to adjust the seat. He wiggled and pushed against the dash only to discover that the seat was already as far back as it would go. He pulled the door shut. It crowded against his right leg and shoulder. He reached back for the seatbelt to find that there was none.

McMurphy guided the key into the ignition, knocked the gearshift into neutral and started the engine. Amazingly it caught on the first try. White smoke billowed out of the exhaust pipe as McMurphy shifted into gear and the car lurched forward. He turned the wheel and steered the car onto the blacktop.

"Where did you get this piece of shit?" Paxton asked.

"I borrowed it," McMurphy answered, checking his rearview mirror.

"Don't you think whoever you *borrowed* it from will report you to the authorities? Every cop and soldier in the country will look for this car."

"The owner will have to untie himself first."

"You could have killed him."

"He's an old man, local farmer. He didn't put up much of a fight."

Paxton glanced at McMurphy then he looked out the front windshield. *So McMurphy isn't as cold-blooded as I thought.* Paxton said nothing more as the Yugo puttered down the road.

Neither Paxton nor McMurphy noticed the old Mercedes panel truck pull out from its hiding place in the woods. The truck turned onto the road and followed the Yugo's smoky trail.

• • •

Back in the woods, Smith assumed command. "Okay, gentlemen. Let's move out," he said.

The airmen picked up all their items. Thompson was lifted

onto Petersen's back, piggyback style, his splinted leg dangling down. Petersen had to lean forward to balance the weight of the pilot. Weil and the loadmaster followed the others. Smith checked the coordinates on the GPS receiver and pointed out the direction. They headed deeper into the woods, farther from the burning wreckage, and farther, they all hoped, from any approaching Serbian patrols.

• • •

Flying low above the Adriatic Sea the two Pave Hawk helicopters full of PJs flew from Italy toward Serbia. The dangerous daylight rescue proceeded with speed and precision. The copters headed directly for the spot that had been tracked on radar as the location of the impact of the largest section of wreckage from the Globemaster.

They headed directly for the spot Smith, Paxton and the others had just vacated.

• • •

The tap-tapping of the Yugo's engine was almost mesmerizing. "How's your Russian?"

"Excuse me?" Paxton said as he turned and stared at McMurphy. His neck still bore the marks from the rope Paxton had strangled him with.

"I read your personnel file. You took two semesters of Russian at St. Mary's University."

"Fucking General Reed." Paxton shook his head and

grimaced. "I can hardly read it and can't speak it worth shit."

"Your transcripts showed that you got top grades."'

"Why are my college transcripts in my personnel file?"

"That's the trade off when you have the Air Force pay for your education."

I had to provide proof of my progress in night classes along with my requests for tuition vouchers. Shit. "I studied hard and sweated out the exams. I did what I had to do to satisfy my foreign language requirement then promptly dumped the information out of my head."

McMurphy smacked the steering wheel. "Son of a bitch."

"Were you expecting me to translate something for you?"

"No. I speak it fluently."

"I don't get it," Paxton said. "If you already speak it, why do you need me? I don't speak Yugoslavian either."

"Serbo-Croat."

"What?"

"The language is called Serbo-Croat not Yugoslavian. I'm fluent in that language too."

"Whatever. I'm a pre-med major, not a linguist."

"This fucks things up." McMurphy looked at Paxton then back at the road. "You and I are supposed to be Russian advisors."

"That's why you picked me? You thought I could speak Russian?" Paxton almost laughed. It was a ridiculous reason to be taken from his family, his job—to be railroaded into a mission that had not yet been revealed to him.

"Reed asked for a pararescueman who could speak Russian.

Yours was the only name that came back."

"So if I had taken a different foreign language class, I would be sitting at home right now?"

"Yes."

General Dickhead Reed had royally screwed up. *I'm gonna die in fucking Yugoslavia because I chose Russian over French.* Paxton punched the door pillar with the side of his fist so hard that the window rattled. "What do we do now?"

"We proceed."

"Are you crazy? What happens when we reach the point where I'm supposed to speak Russian?"

"You're an honors student. Fake it. It's not like you have to fool the Russians."

"Who do I have to convince I'm a Russian advisor?"

"The Serbs."

"This place is crawling with Russians, who are the Serbs' biggest ally. What if we run into some of those bastards? "

McMurphy shrugged. "You'd better hope we don't meet any—or hope that your language skills miraculously recover. Otherwise, you're never going to see your family again."

· · ·

By morning, the news spread through the PJ community at Lackland. Wives of other PJs arrived on Jill Paxton's doorstep with arms full of covered dishes. They brought food and companionship to join Jill in her vigil awaiting word on the fate of her missing husband. She gratefully welcomed them into her home. Someone brewed coffee. Her children were entertained in the backyard. Jill tried to be strong in front of the others. She knew that their husbands went on missions all the time and they could find themselves in her very position. She didn't want to be the one to remind them of the dangers their husbands constantly faced. *But why did it have to be hers?* The weight of not knowing whether he was dead or alive was too much. She broke down and cried.

• • •

The Yugo crested a hill while following a sweeping curve. Looming in the oncoming lane was a series of large green trucks packed with soldiers. Both McMurphy and Paxton caught their breath. *Serbian troops.* Paxton counted the trucks as they rounded the bend. *One, two, three, four … five, six….* Trucks kept appearing from around the bend, one after another. And the open back of each one overflowed with soldiers, rifles pointed in the air. McMurphy hugged the edge of the road to make room for the approaching convoy. It was way too late to turn around.

As the first truck rumbled toward them, it flashed its lights and the driver stuck his hand out the window, palm facing the Yugo, fingers spread, pulsating it toward them, indicating his desire for them to stop. Paxton squeezed his fist until the tension made his arm shake. *Had the farmer untied himself and reported the Yugo stolen?* McMurphy applied the brakes.

"What the hell are you doing?" Paxton asked.

"I'm stopping." McMurphy said. "Try to look innocent."

The lead truck came to a complete stop and McMurphy pulled up next to the driver's window. The truck's engine turned off. McMurphy cranked his window open as the soldiers in the back of the truck looked down suspiciously. The truck driver leaned out of his window and said something loudly to McMurphy in a language Paxton couldn't understand. McMurphy stuck his head out and replied. McMurphy and the truck driver continued to converse as Paxton tried to look innocent. Paxton felt the soldiers' stares, and he heard them shouting taunts. He wished he had taken Smith up on his offer of the pistol.

Paxton realized it would seem suspicious to ignore them. The soldiers were laughing and smoking and one of them leaned over the side of the truck and showed Paxton his rifle. His mind scrambled for the correct reaction.

McMurphy turned toward him and spoke in an indecipherable language. Russian. Paxton watched his mouth in hopes of gaining a clue about what he was saying. He searched his memory for the meanings of the words flooding his ears. In the verbal staccato, Paxton suddenly understood *smile* and *nod*. Paxton followed McMurphy's instructions: He smiled and nodded.

McMurphy turned and stuck his head out the window again and spoke to the truck driver. McMurphy talked to the Serbs in their own language, and then, to keep up their cover, spoke to him in Russian. He stuck his right arm out the window and pointed back the way they had come. Paxton avoided looking at the soldiers.

Suddenly the truck's pre-heater buzzed and the diesel engine cranked to life. The driver ground it into gear and the truck bucked forward. *They're leaving,* thought Paxton. McMurphy cranked up his window and put the car in gear. *And we're leaving.* The soldiers continued their taunts as the truck passed by. McMurphy let out the clutch, gave an absent-minded wave to the men and drove forward. *Seven trucks in all.* McMurphy watched them disappear in his rearview mirror.

"What the hell was that all about?" asked Paxton.

"They were looking for the big plane that crashed. I told them we didn't see any plane, but we saw a big fire in the woods."

"You *sent* them to the *crash site?*"

"We have to keep cover. If I gave bad directions, they might remember the strangers in the Yugo and get suspicious. Right now, the last thing in the world they expect Americans to do after surviving a plane crash would be to dress like mercenaries, speak Serbo-Croat and Russian, hop in a Yugo and drive to Belgrade."

"I see your point."

"Don't worry. Your men will be long gone. Let the Serbs busy themselves picking around the wreckage."

Paxton kept silent, mainly because he couldn't bring himself to give McMurphy a genuine compliment. The asshole was right.

"By the way, your Russian sucks. I could tell by the look on your face that you couldn't understand a word I was saying."

"I understood when you told me to smile and nod."

McMurphy huffed and grimaced.

"What?"

McMurphy glanced at Paxton. "The only reason you understood those words was because I said them in *English.*"

• • •

The convoy of seven trucks filled with Serbian troops passed the Mercedes panel truck that was headed down the small road in the same direction as the Yugo. The trucks were rushing to the crash site and did not bother to stop the Mercedes. The driver of the Mercedes stayed far enough away from the Yugo as to be virtually out of sight, but still close enough to follow the dissipating white smoke trail.

• • •

"Local police are investigating a mysterious death. Fire crews were called to the parking lot outside *The Dugout,* a local watering hole, sometime after three a.m.," the TV news broadcaster said. "After they put out the flames on an older model Toyota, they discovered a body inside the vehicle. The police are asking for your help in locating individuals who might shed some light on the incident."

The television screen cut to three photographs, side by side. The one on the left was a color photograph of Amanda smiling. The other two photographs were black and white still shots taken from the surveillance video. The middle picture was Delevic. The photo on the far right was Labus.

"Please call the Crime Halter's Hotline if you have any information." The number was displayed prominently below the three photos.

The television remained on, with the sound low, in the bedroom of the hotel clerk. Next to his head lay open the novel he had been reading the night before. And he was sound asleep, oblivious to the newscast.

• • •

Paxton rode in silence, reconstructing over and over the incident with the Serbian convoy. He couldn't remember shit about the Russian language. Damn it! He never thought he'd actuallyneed to use what he'd learned. The nearly unbearable tension seemed to have clamped off all but his most fundamental skills. In a crisis, people did not rise to the pinnacle of their abilities, but instead fell to the level of their fundamental training. His whole training philosophy at Superman School was founded upon that principle. That was why he emphasized the fundamentals. His trainees were capable of performing certain critical tasks quite literally in their sleep. He knew it to be true and he was, once again, living it.

But it still pissed him off.

More accurately, he was pissed at himself for his inability to recall. It was like that part of his brain had been walled off. The hurricane shutters had been put up and he couldn't get inside. Why hadn't he spent more time practicing the language? Why hadn't he attempted to retain some of that hard-earned knowledge?

He knew why.

He worked a crazy schedule, training airmen for one of the hardest jobs on the planet. He hardly saw his wife and two young children. He was taking night classes so he could have a career outside the military. The truth was, learning that language was never important to him. It was merely a hurdle that he had to propel himself over, like he had so many other hurdles in his life.

But that hurdle had now become a roadblock.

He had to figure out how to get past the roadblock.

"I'm not clear on our cover story," Paxton said to McMurphy. "If we're Russian advisors, why aren't we wearing Russian uniforms?"

"We're freelance. You and I are former Russian military who got out and now sell our services to the highest bidder."

"Hence the mercenary angle." Paxton nodded. "Okay. *What* are we advising and *who* wants our advice?"

"The less you know, the less you can tell anyone else."

"Why don't you cut the bullshit? I have a top-secret security clearance, damn it."

"I don't care if God named you one of the apostles," McMurphy said. "I'm not telling you shit. Hell, I know *I* won't talk. I'm not so sure about you."

"I know the drill: Name, Rank and Serial Number. That's all they get from me," Paxton said. "Under the UCMJ and the Geneva convention—"

"Are you serious? You have no ID, you're not wearing a United States military uniform, and your foreign language skills suck. If you're captured, you'll be named a *spy*."

• • •

Traffic started picking up on the small road on which Paxton and McMurphy traveled. No other vehicle attempted to stop them. The road widened and occasionally they saw a house or a shop.

McMurphy turned right at one of the intersections and drove into a more densely populated area. He made left and right turns and finally entered a parking lot filled with cars, including Serbian military vehicles.

Paxton peered at the old wooden building with a slanted roof. In the windows on either side of door shone neon signs with swirly letters advertising product names Paxton couldn't read. He stared at the sign featuring an oversized mug with overflowing fake foam. It was unmistakably a neighborhood bar.

"Why are we here?" Paxton asked.

"To get a drink."

"I could use a drink, too."

"Since you don't speak the language, I'll order. What will you have?" McMurphy asked as he climbed out of the small car.

"Just get me a beer," Paxton replied as he exited the Yugo. Outside the bar were several small tables and chairs. The weather was still too cold to make sitting outside comfortable.

Paxton followed McMurphy into the bar. They stood in the entranceway, Paxton on McMurphy's right, slightly behind. The interior was dark, loud, smoky, and surprisingly crowded. The patrons were almost exclusively men; more than half wore military uniforms. Across from the door was a long bar with six men sitting along it consuming drinks. Above the bar was a large photograph of Slobodan Milosevic, the Serbian president. The men not in military uniforms were well dressed compared with the patrons of most neighborhood bars in America. Many wore tweed jackets and some wore ties.

Paxton felt like all eyes were upon them. McMurphy scanned the interior and selected an empty table. Paxton followed. He couldn't have felt more uncomfortable had he been crossing the room naked. McMurphy selected the seat facing the front door, leaving Paxton to sit on the opposite side. The ashtray centered between them looked as if it hadn't been emptied in a week.

People were laughing and talking, but Paxton couldn't understand a word being said. *Am I supposed to be watching McMurphy's back now?* He couldn't ask because he didn't want to be overheard speaking English.

McMurphy caught the attention of the bartender. He said something to Paxton in Russian and got up. Paxton watched him walk to the far end of the bar and the bartender met him there. He said something and the bartender looked at Paxton, then turned and walked toward the center of the bar. He bent down and came back up with two dark bottles, which he opened. He handed the bottles to McMurphy, who paid, and the two men engaged in a brief conversation. The bartender pointed as if he were giving directions. McMurphy returned to the table with the beers.

McMurphy slid one dark bottle to Paxton and leaned in close. Paxton matched his posture. "Change of plans," McMurphy whispered in English.

Paxton grabbed the cold bottle and sipped. The beer was dark and bitter. And refreshing as hell. "What's up?"

"We're not going into town. We're returning to the countryside."

"Why?"

McMurphy swallowed half his beer and banged his bottle on the table. "I have to see a man about a job."

CHAPTER 20

PAXTON AND MCMURPHY FINISHED THEIR BEERS AND l eft the warmth of the bar. Paxton folded himself into the Yugo and slammed the door shut. McMurphy turned the key and the engine whir-whirred to life. The tapping sound in the sewing machine under the hood was worse than ever and Paxton wondered whether there was any oil left in the engine. McMurphy backed the car through its own smoke trail and pointed it in the direction of the road. The interior of the car filled with the smell of burnt oil. They headed away from Belgrade.

The Mercedes panel truck backed out of its spot in the bar's parking lot and turned onto the road, following the Yugo from a great distance.

• • •

Inside the bar, the bartender picked up the phone. He dialed and spoke a few words into the receiver. Then he hung up and returned to serving customers.

• • •

General Rugova arrived at the Stealth fighter's crash site. Nikolic greeted him as he got out of his staff car. Rugova tightly gripped a leather bag in his right hand. Nikolic offered to carry it for him, but Rugova waved him off. The cameras from the international media captured the moment and beamed it around the world via oversized satellite trucks lined up along the muddy road. Reporters speculated about the identity of the man who had just arrived and his purpose. Any report, no matter how insignificant, framed with the backdrop of the downed American fighter plane, was big news among the enemies of the United States be they foreign or domestic.

Crowds still lined up to sit in the cockpit. A Serbian police officer sat on top of the wreckage and worked to keep order. A handful of Serbian troops ringed the perimeter of the wreckage. The soldiers were relaxed, but heavily armed. They kept a close eye on all the gawking people. They intended to protect Serbia's new prized possession.

• • •

McMurphy drove away from Belgrade in the Yugo, but he was not using the same road they had taken to town. Traffic was relatively light.

Paxton could still taste the bitterness of the beer. As McMurphy turned from one road to another, he did not once refer to a map.

"Why don't we work on some Russian phrases? Stuff you think might come up since you're the only one who knows where we are going."

McMurphy nodded.

"Let's start with the basics," Paxton said. "What's my name? I need a Russian name."

"Your real name is John, so you are Ivan, the Russian form of John."

"What's your Russian name?"

"Grigori."

"So is your real name Gregory?"

"No." McMurphy answered too quickly. "Never mind. It's too late for you to start re-learning Russian."

"I'm a quick study. Let's keep working on it. God knows we have nothing else to talk about."

"Your best bet is to keep your mouth shut." McMurphy sighed. "Oh, all right."

The two men worked on key phrases. McMurphy taught Paxton to sound out *Glad to meet you* and *thank you*. Slowly, some of Paxton's lessons returned. Before long, the phrases rolled off his tongue. They added a few more: *Good Afternoon, Yes, No,* and most important, *Grigori, look out*! The goal wasn't to speak Russian like a Russian. It was to sound like a Yugoslavian thought a Russian should sound. Content wasn't as important as delivery. McMurphy wasn't expecting to encounter anyone who spoke Russian.

The road narrowed and became markedly more rural. They passed pastureland, small farms, and lots of old growth European forest. Paxton wished they had grabbed something to eat at the bar. His stomach ached, and he wasn't sure if it was from lack of food or from nerves. Paxton felt the glow of doom grow with every passing mile. After a while, all that broke the silence was the tap-tapping of the engine and the hum of the bald tires rolling on asphalt. The beer had amplified Paxton's weariness. He almost dozed off.

McMurphy slowed down and craned his neck, looking around. Paxton was immediately alert. On both sides of the road were parked cars. Ahead on the left was a dirt road. McMurphy slowed the car and turned onto the deeply rutted path. Mud splashed onto the windshield as the Yugo lurched forward.

They encountered men, women and children, who moved to the side of the road and allowed the Yugo to pass. Some of the people smiled and waved at them. McMurphy and Paxton smiled and waved back. Paxton looked back as they passed one group and the people continued to wave, but they were no longer waves of greeting but instead turned to waving the car's oily smoke away from their faces. The car bounced and splashed down the sloppy road, McMurphy fighting the wheel as the tires plowed through furrows.

Then the sky brightened as the woods thinned out. The road curved and the surroundings opened up to rolling hills of pastureland. Paxton's eyes, however, opened wide at the sight in front of him.

To the left was dense forest. To the right was a wooden fence and a wide expanse of pastureland. Directly in front of them, parked along the dirt road, were more Serbian military trucks than Paxton could immediately count. And not just trucks but troops were there too, surely numbering in the hundreds.

"Shit," Paxton said.

McMurphy said nothing. He slowed the car to a crawl.

Paxton scanned the crowd. Along with the soldiers, there were hundreds of civilians milling about, mostly off to the left side. There were many civilian vehicles there as well.

"What are you doing?" Paxton asked.

"Finding a parking spot."

"Let me guess. You need me to watch your back?"

"You are a quick study."

"And you are an asshole."

McMurphy didn't reply. He found an empty space along the right side of the road and maneuvered the small car between a pickup truck and an old station wagon. He then turned off the motor. There was silence inside the musty interior, except for the crowd's murmurs.

"Let's go," McMurphy said as he popped open his door. Cold air flowed in and the crowd noise grew louder. He got out and stood next to the car.

Paxton felt around for the door latch and pulled it. His door squawked open. The cool air blew on the right side of his face and his eyes teared up, blurring his vision. He climbed out of the Yugo, careful not to hit his head on the low door jam. He stood up, pulled his uniform overshirt down to straighten it out, and looked around.

Parked up the road were several large trucks with satellite dishes. They were not military trucks. Painted in various bright colors, they touted international news organization logos. Paxton recognized at least two news networks among them. He heard the hum of generators in the background. *What is all the fuss about?*

Then he saw it.

Laying flat on its belly behind the throng of onlookers was the wreckage of the Stealth fighter. The flat black paint made the fuselage look cold. He could see only a portion of the plane; the majority of it was blocked by a massive military truck. Civilians stood there, mainly with their backs to him, looking at the strange plane. He could see the faces of soldiers on the plane's perimeter, vigilantly looking outward, rifles at the ready. A line of civilians wound to the side of the aircraft waiting for their turn to climb inside the cockpit. *We wouldn't have been able to cart off the Stealth fighter. Reed knew about this bullshit.*

McMurphy finished surveying the scene and bent over to reach into the car. He folded the driver's seat forward and stretched his arm to the backseat. He then stood up, pulling his worn green backpack out of the car. Paxton heard the familiar metallic clanging. The pack was still heavy given the way McMurphy hoisted it onto his right shoulder. He didn't bother to put his left shoulder through the strap. He reached again into the car and pulled out his AK-74 rifle. He held that next to his side, grasping it by the receiver, the barrel pointing down. He then indicated "let's go" with a jerk of his head and slammed the door. Paxton slammed his door shut, too, and followed.

McMurphy walked across the dirt road toward the bulk of the crowd. As Paxton caught up to him, McMurphy held the rifle out to him. Paxton hesitated, but then accepted it. He imitated McMurphy's carrying style as they continued walking right toward a group of Serbian soldiers. Paxton's throat was tight and his stomach was an ocean of acid. He tried to walk lightly, nonchalantly. The tools in McMurphy's pack clanged with every step.

They passed the side of the truck that blocked the view of the Nighthawk. The cockpit was missing its canopy. The civilians waited patiently for their turn to sit in the plane. A man in a police uniform was seated on the fuselage just behind the open cockpit. From time to time, the policeman tapped the shoulder of the person sitting inside the plane. That person would get out and the next in line would climb in. The procession edged up another step.

Along the right side of the plane was a group of television cameras. Bored camera operators stood behind their equipment. Tangles of wires led away from the cameras to the various satellite trucks. Near the video equipment stood several nicely dressed men and women. Some of them held microphones by their sides or under their arms. *Reporters*, thought Paxton as he scanned the scene. Some eyes followed the two men as they walked up, but the television people were mostly engrossed in preparations for production.

Paxton felt, however, that every soldier was watching him. He did his best to carry the rifle McMurphy had handed him in a non-threatening fashion. He didn't want to give anyone an excuse to blast him away. It occurred to him that he didn't know if the rifle was loaded or not. It didn't matter. Even if the thirty-round magazine were full, he could empty it on full auto and it still wouldn't be enough to save him. The soldiers could cut him and McMurphy down. Besides, there were too many villagers around. Paxton didn't want to start shooting with children running and playing everywhere. Paxton looked around and calculated his odds of survival. The math wasn't on his side.

McMurphy headed toward a group of Serbian officers. They turned and looked at the approaching men. One held a black leather bag in his hand. Their stares were unbearable. It took all his concentration and discipline to walk toward them, even though McMurphy never broke stride. Paxton's ears muffled all the background noise and focused only on the backpack's clanking sound and the thump of his own boots on the muddy grass. The world seemed to move in slow motion. Paxton expected them to give an order to open fire at any moment.

Paxton focused on the officer's ranks. There were two stars on the collar of the man with the bag. *A general.* The man next to him appeared to be a lieutenant colonel. There were also two captains. Four men. Eight eyes staring right at him. *We're supposed to be on their side,* thought Paxton. *Russian advisors. Mercenaries.*

Paxton's mind raced. Despite the chill in the air, he felt sweat drip from his temple down his cheek. *All I have to do is fake it well enough to fool the Serbs,* he assured himself. He scanned the officers. He glanced around as much as he dared. Good news. *No Russians.* Paxton had started his military career on the tail end of the Cold War so he knew what a Russian military uniform looked like.

Paxton adjusted his grip on the rifle as they closed the last ten meters to the Serbs. They were almost to the edge of the semicircle when the lieutenant colonel stepped forward. He reached his hand out, a big smile on his face. "Grigori!"

McMurphy gripped the man's outstretched hand. The tools in the bag clanked in time with each pump of McMurphy's arm. "Vojislav!"

Paxton realized he had been holding his breath. He let it out and forced a smile.

McMurphy and the lieutenant colonel spoke excitedly in Serb-Croat. Paxton stood back, kept quiet, and observed. Obviously, this was some sort of friendly reunion. Catching up on old times perhaps? *How does he know this guy?* After a moment, the lieutenant colonel introduced McMurphy to the other Serbian officers. The general was Dragisa Rugova. He switched his bag to his left to shake hands with McMurphy. Then McMurphy brought the lieutenant colonel to Paxton and rattled off some words in Russian. McMurphy looked at Paxton and placed his hand on Serb's chest and said, "Vojislav Nikolic." Then he placed his hand on Paxton's chest, looked at Nikolic, and said "Ivan."

Paxton and Nikolic shook hands. Nikolic's grip was firm, but friendly. Paxton said, "Glad to meet you," in Russian, just as they had practiced. Nikolic smiled politely, but Paxton realized the man didn't understand a word.

McMurphy and Nikolic continued their conversation. They turned to face the wreckage of the Nighthawk and each took turns pointing to different segments of the fuselage. Paxton shifted his weight trying to dissipate nervous energy. Then McMurphy and Nikolic turned to face each other again. Paxton didn't have to speak the language to discern that the conversation had taken a more serious turn.

Nikolic grasped McMurphy by the upper arm and led him to the general. Nikolic said a few words to the general, who replied. McMurphy spoke and the general opened the leather bag and held it out to McMurphy for inspection. He leaned down and peered inside then reached in and moved around something. He stepped back, nodded, and shook hands again with Nikolic.

• • •

Colonel Ward sat at his desk at Lackland. He had not slept and probably wouldn't until he knew about Paxton's fate. His rubbed his eyes and asked, "How much time has elapsed?"

Sgt. Machette looked at his digital watch. "About ten hours, sir."

"Twenty-six hours before Reed levels the crash site. Any word from Rescue?"

Machette shook his head. "Nothing, sir."

Ward propped his elbow on his desk and leaned his face into his palm.

• • •

The Serbian army convoy arrived in the vicinity of the crash site. They had followed the directions McMurphy had given them on the road earlier and all seven trucks pulled off the asphalt alongside where black smoke billowed up behind the trees. The soldiers piled out of the trucks and lined up awaiting further instructions. The sergeant in charge ordered the men to spread out and search for survivors. He told them to be ready for anything. He said Lt. Col. Nikolic had ordered that every effort be made to capture the downed airmen alive, but he added that he wouldn't lose any sleep if his men killed the Americans. The soldiers cheered and weaved into the piney woods to commence their hunt.

• • •

The Mercedes panel truck rolled cautiously to a halt at the end of the row of parked cars that lined the muddy dirt road. Its lone occupant adjusted the heavy coat sitting next to him on the front seat to make sure that it completely covered his automatic weapon. A scar ran from the corner of his left eye to his earlobe. He could have been mistaken for just another local farmer or craftsman.

He reached over, opened the glove box, and removed an item. He slipped the item into the left pocket of the wool jacket. His pistol already occupied the right pocket.

He locked the van then walked up the row of cars. Casually,

he peered into the Yugo. It was empty. He crossed the dirt road, walking toward the downed Stealth fighter. He disappeared into the crowd in search of his two targets.

• • •

The pararescuemen led by Smith moved through the woods. Smith had elected to take the long way to their rendezvous point. A more direct route would have no doubt been easier, particularly since they were transporting an injured man. That route, however, would have left them without cover for many hundreds of meters at various points along the way. Since it was broad daylight, Smith felt it wasn't worth the risk. So using the map and GPS unit, he devised a more circuitous route, keeping to the natural cover of the woods as much as possible.

Petersen hitched Thompson up to a better position on his back for what must have been the fiftieth time since they set out. Thompson winced with pain each time. The Combat Controller was the current point man for the group. He walked in front, his M4 carbine at the ready. Airman Dobbins was at the rear of the group. He lingered approximately fifty meters from the rest to make sure they weren't followed. He moved from cover to cover, scanning rearward with the optical scope mounted on the top of his rifle. The other two PJs with rifles walked alongside Weil and the loadmaster. Smith had kept Thompson's pistol for himself.

"Why can'twe search for Cue Ball, Sergeant Smith?" Petersen asked.

"It's no longer our mission," Smith replied. "Pax says...."

Shit. Well, it was a day for disobeying orders. "Pax thinks Cue Ball has been rescued."

"He *thinks?* What the hell is that supposed to mean?" Thompson demanded, imposing on their conversation.

"We're canceling the rescue based on a *hunch?*" Petersen asked.

"Sergeant Smith," Thompson said, "I hope you realize that Sergeant Paxton hasn't used sound judgment. We have only his word that Cue Ball is not in danger. I think you ought to reconsider your decision before it's too late."

"We will follow Sergeant Paxton's orders," Smith said, his voice firm.

"We should make sure Cue Ball is safe," Petersen demanded.

Paxton was right. I shouldn't have told them. Now he had to hold off a near mutiny. "Enough!" he shouted, stopping in his tracks. Everyone was so startled, they stopped too. He continued in a controlled tone, "The mission has changed. We are not to search for Cue Ball." He looked each of his men one by one. They saw that he meant what he said. And if Smith believed in Paxton, then they would, too—whether they liked it or not.

"Let's go." Smith turned and continued walking. The others followed and no one else said a word.

• • •

Paxton watched the entire interaction McMurphy had with Nikolic and General Rugova. He could not decipher what was going on, but he did his best to present a blank face. *This is not what I do.* The thought repeated. He felt the adrenaline course through his body. It was the same feeling he got while freefalling. Facing down death always made him feel alive. A strange calmness overcame him. Yet at the same time, his senses were sharply honed.

McMurphy turned and walked away from the little group of officers and stepped up to Paxton. He placed his hand on Paxton's right shoulder, leaned in and whispered in his ear in English.

"Now's the time. Shout a warning if anybody tries to pull anything."

Paxton nodded.

"I'll show you where I want you to stand."

McMurphy leaned back and turned toward the Stealth fighter wreckage. He walked toward the cockpit and Paxton followed. He saw the Serbian officers out of the corner of his eye. They were all watching him. McMurphy pushed himself through the crowd of civilians that stood around the plane. He excused himself repeatedly in their language. The onlookers were filled with curiosity about these two dirty and bloody men.

Paxton walked right behind McMurphy through the hole in the crowd he had made. He gripped the rifle in the proper manner now: left hand supporting the barrel by holding the portion that was covered bythe wooden stock, right hand holding the pistol grip, index finger extended just above the trigger guard. He had the folding stock extended and resting in the crook of his right elbow. He pointed the barrel down.

The two men reached the space between the crowd and the

plane. They stood near the double air inlet on the topside of the right wing just behind the cockpit. As they faced the plane the cockpit was to their right and the tail was to their left. The plane had landed right side up.

The Nighthawk was like a big black flat triangle. Starting at the sharp point of its nose, it spread out at an acute angle all the way to the tips of its swept wings that ended as far back as the rearmost portion of the fuselage. Only the twin tail, which opened in a "V" swept further back than the wing-tips. An angular hump along the middle axis of the fuselage housed the cockpit, engines, bomb bay and fuel tanks. The hump angled up sharply at the nose and then gently tapered from behind the cockpit to the point at the rear of the plane. Unlike most planes that were rounded and aerodynamic, the Nighthawk was a jumble of sharp corners designed not for airflow, but to scatter and confuse radar signals. It was not aerodynamic—it was basically a flying rock. Were it not for its advanced computerized avionics it would be so unstable as to be unflyable. The skin of the plane was covered with layers of radar-absorbing material designed to lessen the strength of radar signals that reflected back to radar antennae. The end result was not invisibility, but a greatly reduced radar signature. To a radar operator, the Nighthawk looked more like a small bird than a fighter plane.

The plane was sufficiently intact that it looked as if it still could fly. The entire structure rested on its flat underbelly and was sunk partially in the muddy grass. Paxton was surprised at the lack of visible damage. He couldn't tell where it had been hit or what brought it down. It could very wellhave been one lucky shot, known as a "golden BB," destroying the computer controlling the stability of the aircraft.

Paxton recalled seeing video footage of a Stealth fighter that crashed as a result of a mechanical failure during a 1997 air show in Baltimore. The pilot of that plane successfully ejected and the fighter started a flat spin on its way to the ground. The plane in front of him looked like it had undergone a similar flat spin, landing right side up and, miraculously, not exploding.

It made him sick to see it lying there broken on the ground. Some of the most advanced technology on the planet, a symbol of American military strength, planted in the mud like an old Chevrolet. It just wasn't right. No Stealth fighter had ever been shot down before. It was like the dawn of a new era. America was less safe. The Nighthawk had turned from a symbol of American strength to a symbol of America's new vulnerability. *And for what?* To stop the Serbs from killing the Muslims who were killing the Serbs and demanding their own country? It had never been proven that the Serbs had engaged in any mass executions or other war crimes. Wasn't this a purely internal matter? Paxton's stomach was tied in knots to see the reality of the wreckage. But everyone else around him was thrilled to see it. Paxton felt like the lone fan for the visiting football team in a stadium full of home team supporters and the home team just scored. He tried to focus on the task at hand. *All I have to do is watch McMurphy's back.* Then he would be taken to Jashari and he could go home.

McMurphy shouted at the civilians standing in front of him

near the cockpit. He motioned for them to move away. They looked confused, but they complied. Soon they were pushed back enough that Serbian officers' view of the Nighthawk was no longer blocked. McMurphy then looked up and said something to the police officer sitting on top of the wreckage. The police officer looked at the group of army officers and Nikolic nodded his head. The policeman tapped the shoulder of the cockpit's current occupant and that person climbed out. The officer halted the next in line from getting in and then spoke. The rest of the civilians climbed down, but they appeared angry about being turned away. McMurphy waved the crowd back from the plane. He wanted to create distance between the civilians and the wreckage.

The commotion caught the attention of the news crews. Some of the reporters were already beaming reports live to the world. The new developments, however, demanded turning the cameras from the on-air personalities to the activities of the two men wearing mercenary uniforms who seemed to have taken over the scene. The cameramen zoomed in with their telephoto lenses.

Satisfied that the crowd was far enough away, McMurphy turned toward the plane. He slipped his left arm through the strap of his backpack so it was on both shoulders, put his foot on the edge of the wing and climbed up. The metallic jangling sounded from his pack with each step. He used the same steps that the civilians had been using to climb up to sit in the cockpit. Paxton watched McMurphy and wondered, just like just about everyone else there, what the hell he was doing.

CHAPTER 21

Jill Paxton acquiesced to the thoughtful demands of her guests that she stop playing the hostess. *The other PJ wives would take care of everything. She should just sit down and enjoy some coffee in her kitchen. They would keep her company. They would help with the children.*

She sat down at the table in the breakfast nook while someone brewed another pot of coffee. The sun shone through the window over the sink and filled the room. A small television was set up on the counter with the sound on low. They watched a twenty-four hour news channel on the vague hope there would news about John's plane.

It was a tight-knit group. Their husbands were all instructors at the PJ indoctrination school. But since their husbands had been actively deployed at one time or another, they were experienced in *The Wait*. Even Melodie Ward, Col. Ward's wife, was there. Ward had never been a PJ, but the Colonel's wife was fond of Jill and wanted to comfort her. They all stood vigil. They tried to talk about things to take her mind off her fears. Everyday things. Striving for normalcy while her life spun out of control.

Nothing they said or did took away the feeling of dread in which Jill was drowning. She mechanically lifted her coffee cup to her lips. She felt as if she was separated from everyone else in the room by a layer of insulation. But it was just her mind attempting to disconnect her from horrible reality.

Then she froze and the half-full coffee cup slipped from her fingers. It fell to the table and sloshed hot liquid on her shirt. She shot up so quickly that her chair tipped over and crashed to the floor.

"Oh my God! John!" she screamed. "He's alive! Look!"

The women followed her trembling finger and turned toward the small television on the counter. One the screen they saw a man in an unusual uniform, dirty and torn at the knee, holding a rifle. Behind the man was a black object. The camera panned back to a well-dressed woman holding a microphone.

"Turn up the sound!" Jill demanded.

Someone reached for the controls and fumbled with the buttons.

The sound blared to life, "…reporting from Yugoslavia. Back to you, Hank."

The woman reporter was gone in a flash and the screen was filled with the face of Hank. He thanked the correspondent and talked about matters pending before Congress.

"You saw him, didn't you?" Jill asked excitedly.

The screen was so small and his time on camera so short it was impossible for the others to be sure they had really seen John Paxton.

"It sure looked like him," one of the women said.

"It *was* him!" Jill exclaimed, tears in her eyes.

"What was that he was wearing?" someone asked.

"He looked injured," another said.

Jill looked at Melodie, reached out and grabbed her by the shoulders, "Call your husband. Tell him John's alive."

• • •

Paxton stood in front of the Stealth oblivious to the fact that his image was being beamed around the globe. He was more concerned about more pedestrian things, such as staying alive. He faced the same direction as the plane, his rifle in front of him. The fuselage was to his left and the crowd and Serbian officers were to his right. He watched McMurphy, the rifle clutched in his clammy grip.

• • •

McMurphy reached the police officer who was seated behind the cockpit opening. "Good afternoon," McMurphy said in the officer's native language.

"Good afternoon."

"Would you be so kind as to step down?"

The officer shook his head. "My orders are to stay on post until I am relieved."

"Consider yourself relieved."

"No," the policeman replied sternly.

McMurphy propped his right boot on the edge of the cockpit. His other foot was on the top of the air inlet. He leaned his wrist on his upraised knee, striking a casual pose. "I have a very special job to do and I don't want you watching."

."Sounds like your problem."

"My employers are over there," McMurphy said, nodding his head in the direction of the Serbian officers. "Either you step down, or I'm leaving and *you* can then explain to them why you interfered with something of great military importance."

The police officer looked at the army officers and scanned the crowd. Sighing, he climbed off the fighter.

• • •

The ousted policeman walked past Paxton, their eyes locked, and then the officer looked away. Paxton moved to a position that blocked the route used to climb to the cockpit. He watched McMurphy take off the backpack and drop it into the cockpit. It landed with a metallic thud. He sat down in the pilot's seat. McMurphy was tall, so his head and shoulders showed above the ledge. He looked down and his arms moved, working on something below the ledge. Then he bent down and disappeared from sight entirely. But Paxton heard the sound of a toolbox snapping open and the sound of tools being sorted.

Now that McMurphy was out of sight, Paxton felt like all eyes were on him. He did his best to look like what he thought a Russian advisor would look like, but there was nothing for him to do. Nothing but stand there and wait. And hope. And pray.

McMurphy seemed to have a good relationship with at least one of the Serbian officers. As long as he played it cool, everything might turn out all right. Whatever McMurphy was doing, the Serbs seemed to be okay with it. He started to feel that ol' confidence he'd felt in the old days. And it felt good. *I can do this.* He thought about his family back home. He would have some great stories to tell his son and daughter when they were old enough. And he'd get to tell the stories even sooner to his PJ buddies. *This whole nightmare will be good for a few rounds of ice-cold beer.*

After a while, the crowd became restless and bored. Some of them left. Engines started and cars drove off. Others, who hadn't wanted to brave the dirt road with their vehicles, walked to their cars parked along the main road. Even the camera crews broke down their equipment in preparation for leaving. Only the diehards, the policeman and soldiers remained.

McMurphy stayed in the cockpit.

Paxton watched the crowd dwindle. Then he noticed among the cars and trucks leaving, one car was arriving. It weaved through the pedestrians and departing vehicles. It turned and drove over the grass toward the semicircle of Serbian officers. It rolled to a stop and its driver turned off its engine. Paxton watched it because he was bored. No doubt it was just another curious spectator who wanted to see the funny-looking plane. The car door opened and Paxton almost dropped his rifle when he saw the man climb out.

He didn't recognize the man. But he damned sure recognized that the man was dressed unmistakably in the uniform of the Russian Army.

• • •

One diehard who had no intention of leaving took advantage of the thinning crowds to move closer to the Stealth's wreckage. He could have been an ordinary onlooker from a nearby village. But he wasn't. He took another picture with his Sony digital camera. He held the camera away from his scarred face and looked at the preview screen. Framed in the small picture was the man holding the rifle. He pushed the button to save the picture along with the others he had already taken. They would be important for his after-action report when he was later debriefed. He slipped the camera back into the left pocket of his wool jacket.

He moved closer so he could get a better shot.

• • •

Jill was so excited she was almost climbed through the phone as she described seeing John on TV to Colonel Ward. Jill was still in her kitchen. She hadn't taken time to change clothes before calling the Colonel. The coffee stain was still wet on her blouse.

Ward sat at his desk on base, furiously taking notes. "Jill, are you sure it was him?"

"Yes, absolutely!"

"And he was standing right in front of the Stealth?"

"I missed the first part of the report. It was something big and black. Odd shape."

Reed had sent Pax to Yugoslavia to recover the plane. So it was possible that Pax had managed to get near it.

"Did you see any other PJs?" Ward asked.

"No."

"I saw some other soldiers standing around, but they weren't PJs."

"Americans?"

"No. Please, you've got to send someone. Bring my husband back."

"We're doing everything we can," Ward said. "You didn't tape it, did you?"

"No."

"That's okay, Jill. Is my wife still there?"

Jill handed the cordless phone to Melodie. "Tell him I'm not crazy. We saw John."

Melodie Ward took the phone. "Honey, we definitely saw him."

"Can you talk without Jill hearing?"

Mrs. Ward smiled reassuringly. Then she acted like she couldn't hear too well. "Honey? Honey? Wait. Let me go to the living room so I can hear you better." She walked out of the kitchen. "Okay."

"Was it him?" Ward asked.

"I don't know. It was so quick. She saw it longer than I did."

"So Pax was standing near the wreckage with Serbian soldiers—and he's still alive? Doesn't make sense."

"The man I saw wasn't wearing a uniform. The colors and pattern were all wrong. And his rifle—well, it wasn't an M-16."

Ward absorbed the information and contained his disappointment. "Listen, dear," he said. "Pax's plane was shot down and all the heavy equipment would have been destroyed. I can't imagine why, if he is alive, he would go near the Stealth. And he wouldn't change clothes."

"Can't you get a copy of the tape from the network? See for yourself?"

"I'll try. Stay with Jill. I'll call if I get any updates." Ward hung up. He then shouted out the open door of his office. "Machette, get in here!"

Sgt. Machette hurried to his desk. "Yes, sir?"

"Get General Reed on the phone."

• • •

Paxton stood next to the wreckage of the Stealth, the confidence that had built suddenly melting away. *The bear never sleeps.* He watched the Russian soldier interact with the Serbian officers. Shit! What was taking McMurphy so long? He was still in the cockpit. He hadn't stuck his head up since he had started—whatever he was doing. He said to watch out for the bad guys. Hell, they were surrounded by the bad guys. Maybe the Russian officer was there to look around, to gather intelligence on the American Stealth technology. Maybe he would leave Paxton alone. Paxton wondered again if McMurphy had loaded the rifle he held in his hands. The magazine was inserted, but that didn't mean anything. Maybe it was empty. It didn't really matter. *You can't shoot your way out of this one, Pax.*

The Russian saluted General Rugova. The officers all exchanged salutes and handshakes. A friendly meeting. The news crews didn't capture that meeting because they were packing their trucks and preparing to leave. Ratings only supported so much exposure of a plane wreck.

The only person capturing the image of the meeting was the scarred man wearing a wool jacket. He stood only ten feet from Paxton and he faced the officers, clicking away with his Sony digital camera. *Nice gadget for a farmer.* Paxton turned his attention to the Russian.

The little group was animated in their conversation. The General pointed at the cockpit several times. Then he pointed directly at Paxton. The Russian turned, following the General's directions and looked at Paxton and smiled. Paxton wanted to avoid eye contact but knew he shouldn't. He looked the Russian in the eye and nodded once.

The Russian said something else to the General. Then he turned and walked in the direction of the Stealth. He was headed right toward Paxton.

• • •

Sgt. Machette tracked down General Reed at Brindisi Air-base in Italy. He was in visiting officers' quarters sitting at the kitchenette table. He was looking at documents with Marshall when the call was put through.

"This is Colonel Ward. Sir, I'm calling to let you know we may have had a sighting of Sergeant Paxton. He may be alive, sir."

"That's good news, Colonel," Reed said. "But your people are handling the rescue, not me. Why are you telling me this?"

"I need more time. The rescue may be trickier than we first anticipated. We believe that Paxton may be in the vicinity of the Stealth wreckage."

Reed perked up. "Was anyone else with him?"

"Half the Serbian army. But we don't know where the rest of his team is. General, it makes no sense. Surely the bulldozer and dump truck you provided were destroyed when the plane went down."

"Did you arrange a rescue mission?"

"Yes, the 255th Rescue Squadron is on its way."

"I'll tell you what, Colonel. You verify that Paxton is alive and well and get back to me. Then you and I will talk about timetables."

"Yes, sir," Ward said. "By the way … can you think of any reason Paxton would change into a different uniform?"

"I have no idea why Sergeant Paxton would change clothes."

"Thank you, General."

Reed hung up the phone and then pushed it across the table to Marshall.

"Get the commander of the 255th Rescue Squadron on the line for me," Reed said. "Ward thinks Paxton was sighted near the Stealth. If that's so, McMurphy is still around."

"That's great news, sir! But why do you need to talk to the 255th?"

"If Paxton and McMurphy are alive and on task," Reed explained, "we don't want rescue teams anywhere near them."

• • •

Paxton froze as he watched the Russian soldier approach him. *What does he want?* He didn't look threatening. Maybe he wanted to engage in small talk with a fellow countryman. *But I'm not a fellow countryman!* Paxton gripped the rifle tighter. He knew it wouldn't take long for the Russian to figure out that he was a phony. *Maybe he already knows.*

Paxton peeked at the cockpit. McMurphy still was out of sight. The only relevant Russian phrase Paxton could yell was "Grigori, look out." But the approaching soldier would understand the words and who knows how McMurphy would react. Paxton looked at the Serbian officers who were watching him. The farmer with the digital camera took more pictures. Paxton did his best to ignore him.

Paxton's empty stomach roiled. *I'm fucked.* How pointless to survive the horrific disintegration of the Globemaster only to be shot because he hadn't kept up with his language lessons. He didn't know whom he was more pissed at: Ward, the doormat; Reed, the puppet master; McMurphy, the nutcase; or himself. Paxton's anger crowded out his fear. They had taken him away from his family and they wouldn't tell him why. *If I survive this,* Paxton thought, *I'm going to kill McMurphy.*

Why wait?

Paxton figured if he was going to die anyway, why not take a few bad guys with him? And he would start with that bastard McMurphy. It would be so easy to switch the AK-74 he held to full auto. He could pepper the cockpit and then the approaching Russian. Then, if the other soldiers hadn't cut him in half yet, he'd spray the semicircle of Serbian officers. That would do it. At least he would die with honor. Not strung up, tortured and shot like an animal. His finger surreptitiously edged over to the selective fire switch. He clicked it to full auto.

He moved his finger into the trigger guard.

Then he hesitated.

Jill and the kids ... he could almost feel their presences. He could see their faces. For him it would be over in an instant. But they would live on, abandoned because he lacked the courage. *Pulling that trigger is the easy way out—for you.*

He took his finger out of the trigger guard. He had to try to stay alive, even if it meant risking torture. The Russian walked up, stuck his hand out and spoke a one-word greeting.

Paxton took his hand off the grip and shook the Russian's hand. "Glad to meet you," he said, just like McMurphy taught him.

The Russian rattled off a bunch of words. Paxton forced a

smile. He stood there, motionless, hoping for his own personal Pentecost. What he needed right then was a tongue of fire to swoop down from heaven, touch his forehead and inspire him to speak in other tongues—preferably Russian.

The officer paused, looking at him.

Paxton nodded, opened his mouth as if to speak then commenced a violent coughing fit. He hacked and wheezed. He forced himself to cough so loud that it felt like razor blades were slicing the inside of his throat. Anyone observing would wonder if he was choking to death. The Russian took a step back, frowning. Paxton rolled his tongue and stuck it out slightly as he was forcing coughs. The sound of his hacking echoed off the Stealth. Paxton's mouth became dry as a desert from his pretend spasms.

• • •

The violent, crazed coughing sounded like a dying walrus. What the hell? McMurphy looked out from the cockpit. His gaze zipped from Paxton, who was apparently determined to expel his lungs, to the Russian soldier watching Paxton with a disgusted expression.

"Can you give me a hand up here, comrade?" McMurphy called down to the soldier in perfect Russian.

The Russian shrugged then stepped on the wing and climbed toward the cockpit.

• • •

As Paxton gradually ended his coughing fit, he turned his head to watch the Russian soldier. When he reached the cockpit, McMurphy stood up on the pilot's seat and handed the ratty green backpack to the soldier. The soldier took it from McMurphy and held it out in front of him like a cafeteria tray. Then McMurphy bent down and picked up something from the floor.

The Russian heaved the bag over his shoulder and climbed off the cockpit. McMurphy descended after the Russian with an object tucked under his right arm. He cradled it like a football. When he reached the ground, he turned toward the Serbian officers.

Paxton straightened, lightly coughing and rubbing his throat. The Russian soldier smiled politely, but didn't attempt another conversation. Paxton looked at the item clutched in McMurphy's hand. It was roughly the shape of an elongated cube maybe a foot long. It had a metal frame riddled with bolt holes. Within the frame was a rat's nest of wires. Visible also were rows of circuit boards. A couple of plugs hung down from cables.

McMurphy and the Russian walked toward the Serbian officers. Paxton stayed put. The farmer with the digital camera snapped some pictures of McMurphy.

When McMurphy reached General Rugova, he presented the device like he was handing the man a trophy. The general handed the black bag to Nikolic and took the object, examining it from every angle. The Russian handed McMurphy his backpack and stepped closer to study the device. Rugova and the Russian engaged in a rapid conversation. Finally, Rugova said something to Nikolic and the colonel handed McMurphy the black bag. He opened the bag and examined the contents thoroughly, then nodded. Everyone shook hands.

McMurphy then turned and walked toward Paxton. He indicated with a jerk of his head that Paxton was to head in the direction of the car. Paxton turned and walked toward the Yugo. He passed some of the soldiers guarding the plane as McMurphy veered to meet him. When they were out of earshot Paxton said in a low voice, "What the hell was that all about?"

"Stop chatting and walk faster."

Paxton gritted his teeth and resisted the urge to throttle the man. "What's in the black bag?"

"Money." McMurphy glanced at him. "I don't think our Russian friend bought your little coughing routine."

Paxton dared a glance over his shoulder. The Russian was talking to Rugova and pointing directly at Paxton. Their expressions were not friendly. "Shit."

"That about sums it up."

"Are we going to see Jashari?" Paxton asked as they strode past one of the television satellite trucks.

"As fast as humanly possible."

Part III

CHAPTER 22

PAXTON MENTALLY CLIMBED THE STEPS TOWARD awareness from deep slumber. He felt the softness of the bed beneath him. It felt so good—so comfortable. So safe. His eyes were still closed, but through his eyelids he was aware of the bright morning sunshine pouring in through his bedroom windows and splashing across his face. He savored the contentment he always found in the twilight between dreams and awakening.

Sleep enveloped him, clinging like a new lover. He felt like he had sunk into a sagging hammock and couldn't move his arms or legs. He must have been especially exhausted to sleep in—he usually got up before dawn. Must be an off-duty weekend. He felt the urge to roll over and hold Jill close, but that would take too much effort. He couldn't move. Hmm. Maybe later....

Slowly, Paxton became aware of movement in his bedroom. Someone had crossed momentarily in front of the sunlight. *No more sleep now—the kids are up.*

Through the fog he heard a voice say, "Wake up."

John, Jr. There was energy and excitement in his voice.

"Hey," his son prompted.

He didn't have the energy to open his eyes. Oh, wait. Was this the weekend they were supposed to go fishing? *That's it. Fishing.*

Just like he promised himself back in Yugoslavia—he was going to do those things that he'd neglected. Fatherly things. Paxton struggled to wake up. A new sensation encroached on him—a dull ache in his head. *Ouch.*

"Hey, get up!" He felt John, Jr. pat his cheek.

A survival instinct beckoned him to return to dreamland. His headache would worsen once he opened his eyes. But he didn't want to disappoint his boy.

"No more sleep!" the voice insisted. "Hurry up!" More smacks rained on his face. "I said wake up, asshole!"

What the hell?

His face was slapped again. It stung. Paxton's eyes shot open. The sunlight was incredibly bright. It sent spikes into his eyes all the way through the back of his head.

"He's up."

Paxton blinked, trying to focus. Everything was blurry. He felt like his brain had swelled too big for his skull. He squinted against the light. The sun was in the room with him, floating above his head. He felt the heat on his cheeks. He rolled his head to the right, turning away from the light, nose and mouth against his upper arm, which stretched out over his head. A musty smell filled his nose and mouth as he felt the rough texture of the mattress. *No sheets.*

His exposed left cheek sharply stung as it was smacked again. Then a face lowered into his field of view. Familiar. He searched his memory. Where had he seen that face before? Paxton croaked out a name, "Nikolic?"

The hovering face smiled grimly.

I'm not at home. Regret arrowed through him. *Where am I?*

Nikolic pulled out of his line of sight, allowing him to see the plain concrete wall. Two men stood against it, watching him. Their faces seemed strangely familiar too. The bigger man with the pig eyes … oh yeah. *Rugova.*

Who was the other man? When Paxton tried to retrieve his name out of his aching head, all that came back was: *Russian.*

Fuck! I'm captured!

Paxton opened both eyes wide and bolted upward. Pain shot through his wrists and shoulders as his body snapped back to the crappy mattress. The metallic sound of chains rang out. His arms were stretched over his head and his wrists bound. He rolled his head to look up at a steel frame headboard. His arms were handcuffed to it.

The "sunlight" was a bare bulb in a floor lamp aimed directly at his face.

He tried to kick his feet off the bed but his efforts were thwarted. His ankles were chained to the foot of the bed. He twisted violently from side to side trying to break loose. But all he managed to do was strain his muscles and rub his skin raw.

Where am I? Paxton's mind raced. *What happened?*

McMurphy had handed the electronic device to General Rugova. Nikolic gave McMurphy the black bag full of money. Then he and Paxton had walked toward the Yugo ... and nothing. *What was going on?*

Paxton glanced around the room. The bright bulb was painful. No matter what direction he looked, he could never get complete relief from it. On his left was a barred window. Below that, he saw the end of another bed. Chained to the steel piping were two muddy boots. He strained to see the occupant. *McMurphy.* The man's face was bloody, but his eyes stared right at Paxton. His expression appeared to convey a message, but Paxton couldn't interpret it.

Nikolic's face hovered over his. "Who are you?"

Groggy, Paxton blinked up at him. Something was odd, but he couldn't put his finger on it.

Then it struck him.

English.

They were supposed to be Russian advisors. He had stark memories of struggling with Russian to keep up appearances. *How does Nikolic know to speak English to me?*

"Who are you?" Nikolic repeated.

"Don't tell him shit," McMurphy yelled in English.

Something else was going on here. Paxton looked at McMurphy. He appeared more serious than he had ever seen him—and for McMurphy, that was saying something.

"I'm talking to you," Nikolic boomed.

Paxton faced Nikolic, who stood over him. He remained silent as he assessed the situation. McMurphy had dragged him into hell. They weren't in uniforms. They were both speaking English. His heart thudded in his chest. *I'm not a spy.*

Nikolic struck him again. "Identify yourself!"

"Don't do it!"

"Shut up!" Nikolic shouted at McMurphy.

A member of the United States Armed Forces, he had rights. Article V of the Code of Conduct required that he give name, rank, service number and date of birth. He was to evade answering other questions to the best of his ability.

If Paxton properly identified himself as a member of the United States military, there was a chance, though slim, that he would be treated as a POW. If he continued with McMurphy's charade, a spy's death awaited him. He would never see his family again.

But McMurphy was insisting that he not say a word. Why?

Damn it. Paxton qualified for POW status under the Geneva Convention, which prohibited torture, other inhumane treatment of POWs, and execution. Violation of the Geneva Convention was a war crime. POW status would keep him alive.

Why would McMurphy want me to violate the Code of Conduct?

If Paxton identified himself, and the Serbs granted him POW status, they might report to the International Red Cross that they were holding him as a POW and doing so would expose Reed. The General and McMurphy had obviously cut a side deal with the Serbs—something to do with that black box and the Stealth. *McMurphy is trying to protect Reed.*

Paxton looked at the ceiling, eyes forward. "I'm Senior Master Sergeant John Paxton—"

"Shut up, Sergeant!" McMurphy demanded. "Just shut your fucking mouth!"

"I'm a pararescueman with the United States Air Force." Paxton rattled off his Social Security Number, which was also his service number, and his date of birth.

Nikolic took notes. "What was your mission?"

Paxton stared at the ugly concrete ceiling.

"How many men were with you?"

Paxton said nothing.

"What is *his* real name?" Nikolic asked, pointing to McMurphy.

Paxton was tempted to expose McMurphy, but he kept his mouth shut. *I will evade answering questions to the best of my ability.*

He heard the clomp of boots across the bare floor, then General Rugova appeared at his side. "I strongly advise that you answer the questions of Col. Nikolic," he said in clear English.

Paxton wondered if he was the only one in the room who didn't speak multiple languages. He kept silent, his eyes glued on the ceiling.

"Very well." Rugova crossed the room and opened the door. Over his shoulder he said, "We shall return. When we do, you will talk." He left, followed by the Russian and Nikolic. The door slammed shut and a lock clicked into place.

Paxton looked at McMurphy. "This sucks."

McMurphy's expression was filled with disgust. "You're not planning on telling them anything *else* are you?"

"Well, I might tell Rugova to try a breath mint, but other than that you made sure that I don't know anything."

McMurphy rolled his eyes, but his lips tilted slightly. "Paxton, you're an asshole."

"Yeah? Look who's talking."

CHAPTER 23

THE 255ᵀᴴ SQUADRON HEADQUARTERS, HOUSED IN A hangar, was on the other side of Brindisi Airbase. Inside the hanger sat a partially disassembled helicopter. Mechanics were on top tinkering with the turbine engine under the close supervision of the crew chief. They were so focused upon their work that they didn't even notice that a two-star general had walked into their work area.

Or maybe they ignored him.

Marshall and Reed proceeded to the office located in the corner and stepped through the door. The sergeant on duty behind the desk bolted to his feet and barked, "Tench-hut!" The sergeant stood there sharply at attention. His BDUs were crisply starched. Reed noted his Pararescue patch sewn neatly in place.

"At ease, Sergeant," Reed said.

As the sergeant assumed the parade rest stance, a colonel stepped out of his inner office to greet Reed.

"Welcome to the 255th, sir," the colonel said politely.

"Thank you, Colonel…" Reed examined his name patch. "Hicks."

"Come on back to my office," Col. Hicks said. "Can I get you and your aide some coffee?"

"Yes, thank you."

"Coffees all around," Hicks said to the sergeant behind the desk. "This way, gentlemen."

Marshall and Reed followed Hicks into his cramped office. They sat—Hicks behind his desk, Reed and Marshall in two uncomfortable metal chairs.

Reed got right to the point. "You have a team searching for PJs led by a Senior Master Sergeant Paxton. You've probably heard that Sergeant Paxton might have been sighted in the vicinity of the downed Stealth fighter."

"Yes, sir."

"Paxton's distraught wife claimed that she saw her husband on CNN." Reed shook his head. "The person she identified as Paxton was not wearing a United States Air Force uniform and he was standing near Serbian soldiers."

"Your point, General Reed?"

"You're dividing your efforts now … putting your team at high risk with very little hope of finding Sergeant Paxton."

"With all due respect, sir, pararescuemen are always at high risk. You've already called us off once. Is that what you're here to do again?"

"Call off the rescue?" Reed chuckled. "No. I'm here to offer my help."

The sergeant entered, carrying three coffees. He distributed them and disappeared, closing the office door behind him.

Reed looked at Hicks. "I can … adjust the risk-reward ratio in your favor."

"I'm listening."

"I have a man on the ground in that area. Let me contact him and send him to determine whether or not the person sighted is Sergeant Paxton. Focus your men on locating Sergeant Paxton's team. If they survived the crash, they're probably holed up somewhere around the wreckage of the Globemaster. My man is undercover and in the same area as the Stealth. If he finds Paxton, I will contact you and your men can go get him."

Hicks sipped on his coffee, staying silent for several moments. Then he nodded. "We will do it your way, General. But I need you to tell me the name of your man on the ground."

"No problem," said Reed. "His name is McMurphy."

• • •

Jill Paxton pulled herself together. The sight of her husband on the television had given her new hope—and new fears. She was grateful that he was still alive, but she didn't understand what he was doing. Obviously, he wasn't rescuing the pilot, but at least he didn't appear to be a prisoner. All she could do was trust him and his commanders. What other option did she have?

She convinced the other wives to go home. She promised to call the moment she learned anything. She declined several offers to stay with friends. She wanted to make life as normal as possible for her kids and that meant staying home and keeping to a routine.

John is alive. She'd seen him with her own eyes—on a live newscast from halfway around the world.

Colonel Ward assured her that he was directing the rescue forces to the site of the downed Stealth fighter. They would find John and rescue him the way he had rescued so many others.

All she could do now was take care of her children and sit and wait.

And pray.

• • •

Paxton tested the sturdiness of the handcuffs around his wrists for what must have been the hundredth time. Unfortunately, they were solid. He was stuck there in the strange room, helpless, with a grumpy McMurphy for company.

General Rugova and the others had not yet returned. From time to time he heard voices through the locked door. Paxton let his mind drift. *Did McMurphy sell the Stealth's hardware to the Serbs? Did I witness treason?*

He looked at McMurphy, who was sound asleep. *How the hell could he nap?* What was that old saying? Only the innocent sleep?

Nothing made sense. Would Reed, a two-star general in the

Air Force, be involved in treason? *Anything's possible.* The mission that didn't officially exist. The confiscation of Paxton's identification. The blocking of his efforts to contact Jill. The mercenary uniforms. *It sure would explain the need for secrecy.*

But would Colonel Ward be involved? No. Paxton knew his commander well, and he would be the first to step up and stop it. *What does Ward know?* Ward believed Paxton was here to recover the wreckage of the Stealth. An odd mission for a PJ but not unprecedented. PJs were often utilized to recover items of military importance, but usually in conjunction with a bona fide rescue. *Grab the codebook when you pick up the pilot.* But recovering a whole plane? This mission stunk from the beginning. *As far as Ward knows, I was killed when the Globemaster crashed.*

Oh my God! Jill!

Paxton yanked at his chains futilely. No one knew there were survivors. If a rescue team had been dispatched to the Globemaster wreckage, they wouldn't find anyone. *We look like dead men.* Paxton looked at his chains and those holding the sleeping McMurphy in place.

We are *dead men.*

I've got to get out of here!

Was he going to be killed over money? It seemed absurd. The bag didn't seem nearly big enough to carry any truly significant amount of cash. Hell that bag couldn't hold more than about one year's worth of a Major General's retirement pay. It was one thing to give his life in defense of his county. And it was quite another to be tortured and executed to protect some Pentagon prince.

If McMurphy made a deal with the Serbs, why was he captured and chained up? Did the Serbs just want the device and the money? A double cross? That made no sense. If they didn't want to pay, why didn't they just shoot McMurphy the moment he handed them whatever they wanted?

Paxton agonized over all the possibilities. His mind reeled with the all the scenarios. But each one led to the same chilling conclusion.

Both he and McMurphy were now liabilities—to *both* sides of the equation. They had outlived their usefulness. They were a millstone to the Serbs because, if you steal the enemy's code, the last thing in the world you want is for the enemy to find out you have it.

And should they somehow escape, the Serbs would have something to hold over Reed's head forever. Paxton knew enough about Reed to realize he wouldn't allow that. So it was in Reed's best interest for them to be eliminated as well. And if done by the Serbs, so much the better. Plausible deniability. But how would Reed get the money? Paxton had no idea but assumed that Reed had that figured out as well.

Images floated through his mind. The Yugo. He glanced back at the semicircle of Serbian officers. General Rugova was shouting and pointing at them. Paxton didn't speak a word of Serbo-Croat, but it was nonetheless clear the general was shouting orders for his men to stop them. Soldiers came at them with guns raised. Ran for the Yugo ... blocked by soldiers. Guns pointed at him. Surrounded and grabbed. His rifle snatched from him—the leather bag snatched from Mc-Murphy. Shouting. The butt of a rifle struck the back of Mc-Murphy's head. He crumpled like a rag doll. *Here it comes.* Searing light … pain … blackness.

The Serbs could have easily killed them.

So why hadn't they?

• • •

Mid-air refueling was incredibly dangerous. Even in peacetime the risks were great. War multiplies the hazards. The crews of both the fueling aircraft and the aircraft receiving fuel were at risk. It was possible that both aircraft could collide into each other. This was particularly so when the aircraft receiving the fuel was a helicopter. The fuel-ladened turbo-prop HC-130P had to fly at its slowest speed, which made it unstable and in danger of stalling. On the other hand, the helicopter receiving the fuel had to fly at its maximum speed just to keep up.

The helicopters carrying the team of PJs out of Brindisi Airbase were refueling for the second time. The decision was made to refuel over the Adriatic Sea because the slow speeds and limited maneuverability during the connection made for an easy target. So the HC-130P met the helicopters over the water. Long hoses trailed behind the wings of the plane.

The first helicopter successfully connected to the fuel hose on its second try. The HC-130P dumped fuel from its tanks into the helicopter. The second helicopter approached the hose that trailed the other wing of the HC-130P. The helicopter's pilot focused on the flopping cup at the end of the fuel hose. He edged the fuel boom toward it. He timed it and stabbed the controls forward ... and missed.

The PJs in the back of the helicopter were silent. They all knew the stakes. If they failed to refuel, they would either have to set down in enemy territory or splash down in the angry Adriatic Sea. Neither option seemed particularly appealing.

The pilot tried again.

Again he missed.

Fuel was critically low on the second helicopter. A decision would have to be made if a connection wasn't made soon.

Tension gripped the seasoned warriors.

The helicopter pilot aimed again. He held the copter level and throttled up the forward speed. The boom inched close to the spinning hose. Both the pilot and co-pilot held their breaths. The pilot feathered the controls to counteract the vortices churned up by the HC-130P's wings and props. He throttled up a little more.

Contact!

The helicopter's boom successfully connected to the fuel hose. The HC-130P dumped the much-needed fuel into the second helicopter.

Once the refueling operation was completed, they proceeded with their newest orders from Col. Hicks.

Focus search for survivors of the Globemaster's crash.

Do not expend resources or men looking for the Stealth or for Sergeant Paxton.

CHAPTER 24

THE STAFF CAR ROLLED TO A STOP IN FRONT OF THE
nondescript building tucked away in the thick Serbian forest.
One of the soldiers standing outside the entrance scurried to
the back door of the car and opened it. He stood back and saluted as Nikolic, carrying a briefcase, and the Russian soldier
Sergov got out. Then General Rugova climbed out of the car.

The one-story concrete block structure appeared to be at
least fifty years old. It could have served as a garage or workshop. In the front was a steel door, a garage door and two
windows. There were three more windows on the side of the
building. Steel bars covered every window.

Three soldiers, including the one that opened the car door,
stood guard outside the steel door. Only Rugova's most trusted men were present. This location was unknown to most of
the Serbian military. The secrecy helped avoid interference

that usually came from the Belgrade bureaucracy. Rugova didn't have much patience for interference.

Rugova walked into the building, followed by Nikolic and Sergov. Men inside bolted to attention at the sight of the general. On a large workbench were tools and testing equipment. Centered on the workbench was the electronic box McMurphy removed from the Stealth fighter. Various wires were connected to the box leading to testing equipment.

"Was I right?" Rugova asked.

"Yes, sir." replied one man.

"Excellent. Let's see if our guests are ready to talk."

One soldier walked to the wooden door on the far wall and unlocked it. He swung it open and stepped aside. Rugova, Nikolic and the Russian entered after him.

Paxton and McMurphy were chained to their beds, just as Rugova had left them. The bright unshielded bulb shone in Paxton's eyes. Once they were all in the room, Nikolic closed the door behind them. McMurphy stirred awake, but Paxton glared at the men.

"Ah, Senior Master Sergeant Paxton," Rugova said conversationally. "Are you ready to have a conversation?"

Paxton said nothing, but his eyes conveyed fury.

"Nothing to say? Hmph. In a matter of moments, you will be dying to tell me everything."

• • •

Paxton studied General Rugova. What information did he want? The Serbs already had the entire wreckage of the

Stealth. McMurphy had already extracted and given them the mysterious black box. He doubted the Serbs were looking for the latest rescue techniques employed by pararescuemen. Maybe he could explain the intricacies of Organic Chemistry since he had been studying for that course when he'd been pulled away by Reed.

Rugova stepped closer to the bed. Nikolic and the Russian stood in the background near the wall. "Let's start from the beginning. Who sent you?"

"The Easter Bunny," Paxton replied.

"I see you want to play with me. I don't like games, Sergeant Paxton. Tell me … how many came with you? Where are they?"

"I want a lawyer."

"I don't think you should be making jokes, a man in your position." Rugova sighed heavily and turned toward the two along the wall. "Nikolic," he said, holding his hand out to his assistant.

Nikolic reached into his briefcase and pulled out a file folder. Rugova took the folder and opened it. He flipped through papers in the file and periodically looked up at Paxton. Rugova removed a cell phone from a clip on his belt. It was an older model, fairly large and boxy. After a moment, Rugova spoke loudly into the phone in Serbo-Croat, but the word "Paxton" was recognizable. He glanced at his watch, uttered a few more words and pressed the end button. He returned the phone to his belt.

"Who sent you?" asked Rugova

"Your mother."

Rugova's jaw clenched. "If you do not wish anything to happen to your family, you will answer my questions."

Dread pounded through Paxton. "I don't have a family."

Rugova smiled. "Yes, you do. And we know where they live." He looked in his file again. "324 Casa Verde Way, San Antonio, Texas."

Paxton's blood ran cold. He clamped his lips shut and stared at the ceiling.

"It's amazing what you can find on the Internet. You told us your social security and date of birth. Tsk. Tsk."

Rugova leaned over Paxton, his eyes as hard as black marble. "I pulled your credit report. I found a base newsletter online that touted your promotion to Senior Master Sergeant—congratulations, by the way. I found your property taxes for your home. I know that you have a wife named Jill and two children…" Rugova referred to his file again. "John, Jr. and Megan."

Paxton seethed with rage, but he forced a chuckle, "You've got the wrong John Paxton, General. I'm not married and I have no kids."

"Oh, then how do you explain this?" He reached into the file and pulled out a piece of paper. He held it in front of Paxton's face.

It had been folded twice and was stained with sweat. Across the middle of the piece of paper were numbers. He recognized them as the GPS coordinates for the crashed Stealth—written by his own hand. Above the numbers were the words, "My dearest Jill. I'm so sorry I wasn't able to say goodbye to you or the children before I left."

"Why were you carrying this in your top pocket?" Rugova asked. "What are the odds that there are two John Paxtons who are pararescuemen, recently promoted to the rank of Senior Master Sergeant, and married to women named Jill?"

Paxton squeezed his eyes shut. Writing the letter to his wife seemed like something he'd done in another lifetime. He planned to have it delivered to Colonel Ward. In case he was killed in action, he wanted to explain to his wife why he had left without saying goodbye. He had to tell her and his kids that he loved them—just in case he never made it back.

"Oh well, maybe you are right," Rugova said offhandedly. "Perhaps you do not live in Texas. But my assassins are ready to kill the family who lives at 324 Casa Verde in San Antonio."

Paxton bit his bottom lip so hard he drew blood. *Goddamned McMurphy was right again. I should've kept my mouth shut.*

"Won't you feel badly that an innocent woman and her two kids will be killed because of you?" asked Rugova. "Or do you not care if we splatter their brains all over that pretty little house?"

Paxton lunged against his restraints. "You son of a bitch!" he shouted. "I'll kill you before you can give the order to kill my family!" He struggled against the chains, burning with rage.

Rugova's smile broadened. "My dear Sergeant Paxton. You don't seem to understand the situation. Killing me will do you no good. Once dispatched, my assassins will proceed unless I personally call them and tell them to stop. They answer to no one but me. The only way to save your family is to answer my questions."

"Fuck you!" Paxton yanked at the chains with all his might, screaming in fury when they held fast.

"Ah, I understand. You need time to think," Rugova said calmly as he waved at Nikolic and the Russian. They quickly exited the room. Rugova turned on his heel and walked toward the door. The big Serb paused and looked over his shoulder. "Time is not your friend, Sergeant Paxton. You see, I've already given the order."

•   •   •

Borislav Delevic snapped his cellphone shut. He looked at Labus. "Get packed. We have a job to do."

"Where ?"

"San Antonio, Texas."

CHAPTER 25

A VILLAGER WITH A SCARRED FACE KNOCKED ON THE house's front door. He was let inside and taken to the living room. Sitting at a chair in front of the fireplace, sipping a cup of coffee, was Jashari.

"I bring news of the Americans," the man said. "They have been captured by the Serbs. The manner in which they were captured was most unusual."

"What do you mean, Hashim?"

"Two of them somehow obtained a car. They drove to the wreckage of the other American plane."

"The Stealth fighter?"

"Yes."

"What did they do there?"

Hashim recounted what he had seen. He told how the two Americans interacted with Serbian officers and how they were granted unfettered access to the wreckage. He described how one climbed inside the cockpit and came out with a piece of equipment.

"What sort of equipment?" Jashari asked.

"I have photos." Hashim produced his digital camera and turned on the small screen. He surfed from image to image. "Here is the best picture. The Serbs must think it important. I think they paid the Americans for it. But when the Americans tried to leave, the Serbs attacked them."

"*Attacked?*" Jashari stared at Hashim.

"They surrounded them and beat them unconscious. Then they loaded them into the back of a truck and drove off." Hashim gave the camera to Jashari. He smiled proudly. "I followed them."

"Very good, Hashim. Where did they take the Americans?"

"To a building in the woods—outside of Belgrade. They have the Americans chained to beds. I believe they will be interrogated."

"It is likely." Jashari looked at the camera on his lap as he sipped his coffee.

"That device is also there. I saw it on one of the workbenches."

"Interesting. Hmm. You've done well, Hashim. I will return the camera after I download the pictures to my computer. We must find out about that black box."

"Of course." He hesitated. "The Americans … are we going to rescue them?"

"No," Jashari said. "There is nothing in it for us."

• • •

In their Lake Mary hotel room, Labus closed the door behind him and handed Delevic the empty shipping box and newspaper. Their disassembled weapons were laid out on the bed.

Delevic crumpled up the newspaper and shoved it into the box. Then, one at a time, he placed their weapons inside the box. First was the MAC-10 machine pistol since it was the largest. Its folding stock had been retracted and the custom silencer had been unscrewed from the stubby barrel. He then lay the silencer in the box along with two thirty-round magazines. He had removed all the bullets from all the magazines. He wanted to make the package as light as possible. More ammunition could be easily purchased once they arrived in Texas. More crumpled newspaper was stuffed into the box. Then he put in his pistol, followed by Labus's, and more crumpled newspaper. He closed the lid.

He shook the box; nothing rattled. He filled out the overnight delivery service label, listing himself as the recipient, a guest at the hotel he had booked a few minutes ago. He affixed the label to the front of the box and taped it shut. Glancing at his watch, he said in his native Serbo-Croat "Let's get going. We must ship the package before we go to the airport."

Labus picked up the box. "Boris?"

"Yeah?"

"What do you think the women are like in San Antonio?"

Delevic grinned.

• • •

Smith double-checked the GPS receiver unit against his map. Everything checked out. They had arrived at their destination. He surveyed the location. The growth seemed dense enough to sufficiently conceal them from both the ground and the air. "Okay, gentlemen. Welcome to your new temporary home."

Petersen gently lowered Thompson down off his back. "Home, Sweet Home."

"What do we do now, Sergeant Smith?" one of the other airmen asked.

"We get as deep in cover as we can. Then we sit and wait," Smith replied.

• • •

Detective Margolis looked over his notes again. *Dead end.* He had followed up on all the calls of possible sightings of Amanda and the mystery men prompted by the story on the local news. Most of the people who reported seeing Amanda had seen her at times prior to her disappearance. Nobody had claimed to see her after she left the bar on the night she died. The still frames of the men were too grainy to be useful. The bar's system, while advanced, had inadequate mega pixels for the desired resolution.

To solve this case, he needed to employ a different strategy.

• • •

Paxton yanked on his chains, furious. His world was crumbling. Was his family really in the sights of an assassin? No. No! He looked at McMurphy, who lay on his bed like he'd checked into a resort hotel.

"This is all your fault!" Paxton yelled.

McMurphy looked at him, puzzled. "How is this *my* fault?"

"Because I wouldn't even be here except for *you*."

"I think I already told you that *I* didn't pick *you*." McMurphy shot back. "Hell, if I were picking, I certainly wouldn't have picked you."

"How are you gonna get us out of this clusterfuck, McMurphy?"

"Me? You screwed up everything."

Stunned, Paxton stared at him. "What the hell are you talking about?"

"If you had stayed out of my stuff, we wouldn't have fought, and the gun would've never been fired. The Globemaster wouldn't have crashed." He snorted in disgust.

"McMurphy, you are unbelievable! Next you're going to say our being captured is my fault."

"It is."

Paxton was speechless.

"The Russian soldier blew the whistle on us 'cause you couldn't have a simple conversation. Thanks for fucking up my mission."

"I don't give a shit about you or your mission, you arrogant asshole! I've got more important things to worry about. Like the death threat directed at *my* family—or had you forgotten?"

"That's your fault, too."

"*What*?" Paxton was incredulous. "You've got to be shitting me!"

"I told you not to tell Rugova anything, but you did. Now you've jeopardized the lives of your family."

"He doesn't have a hit team in the States."

"I speak Serb-Croat, remember? When General Rugova made that phone call, he told someone details about your family and your home. He told them to take care of it as soon as possible."

"It's a bluff." Paxton's heart pounded furiously. *Jill. The kids. No way to warn them, to protect them.*

"Bluffing is not Rugova's style."

Paxton glowered at McMurphy. "I don't believe anything that comes out of the mouth of a traitorous son-of-a-bitch."

"Traitorous?" McMurphy had the audacity to look hurt. "What the hell are you talking about, Sergeant Paxton?"

Paxton was confounded. "You took something from the Stealth and sold it to the Serbs. That's giving aid and comfort to the enemy—the definition of treason. My family is in danger because of your damned greed. I swear I'm going to kill you myself. And General Reed too."

McMurphy stared at Paxton then shook his head. "No one's a traitor. Smart as you are, Paxton, you still have no clue what's going on."

"Then tell me what you and Reed are doing."

"No."

"What's wrong? Can't come up with any more good lies?"

"I can't tell you the truth." McMurphy looked at him with pity in his eyes. "You just might sell out your country to save your family."

• • •

In the rental car, Delevic and Labus merged onto the highway and headed toward the airport.

"So who are we puttin' the hit on?" Labus asked.

"Sergeant Paxton isn't being cooperative. The targets are his wife and two young children." Delevic answered.

"Paxton? Is he a hotshot pilot?"

"No. Pararescue."

Labus nodded, though he didn't really care. "Is his wife pretty?"

"She won't be after we're finished."

CHAPTER 26

PAXTON AGONIZED AS HE STARED AT THE WALLS AROUND him. Trapped. Chained to a bed inside a building in the middle of Yugoslavia. Somewhere the rest of his team, along with the injured Globemaster pilot and his crew, were hiding out. Had they been captured or killed? Maybe Cue Ball, the Stealth fighter pilot, was still waiting for rescue. *Maybe I miscalculated and no one had rescued him.*

He kept trying to suppress the thoughts of the horrific possibility that a Serbian hit team was on the way to his house. *Surely it's a bluff.* The Serbs had advance notice of the coming NATO bombing campaign, so it was possible they pre-positioned agents inside the United States. Once inside the U.S. they would be able to move about freely. *A sleeper cell waiting for orders to attack.* Paxton realized it was technically feasible. McMurphy's words kept coming back to him: *Bluffing is not*

Rugova's style.

Paxton thought about Jill, John, Jr. and Megan. He always knew the possibility existed that he would never see them again—because he was the one who risked getting killed. His mind could not grasp the hellish idea that his wife and kids might be killed because of him.

He had to do something. But what? His mind reeled. How could he get free? What were his options? Was there any way to get word out? A warning back home? There had to be a way. He would find a way, or die trying.

Get rid of the anger. Think clearly. He had to remain cool. He was trained for that. He trained others to do that.

But the stakes had never included the lives of his family.

Pull yourself together.

The door lock clicked open and the door swung inward. Paxton and McMurphy both looked over and saw Nikolic come in. His face was ashen. He crossed the room. Two Serbian soldiers followed him, their rifles at the ready. Rugova wasn't with them.

"Sergeant Paxton, the assassins are on their way to pay a visit to your family. Are you ready to talk?"

"Fuck you," Paxton said without hesitation. McMurphy was wrong. *I won't sell out my country.* Even if he cooperated, he had no guarantee the Serbs wouldn't kill his family. Besides, he had nothing to tell them. The only information of value he had was the location of his team—and there was no way he would give up their location.

"So that's a no." Nikolic looked at McMurphy. "What about you, *Grigori?*"

"I've got amnesia," McMurphy said.

"I think the problem is you two are together. You are giving each other comfort and support," Nikolic said.

Paxton snorted.

Nikolic looked back and forth at McMurphy and Paxton as if he were trying to pick between them. "You, Grigori. You will come with me."

"Where are we going?" McMurphy asked.

"I have something special planned for you." Nikolic pulled out a pistol and aimed it in McMurphy's direction. Then he barked some orders in Serbo-Croat to the soldiers, waving his pistol horizontally for emphasis. One soldier unslung his rifle and pointed it at McMurphy. The other soldier pulled out a key and walked to McMurphy's bed. He methodically unlocked each of the four locks and McMurphy slowly sat up, shaking his hands in an attempt to restore circulation. Both the soldier and Nikolic aimed their weapons at McMurphy, ready for any quick moves.

There were none.

McMurphy sat on the side of the bed, dizzy from being in one position for so long.

"Get up!" Nikolic ordered.

The nearest soldier kicked McMurphy in the shin. McMurphy grabbed his leg and eyed the soldier coldly.

"Move it!" Nikolic yelled.

McMurphy dragged himself to his feet. The soldier pointing the rifle maneuvered behind McMurphy and prodded him with the barrel. McMurphy stumbled toward the door.

Nikolic backed away, his pistol leveled, allowing McMurphy to pass in front of him. McMurphy passed the foot of Paxton's bed. He glanced at Paxton and continued out the door. The two soldiers followed him.

Nikolic turned to Paxton. "You are sure you're not ready to talk?"

Paxton was silent.

"Very well." Nikolic walked out the door and shut it behind him. Paxton heard him locking it. Paxton lay there, all alone in his agony.

• • •

Delevic and Labus passed easily through security at the Orlando Airport and went to the airport bar. They sipped drinks and made small talk while waiting for the boarding call to their flight to Texas. Their tickets, purchased under assumed names, were safely in their pockets.

• • •

Sitting at his desk, Detective Margolis turned the problem over and over in his head. *I'm missing something.* Earlier that evening Amanda was not in the car. Later her skeleton was found inside it. The witness claimed she had gotten into the dark-haired man's car. They were cozy. Having drinks. Maybe the suspect talked Amanda into going out with him. So … she went somewhere with him and returned to the parking lot later.

She was alive when she got into the Toyota because of the way her hand gripped the steering wheel. Was there an altercation in the parking lot? *The man drops her off, maybe he tries something Amanda doesn't like, and things get out-of-control.* Or maybe the guy isn't a gentleman. Maybe Amanda finds her own way back to the car.

Taxi. He opened the phone book and telephoned taxicab services. He questioned the dispatchers about any drivers who would have been in that area in the middle of the night.

He struck gold with the third taxi company.

"One of your drivers dropped off a fare in that parking lot at three a.m.?" Margolis frantically took notes.

"Yes, a female," the dispatcher said.

"Where did the driver pick up the woman?"

The dispatcher rattled off the name of a local hotel.

"Please give me the name of the driver and let me know how he can be reached. It is vital I speak with him," the detective said.

The dispatcher gave the contact information for the driver and Margolis jotted it down.

"Thank you so much," Margolis said as he hung up. He grabbed his folder with the photos and headed to his car.

• • •

Delevic looked at his watch. The plane didn't board for another twenty minutes. He ordered another round for himself and Labus.

• • •

General Reed summoned Marshall to his temporary quarters at Brindisi Airbase, Italy. "Have we had any contact from McMurphy?"

"No, sir."

"But we do have a good signal?"

"Yes, sir."

"Why isn't McMurphy reporting in?"

"Maybe he got tied up, sir," Marshall offered.

"If we don't hear from him soon, we will proceed anyway."

"Yes, sir."

• • •

Detective Margolis arrived at the hotel. He entered the glass doors of the tiny lobby. Behind the counter the motel clerk looked up from a paperback. "Can I help you, sir?" he asked with a Middle Eastern accent.

"My name is Detective Margolis of the Lake Mary Police Department." He showed the clerk his badge and identification. "Have you seen this woman?" Margolis handed the clerk a photo of Amanda.

The clerk looked at it. "Yes, sir. I called a taxicab for her."

"Was she with anyone?"

"No."

"How about these two?" Margolis said as he handed him the grainy photos of the two men.

"Those men were guests of this motel. They checked out

earlier today."

"I'll need their names and contact information. Do you know where they were going?"

"No, sir."

"Has their room been cleaned yet?"

"No, sir. We only have one maid and she's sick today." The clerk grabbed his master key card, put up a "Be Back in Five Minutes" sign, and came around the desk. Then he led the detective to the room and opened the door.

The beds were messed up. There were towels on the bath-room floor.

"Ok. Don't touch anything. I'm calling in forensics."

• • •

The boarding call was sounded over the airport loudspeaker. Delevic paid the bill, and he and Labus proceeded to the crowded gate. They waited in line patiently and handed the agent their boarding passes. They then walked up the jetway and onto the aircraft.

Delevic allowed Labus to have the aisle seat since he was larger. He peered out the window and buckled his seatbelt. In a matter of hours, they would arrive in San Antonio.

• • •

Paxton's imagination ran at full speed. He tried to crowd out worries about his family with plans of escape. But escape seemed impossible. He looked around the room. Even if he found a way out of the handcuffs and chains that secured him to the bed, he would still have to find a way through the window or out the door. The door was made out of heavy wood and locked from the other side. Could he pick the lock? With what? It wasn't like on television where the hero simply jiggled a piece of metal in the lock. It took skill. And even if he could pick it, he knew there were armed guards on the other side of the door, and probably more surrounding the building. Burglar bars covered the window and he had no hacksaw. It was unlikely he could force them apart with brute strength.

He didn't even see a way out of the cuffs. Perhaps if he managed the smash his hand repeatedly with sufficient force, he could break the bones and slide this hand out of the cuff. But then he still would have to figure a way out of the leg irons. And that would leave him with broken hands, making it more difficult for him to attack his captors with any chance of success.

No. It appeared that Paxton would have to sit and wait. Wait and be ready for when an opportunity came along.

• • •

"Sergeant Smith, it's been more than twenty-four hours," Peterson said. "And no sign of Sergeant Paxton."

"I *know*."

"What are we gonna do?"

Smith had been agonizing over this; now it was decision time. He didn't want to leave Paxton behind. He wanted to wait for him, give him more time. Clearly something bad had happened. Paxton would have shown up otherwise. Maybe they should go out and look for him. But he had an injured man to worry about. And Paxton said not to look for him. The decision was already made. He had his orders.

Smith gazed at Peterson. "We're going home."

The men packed up everything, including the injured pilot, examined the map, and headed on foot toward the Bosnian border.

CHAPTER 27

JASHARI WAS ON THE SECOND-STORY BALCONY, contemplating the skyline. The satellite phone was quite a useful device. He could call anywhere in the world that had a working telephone number. So he took advantage of that wonderful feature.

He didn't limit himself to calling only the Americans.

Summoning his trusted lieutenant Hashim, he asked, "You remember where the device removed from the Stealth plane is hidden?"

"Yes." Hashim nodded. "I remember very well."

"We have a potential buyer." Jashari answered. "You see, that device is designed to defeat advanced radars—an anti-radar. Apparently the Chinese have developed a radar that better detects the Stealth. The device you saw somehow confuses that new system. The Chinese and the Russians are scrambling to get their hands on the anti-radar so they can reverse engineer it. Our old nemesis General Rugova is shopping it to the highest bidder. His government doesn't know about his little auction."

"So what does that mean for us?"

"Our buyer is willing to give us weapons in exchange for it. Weapons we can't get anywhere else. Lead a team to the building, get the device and return here."

"What about the Americans?"

"Bring them, too. They may prove to be useful. But they are not the priority. If you cannot free them quickly, leave them to their fates. I want that device."

"Be it Allah's will … you shall have the device."

Jashari smiled.

• • •

Marshall entered Reed's temporary quarters. The general was seated at the table reviewing documents. He looked up. "Yes?"

"Sir, we have a new intercept from the tap on Jashari's satellite phone."

What was the content?"

"They are working on the translation. It should be ready within the hour."

"Thank you, Marshall. Get back to me once it's in English."

• • •

The plane carrying Delevic and Labus landed at the San Antonio International Airport. The two men retrieved their bags and picked up a rental car. The clerk used a red marker to draw the way to their motel on a city map. Delevic climbed behind the wheel, and Labus plopped himself into the passenger seat. Delevic sped off into the light traffic.

It took only twenty-five minutes to get to their motel. Delevic checked them into their room using his false identification. The room looked like every other motel room they'd ever been inside. Delevic laid his bag on the twin bed nearest the door.

Labus availed himself of the bathroom while Delevic sat on the edge of the bed and studied the city map provided by the rental clerk. He plotted out the best route from the motel to the Paxton residence. Based upon his experience driving from the airport, he figured it would take a half hour to drive to the target destination. They would make a dry run to make sure they knew the route in and the route out. They didn't want to get lost while they escaped.

Next Delevic opened the thick phone book and looked up a pizza place. He called and asked how late they delivered tonight. The answer was midnight. Perfect. Then he looked up sporting goods stores. He opened the desk drawer and pulled out a note pad and pen. He jotted down the addresses of several stores. He wanted to spread out his buys to avoid raising suspicion. It was time to replenish their ammunition supply.

Their weapons would arrive tomorrow.

• • •

General Rugova summoned Nikolic to his private office.

"You wanted to see me, sir?" Nikolic asked.

"Blow up the Stealth fighter."

"Sir?"

"Destroy the wreckage, Colonel." Rugova smiled. "The anti-radar device is more valuable to our bidders if no one knows they have it. If the plane is obliterated, the Americans will assume the device has been demolished, too."

"What about the plane's value to our country?"

"Pah! Who cares! Politicians in Belgrade are getting fat off my work. It's time I get my share."

"Sir…"

Rugova waved away Nikolic's protests. "Keep it secret. Use only your most trusted men. And make it look like the Americans did it."

"Yes, sir."

"Have either of our guests decided to talk?"

"No, sir."

"Sergeant Paxton better find his voice. Unless he starts talking, Delevic and Labus will kill his family tomorrow."

• • •

Paxton was losing track of time. How long had he been chained up? He didn't know. Minutes seemed like hours. Had it been three days since he last saw his team? Have they left the country or been rescued? Maybe they would be in contact with American forces. But they had no idea where he was.

He looked at the window. Night had fallen and his room was cast into almost complete darkness since Nikolic had switched off that blasted light bulb.

Frustration knotted him. All he could do was lie there, immobile, and think. Think and worry. He tried everything to block out the bad thoughts. But the bad thoughts were always there.

He wondered about his family. What were they doing? What were they thinking? Were they still safe?

• • •

Jill Paxton placed the steaming bowl of soup in front of her son. "Here you go, dear."

John, Jr. munched on a peanut butter and jelly sandwich. It had been carefully cut from corner to corner into four pieces. The crust had been lovingly removed. Jill watched him eat his simple dinner. She tried to push back the worry—the constant wondering when the phone would ring with news of John. She focused on the present, the known. She focused on mothering her babies.

Her daughter was seated in her high chair pulled up next to the table. She wiped her little arm back and forth across the high-chair table, pushing all her Cheerios to the floor. Both Megan and John, Jr. thought it was hilarious. Jill sighed at the mess to be cleaned up but smiled at the sound of her children giggling.

. . .

Reed answered the phone gruffly, "Reed here."

"General," Marshall said. "I've gotten the translation from the tap on Jashari's satellite phone."

"Excellent. What did you find out?"

"Sir, you're not going to like this."

. . .

The sun was setting as Delevic and Labus drove slowly through the neighborhood. Labus checked the numbers on the houses against the address written on the piece of paper he held while Delevic drove.

"There it is," he said. "324 Casa Verde Drive."

Delevic stopped the car. He and Labus looked out the driver's side window at the stucco two-story house. The lawn was nicely landscaped as were all the lawns in the neighborhood. The porch light was on as well as a light in an upstairs window. Parked on the driveway in front of the garage door was a medium-sized Ford SUV. Delevic checked his notes again. A quick check of the license plate number confirmed Rugova's information. "Casa de Paxton," Delevic said with a smile.

"Too bad we don't have our guns," Labus said. "We could do it right now. This is going to be easy."

"Yeah. But we have a couple things to do first." Delevic said. He pulled away from the curb and drove away.

• • •

The Mercedes panel truck was followed by a rusty cargo van. Both vehicles shut off their headlights and slowed to a stop on the side of the road. There was complete darkness except for the red glow of brake lights. Hashim shut off the engine, grabbed his machine gun from under the heavy coat on the front seat, and got out from behind the wheel of the truck. Several other soldiers piled out of the back of the truck and the van. The soldiers were dressed in green fatigues with black watch caps on their heads. They all gathered around Hashim, weapons at the ready. He quietly reviewed the plan with them. Then they checked their weapons.

Strapped over Hashim's shoulder and leveled at waist height was his MP-40 submachine gun. He pulled out the magazine and felt in the darkness the first 9mm parabellum round. He pushed down on it with his thumb and the spring pushed it firmly back. Earlier, he had loaded thirty rounds into the magazine—two short of its capacity. Leaving a couple rounds out was the best way to avoid jams because the MP-40's magazine spring wore out quickly. It was a constant problem with the World War II-era weapons even when they were brand new. Satisfied, he pushed the magazine into the bottom of the weapon. The magazine was located almost a foot forward of the trigger and acted as a front grip to counter the relatively low recoil generated by its blowback operation. He pulled the charging handle back with a click, leaving the bolt open. Most of the other soldiers were similarly armed and prepared for battle in a like manner.

"Let's go," Hashim said softly, and the other soldiers followed him silently up the dirt road that led to the nondescript building.

The KLA soldiers moved quietly and professionally up the road. They slowed as they approached the first bend. A swath of light bathed the ruts of the path. Hashim raised his hand for the others to stop. He crept to the right side of the road, which was the inside corner of the curve, and peered around the bend.

He had a clear view of the workshop, which was approximately seventy-five meters from his position. He noted the floodlight. No one could approach on the road without being illuminated. Serbian soldiers were positioned on each side of the front door. They stood casually, leaning their backs against the concrete block. Their rifles were slung in front of their bodies pointing downward, ready to be raised and fired. The guard on the left was smoking a cigarette. Any attempt to approach the building from the road with the two guards so positioned would be suicidal.

Hashim scanned the area. He did not see any other soldiers. He called out in a hushed tone for one of his soldiers by name. The soldier scurried to his side. He pointed to the guards and whispered his orders. The soldier unslung his RPG-7. He crouched down on one knee and leveled the long thin metal tube of the rocket-propelled grenade launcher on his right shoulder. Then he slapped out the front iron sights and waited, ready to fire.

Hashim joined the other soldiers and briefed them on the adjusted plan. Satisfied his men were ready, he gave the order to fire.

A bright orange flame shot out of the back of the RPG as the warhead whooshed off the front of the tube. The grenade streaked in a low arc toward a point directly between the two Serbs, leaving a glowing smoky trail in its wake. The grenade struck the front door of the workshop and instantaneously detonated with a brilliant flash. Half an instant later, the shockwave from the explosion arrived at the KLA soldiers' position with a bone-jarring thud.

The shrapnel generated by the grenade's explosion sliced through the bodies of the two Serbian guards faster than the speed of sound. They were dead before their bodies landed.

Without hesitation, Hashim and his soldiers rounded the corner and ran headlong toward the building. As they ran, they fired long steady bursts from their MP-40s into the newly created opening where the front door had been.

• • •

The incredibly loud explosion jolted Paxton from fitful sleep. His bed had been jarred across the floor. For a moment, he had forgotten where he was and tried to bolt upright. The chains jerked him back to the bed. An instant later machine gun rounds pierced through the wooden door. A spray of splinters impacted the far wall. The bullets passed over his supine body. Had he successfully sat upright, the rounds would have struck his chest.

He heard screams and more staccato of the MP-40s. Then he heard return fire. Another burst of machine-gun fire shattered the door. Paxton flattened himself against the bed as the rounds ricocheted around the concrete chamber. It seemed as if he would be cut in half by machine gun fire as he lay there chained helplessly to the bed. There was more return fire from the outer room. It seemed as if all hell had broken loose, and he couldn't even get into the fight.

But who was attacking?

Had someone come to rescue him?

He did not recognize anything that sounded like American weapons.

His thoughts were interrupted as another torrent of machine-gun fire sprayed the room. He squeezed his eyes shut against the flying particles of wood and concrete. Dust filled his mouth. The smell of gun smoke wafted in—along with another unmistakable smell. Blood.

The machine guns sounded like they were getting closer by the moment.

A sustained eruption of automatic fire buzzed in the next room. He opened his eyes. The muzzle flash blazed into Paxton's room through the holes in the door like a strobe light. A short-lived scream was replaced by a moan and thump on the floor. Then there was shouting and the shooting stopped.

Paxton held his breath, waiting for it to resume any second. But it didn't.

The only sound was the echo of gunfire in his head.

Light filtered through the holes in the door, illuminating

streaks of dust. He heard voices again in the next room. He couldn't make out what they were saying, but they sounded calm and in control.

The lock of the wooden door rattled. There was a click and the doorknob turned. The door swung back and a man dressed in green fatigues stood there lit by the overhead fixtures in the outer room. Paxton saw the scar on his face and immediately recognized him as the farmer who had been taking photographs around the Stealth.

"You?" Paxton said, unable to hide the surprise in his voice.

"My name is Hashim," the man said in broken English. "I have been sent by Mr. Jashari."

"Oh my God!" Paxton exclaimed. "Am I glad to see you!"

"What is your name?"

"Paxton," he croaked, as dust coated his lungs. "Senior Master Sergeant John Paxton of the United States Air Force."

"What is your purpose in our country?"

"I wish the hell I knew," Paxton replied. "Look, get me out of these things. We've got to contact NATO right away. It's an emergency."

The man examined a set of keys in his hand. He seemed to be unfamiliar with them. As he stepped closer, Paxton could see that they were covered in blood. He had apparently extracted them from one of the presumably dead Serbian guards. He fished through them until he found the right one and unlocked the handcuffs restraining Paxton's arms. He then unlocked the shackles from Paxton's ankles.

Paxton sat up in the bed a little too quickly. He had to

steady himself with a hand flat on the bed until the room stopped spinning.

Once Paxton gathered himself, he stood up cautiously. His legs were a little unsteady, but he was ready for action.

"I've got to contact my commander immediately," Paxton said.

"We must bring you to Jashari."

Paxton shook his head. "No, you don't understand. This is a matter of life or death."

Hashim shook his head.

Shit. Paxton ran through his options, but being that the KLA soldier was armed and he wasn't, he didn't have a choice. "Fine. Jashari first. Let's go." Paxton headed for the door.

Hashim hesitated, picked something up off the bed and then followed him out.

The outer room was a mess. The front door had been blown off its hinges. The force of the blast had knocked over the workbench that had been in the center of the room. The concrete floor was littered with tools and equipment. Three men dressed identically to Hashim stood in the room holding their own machine guns. The bodies of two Serbs lay in pools of blood, rifles next to their lifeless forms. Paxton turned around. The back wall was riddled with bullet holes. He looked for McMurphy, but he wasn't among the living or the dead. Nikolic evidently had removed him from the building entirely. But to where?

Wires and testing equipment were strewn about. On the floor was McMurphy's ratty green backpack. It lay there flat and empty. Next to it was his metal toolbox. The lid to the toolbox was open and McMurphy's tools were scattered. Styrofoam peanuts scurried across the floor propelled by the cool night breeze coming through the blasted hole.

Then he saw it.

The strange electronic device McMurphy had removed from the Stealth was laying where the top of the workbench met the floor.

Paxton couldn't believe it. Finally some good luck. Apparently the Serbs had brought the device here to test it. It was still attached to an oscilloscope-type box that lay upside down next to it. And now McMurphy was gone, and Jashari had sent KLA soldiers to rescue him. *Rugova and Nikolic will be surprised when they come back and find their guards dead and their precious device gone.*

The object was the proof he needed to convict Reed for his treasonous acts. He would have Hashim take him to Jashari; they could contact NATO forces and prevent an attack against his family. Then they could pick up Smith and the others and go home. He hurried to the workbench, grabbed McMurphy's empty pack and reached down to pick up the device.

The ominous sound of charging handles being pulled back simultaneously on no less than three MP-40 submachine guns echoed in the room.

Paxton froze, bent over, his left hand on the device and the bag in his right. He slowly turned to look up. Three KLA soldiers had leveled their weapons directly at him. "What the....?"

"What do are you doing, Sergeant Paxton?" Hashim asked in broken English.

"I'm retrieving property that belongs to the United States Air Force."

"I don't think so," Hashim said. "That piece of equipment is now the property of the Kosovo Liberation Army."

Paxton ignored the guns and stood up angrily, turning to face Hashim. The machine guns followed his every move. "What the hell are you talking about?"

"It is, as they say, the spoils of war." Hashim said, holding up a pair of the handcuffs that had secured Paxton to the bed. "Place your hands behind your back."

Paxton glanced at the soldiers who aimed their weapons at him. He would be mowed down before he could lay a hand on Hashim. He had to stay alive. Not just for his sake, but for his family's.

He would go see Jashari and straighten everything out with him. These men were following orders. The sooner he cooperated, the sooner he could talk to someone who could get word to Jill. Paxton turned his back to Hashim and put his hands behind him.

Hashim clapped on the handcuffs. The cuffs lined up perfectly with the marks on his wrists that were a result of his earlier struggles against captivity. Terrific. Now he was being secured by his third jailer since the start of this mission.

"Hashim," Paxton said, "Don't you think the United States military will have something to say about the KLA's claim of ownership?"

"You think so?"

"I *know* so."

"Well, Sergeant Paxton," Hashim said, "I very much doubt the United States military is ever going to find out we have it."

CHAPTER 28

As MUCH AS PAXTON DIDN'T WANT TO COOPERATE, HE didn't see where he had much choice. He was unarmed, surrounded by men with Nazi machine guns. He was somewhere in a strange war-torn country, his exact location a complete mystery. He didn't speak the language. He was separated from the rest of his team on a mission that didn't officially exist. He had been forced to help two traitors sell presumably top-secret electronics to the Serbs. He had no clue what day of the week it was, let alone how many days had elapsed since he had last seen Smith and the others. He didn't know whether the Air Force was looking for him or even knew he was alive. He was incredibly tired and hungry. And he was once again restrained.

Now he was a prisoner of the Kosovo Liberation Army—the very people the United States was trying to protect from Serbian atrocities. *I'll go with these guys and straighten everything out with Jashari. He's supposed to be my ticket home.* Paxton grimaced. *My ticket home according to Reed,* he thought bitterly.

What choice did he have? Even if Jashari planned to kill him, maybe he would at least have the decency to allow him to call and warn his family and say goodbye.

Say goodbye.

Goddamn Reed never let him even say goodbye.

Paxton's hands balled up into fists behind his back.

"Let's go, Sergeant Paxton," Hashim said.

Time to go. Time to leave this prison. There certainly was no reason to stay here. The Serbs could return at any moment, and they would surely kill him.

Paxton decided to take his chances with the KLA.

Things couldn't possibly get worse.

One of the KLA soldiers picked up the device and placed it inside McMurphy's pack. Then he slipped the pack onto his back. They all crossed the room, stepping over the body of a Serbian soldier as they left the building.

Outside Paxton felt the cool clean air. It was refreshing after the concentrated smell of gunpowder and death. Paxton looked around. The sun was just coming up, light streaming through the dense trees. Two more KLA soldiers stood outside. Paxton saw the bodies of Serbian soldiers lying twisted and bloody on each side of the doorway. The barrel of a machine gun prodded Paxton in the back and he started walking.

Paxton walked down the dirt road followed by his captors. Along the way, he passed three dead KLA soldiers. The group rounded the bend and made their way to the two vehicles parked by the side of the paved road. The lead vehicle was a Mercedes panel truck. The second vehicle was a van. Hashim opened the back of the truck and indicated that Paxton should get in. Paxton climbed inside, grimly resolved.

There were no seats in the back of the truck. Two KLA soldiers got in behind Paxton, including the one carrying Mc-Murphy's pack. Paxton lowered himself until he was sitting on the bed of the truck, his legs pointing toward the back doors and his back to the front wall. The door slammed shut.

The truck rocked as someone got into the front of the truck. The engine started and the vehicle lurched forward.

The two KLA soldiers in the enclosed back sat cross-legged with their weapons across their laps. They never took their eyes off Paxton. The green backpack was placed on the floor between them.

Paxton looked at the soldiers and then at the pack. If the KLA had no intention of letting the United States military find out they had Stealth technology, then he was screwed. Since *he* knew they had it, his expected chances of survival had just gone to zilch.

• • •

In Reed's temporary quarters in Italy, Marshall looked visibly shaken as he approached the table. "Jashari has learned about the anti-radar device. He had an agent who photographed Mc-Murphy removing it from the Stealth and he made some calls. He found out that General Rugova was shopping the device to the Russians and the Chinese."

"The usual suspects. So what?"

"Jashari decided to take the device for himself and sell it."

"Take it from Rugova?" Reed laughed. "How does he intend to do *that*?"

"He found out where Rugova is hiding the device and sent an assault team to recover it."

"Shit. That's gonna screw everything up," Reed said. "Who does he plan to sell it to?"

"That's where it gets really bad, sir." Marshall meet Reed's gaze. "Jashari is working a deal with Iraqi agents."

"Iraq!"

"Yes, sir."

"Having the device alone won't help Iraq shoot down Stealths. The device defeats advanced radar. To reverse engineer the anti-radar and then modify systems to counter the device … that's a very high-tech undertaking. I'm not sure their scientists are up to the task. Not with the post-Gulf War sanctions in place." Reed stood up and paced the room, deep in thought. "Iraq has lots of money. Oil money. Why wouldn't they let the Russians or Chinese get the device, do all the technical stuff and then buy the new radar from them?"

"Maybe it's not worth money."

Reed looked up. "A trade. Something he wants more than money."

"Nukes?"

"I don't think the Russians or the Chinese would be so stupid as to turn Iraq into a nuclear power. Russia and China are permanent members of the United Nations Security Council.

As permanent members, they have veto power, so they can stop any U.N. action in its tracks."

"I'm not sure I follow," Marshall said.

"What if the Iraqis offered the device in exchange for a promise to veto any U.N. resolution to take action against Iraq? Hell, Saddam could wield enough power through those countries to perhaps even get the U.N. sanctions lifted. He'd be back in business then." Reed paused, his brow furrowed. "The device will end up in the hands of the Russians or the Chinese—just not in the way we thought. This doesn't change much."

"What about all that with the U.N.?"

"That's not our department. I'd say that's for the politicos to worry about. No, we're pretty much where we were before," Reed said.

"Not exactly."

"What?"

"Well there's more bad news."

"What else, Marshall?"

"Jashari isn't going to be paid in cash for the device."

"And what does our friend Jashari want?"

"One-hundred liters of Tabun," Marshall said.

"Son of a bitch!"

Tabun was a chemical warfare agent also known as GA. It was a colorless, tasteless liquid nerve agent likely used in the Iran-Iraq war. Nerve agents were the most toxic and fast-acting. If heated, it became a vapor. In many ways it was similar to Sarin and VX, but it was much more persistent than Sarin.

People were exposed to Tabun either by skin contact, breathing its vapors, or intake of poisoned food and water. It was highly toxic and symptoms appeared seconds after exposure. Tabun impacted nervous systems by interfering with the "off switch" for nerve impulses. Muscles and organs were over-stimulated to the point of failure. Agonizing death followed.

"Sir, I think we should pull the plug."

Reed shook his head. "We've come too far to turn back now. We can't return to Washington empty-handed."

"Would you rather explain to Washington why Jashari and the KLA are in possession of Tabun, sir? This is a stupid game of 'the enemy of my enemy is my friend.' But you and I both know what Jashari and his men are like. He is interested in a lot more than an independent Kosovo."

Shit. Marshall was right. Still, it was hard to kill one's darlings. He had gotten so close. It almost worked. Marshall was smart. That's why Reed had picked him as his assistant. Better to cut his losses and try again another day. But he had to get rid of the evidence first.

"Are we getting a good reading of coordinates from the device?" Reed asked.

"Yes, sir. The transmitter in the device is pinging with its updated GPS coordinates every sixty seconds."

"Are there any air assets in the vicinity?"

"Yes, sir. There are plenty of sorties being flown. It will be a simple matter to divert a plane or two. Just say the word."

Reed sighed. "Do it. Pull the plug. Let's get an air strike on the Stealth wreckage so no one will know the device is gone

and another on the device to destroy it and whoever has it."
Reed sat down dejected, as if it sucked all the life out of him
to give the order.

"Right away, sir." Marshall looked at his boss. "You're making the right decision, General. We almost pulled it off."

"I know. But you're right, Marshall. We can't afford to let
Tabun fall into the hands of Jashari's KLA crazies."

• • •

The San Antonio police officer stood in the morning sunlight examining the broken glass on the ground. There was
no doubt as to how entry was gained. He jotted notes on the
report clamped to his clipboard. He looked at the man standing next to the door. "So what is your title?"

"I'm the general manager."

The officer's pen scratched across the multipart form. He
looked at the sign in the window advertising pizza delivery
and he wrote down the phone number. "What was taken?"

The pizza manager scratched his head and said, "Only
things that seem to be missing are a couple a uniforms, one
car topper and an insulator bag."

"Insulator what?"

"Insulator bag. It keeps the pizza hot while it's being
delivered."

"Oh, I know what you're talking about." More notes. "How
much cash?"

"No cash was taken. When the night manager closes, he

puts the cash in the floor safe to be deposited in the morning. When I got here this morning, I saw we had been broken into and that was the first thing I checked. The safe wasn't touched."

The officer shook his head. "Kids. Look, I'll give you the report so you can notify your insurance carrier. That's about all we can do."

• • •

Lieutenant Petrov stumbled out of his tent as he heard the distant sound of the Pave Hawk helicopters thumping in the distance. He cocked his head to the side. *No doubt about it— the Americans were coming.*

"Sergeant Jovanov!" Petrov shouted at the command truck. No answer.

"Sergeant!" Petrov lumbered toward the stairs, taking big steps over the cables.

The sound of the copters kept changing pitch as if they kept reversing direction.

At the top of the steps, Petrov yankedopen the door and pushed inside. Jovanov turned away from the dormant radar screen to look at his boss.

"Helicopters are coming!" he wheezed. Petrov was breathless and sweating from the exertion. "Turn on the radar and prepare to shoot them down."

"Yes, sir."

Petrov turned and blasted out the door on his way to get sick.

• • •

Miles away the Pave Hawks full of PJs out of Brindisi continued their grid search, unaware that the fire-control system of the SA-10 Grumble was warming up in their honor.

• • •

Smith heard the Pave Hawks too. He was crouched next to Peterson under some heavy brush. They were looking in the direction from which the sound was coming. Then Smith studied his map and GPS receiver. He had to find a safe route. The rescue helicopters were working their way toward them. Unfortunately, between the helicopters and their position, directly in front of them lay the SA-10 Grumble launch complex. They had stumbled across the missile site as they worked their way toward Bosnia-Herzegovina.

He needed to find a way to move his men, including the injured Thompson, who were hiding further back in the woods, around to the other side and remain undetected. The Pave Hawk crews didn't know they were there. They were just performing a standard search. He would have to figure out how to signal them so they could be rescued.

Smith had no means to contact the helicopters. He couldn't radio his position to them.

Or warn them.

• • •

The ride in the back of the Mercedes panel truck was very uncomfortable. Paxton couldn't see much through the two rear windows, but he could tell the terrain was getting more mountainous. He felt every bump the truck hit. There was no padding under him or behind him. Several times Hashim hit the brakes hard and Paxton's body weight jammed his hand-cuffed arms between his backside and the metal wall that divided the driver's cab from the cargo hold.

He looked at the two KLA men riding in the back of the truck with him. McMurphy's green backpack still was between them. Here he was riding in the back of an old truck through the mountains of Yugoslavia. War was raging around him—a war that had been raging for a very long time indeed. A war that pitted one ethnic clan against another. A war based upon religion. And his guards were armed with the very same MP-40 machine guns the Nazis carried when they controlled this country fifty years ago.

Paxton felt like he had awakened in the middle of an Alistair MacLean novel. Only this time the United States had changed sides. *We're helping the side that fought with the Germans against the Serbs.* Considering his circumstances, he wondered if that had been a wise choice.

Nevertheless the men riding with him were his allies. Supposedly. *Better make the best of it.* "Do you speak English?" he asked.

"I do," one of the men replied.

"My name is John Paxton. What is yours?"

"Moriz," the man said gruffly.

Not very friendly. "Lovely country you have here, Moriz."

"It's *not* my country."

"Where are you from?"

"Chechnya."

"Chechnya?" Paxton repeated quizzically. *He came a long way from the breakaway Russian Republic.* "What made you come to Yugoslavia?"

"To fight jihad."

The words left Paxton cold. The truck bounced around some more. Paxton was silent. Suddenly it didn't seem he would be very successful in his negotiations with Jashari. "You joined the KLA?"

"No. But I fight with KLA."

The truck shimmied some more.

Paxton nodded. "You're a freelancer."

"What do you mean, 'freelancer'?"

"Freelancer means you're on your own. You don't fight with any particular organization," Paxton explained.

"No. We are not, as you say, 'freelancers.'"

"You're not?" Paxton leaned forward. "You're saying Hashim organized you?"

"No, Hashim is a member of The Base, too."

"What's The Base?"

"The name of our organization." The man stared at Paxton as if questioning his intelligence. "In Arabic we are known as *al Qaeda.*"

• • •

The Serbian soldiers quickly and efficiently executed Nikolic's orders. They told the remaining Serbian villagers to go home and not to return. They packed the Stealth wreckage full of high explosives. No one was allowed to question why. The military vehicles were moved a safe distance away.

• • •

The phone rang in Reed's quarters. Marshall answered it. He spoke for a few moments and then hung up. "Sir, Aviano has directed an air strike in accordance with your orders. They'll strike the Stealth first. Then they will bomb the latest coordinates transmitted by the anti-radar device."

"Did they ask any uncomfortable questions?" Reed asked.

"No, sir. They've been itching to bomb the wreckage for quite a while now. Ironically, they don't want the technology stripped and sold. They didn't understand why you nixed the orders to bomb it in the first place."

"Very good. Will the bomb be sufficient to get rid of our little problem with the device?"

"They are using a 500-pounder. That should be more than sufficient to destroy any evidence of the device and kill anyone in its vicinity."

"That's…." Reed's statement was interrupted by the ringing of a phone. But this time it wasn't the desk phone. It was Marshall's cell phone. He unclipped it from his belt and opened it. "Hello?"

Reed looked at Marshall in silence. Marshall's eyes widened. He held the phone out to the general. "Sir, it's for you."

"Who the hell is it?"

"McMurphy."

CHAPTER 29

THE LONE F-16 AVIANO COULD SPARE FOR GENERAL
Reed's mission of destruction streaked across the Yugoslavian
sky toward the GPS coordinates for the Stealth fighter wreckage provided by Screwdriver. The jet was outfitted with two-
500 pound GBU-12 Paveway II laser-guided bombs. One was
designated to take out the Stealth wreckage; the other designated to take out the anti-radar device. The pilot felt particularly vulnerable flying a daylight mission, especially apart from
the rest of his squadron. But he had a job to do. Take out both
targets and then it would be Miller Time.

The pilot made a cautious pass over the site of the Stealth
wreckage. He observed the wreckage through his targeting optics. Despite earlier reports to the contrary, he was pleased to
see that the downed plane was not covered with curious people. In fact, it appeared to be abandoned. Good. No collateral

damage. It would be a nice clean strike.

The pilot switched on the target acquisition laser and feathered the crosshairs until he painted the center of the Stealth with his high-powered laser. He made final systems checks, armed the bomb and triggered its release.

The plane barely shuddered as the 500-pound object dropped off its belly pylon. The fighter's fly-by-wire computer system instantly adjusted to compensate for the change in weight and aerodynamic shift.

The pilot continued to keep the laser steady on the target as he tracked the glide path of the falling bomb. The guidance system in the GBU-12 acquired the reflection of the laser off the Stealth's fuselage and its fins adjusted to aim for the target so designated.

The 500-pound high explosive payload to be delivered by the falling munition promised to pulverize the remains of the Stealth. There wouldn't be a piece big enough to be of use to any enemy.

Unlike the bombs of World War II that basically fell more or less straight down, the design of the GBU-12 bomb caused it to glide to its target, utilizing the forward momentum imparted upon it from the F-16. The plane's radar indicated there were no threats from the air in the area, so the pilot watched the video screen of the bomb-drop. He wanted to keep the laser properly lined up on the target, constantly compensating for the flight path of the F-16. The pilot flipped a switch and the video display in the cockpit switched from live video from the plane's gun camera to live video from a doomed video camera in the nose of the falling bomb. With each passing second, the wreckage of the Stealth grew in the center of the screen as the bomb raced to its final destination. On the screen a digital counter displayed in real time the bomb's height and distance to target.

The counter indicated that the bomb was passing through the 5,000 feet of altitude mark when the image on the video screen erupted into a bright flash. At first the pilot thought there was a malfunction. Strangely, the video clearly showed a ball of fire where the Stealth wreckage used to be.

But it wasn't his bomb that caused the destruction. The GBU-12 was still transmitting live video of the flames and smoke rushing up to meet it. An instant later the video screen turned to snow.

"What the!" was all the pilot could say.

There was no way he could have known that on the ground Nikolic's men had just detonated the explosives they had so carefully placed inside the Stealth wreckage. The stunned Serbian soldiers stood and watched in amazement as the first explosion was almost immediately joined by a second explosion as the GBU-12 struck its mark.

• • •

"You're sure there's no way to call McMurphy back?" Reed was furious.

"No, sir. The number's blocked. Nothing shows up on caller ID," Marshall examined his phone.

"Goddamn it! The call cut out soon as I heard his voice."

"What'd he say?"

"Just that we have to help Paxton's … *something*. I've no idea what he was talking about. How the hell are we supposed to help Paxton? We don't know where he is!"

• • •

Smith was about to give the order to his men to move out when a large man burst out of the command truck and stumbled down the stairs. Petrov had his hand over his mouth and was headed right for Smith's team.

Smith stiffened. Petrov suddenly stopped and threw up.

The sound of the copters grew louder and hydraulics hummed as the targeting radar dish turned toward the sound.

Smith's mind raced. His team was about to be discovered by the Serbs, and the rescue helicopters were about to be shot down. He fingered Thompson's pistol.

Petrov finished retching and stared into the woods. His eyes suddenly widened. He took a hesitant step toward Smith's team and then turned. He screamed as he ran toward the command truck.

Shit, they were discovered.

Smith raised the pistol and pulled the trigger twice. Petrov dropped and lay motionless.

The door to the command truck opened and Jovanov peered out. The PJs fired their rifles and he ducked back inside as the rounds struck the side of the truck.

Several Serbs appeared out of other vehicles and tents. They fired their weapons toward the sound of the incoming gunfire. The PJs returned fire from their concealed positions with devastating accuracy. The Serbs appeared surprised and unprepared for the sudden assault. They died as a result of their lack of vigilance. Those who were not cut down turned and ran into the tree line.

The firefight lasted no more than three minutes. The quiet was interruptedonly by the sound of the approaching helicopters. Several Serbs lay on the ground dead or dying. The PJs scanned the site with their nearly empty rifles. Nothing moved.

The protective cap opened on top of one of the missile cylinders.

"Shit! Stop 'em!" Smith jumped up out of the brush and bolted toward the command truck. The four PJs with rifles followed.

Smith leapt up the stairs and yanked the door open. Jovanov sat alone at the launch controls unarmed. Smith raised his pistol and fired off five rounds.

Jovanov, eyes wide, sat shaking and staring at Smith. The smell of ozone and gunpowder filled the air as sparks and smoke pored out of the five holes Smith had made in the launch control panel.

Smith shifted his aim to the terrified man. "Get up!"

Jovanov raised his hands.

"Up! Up!" Smith gestured until Jovanov stood up.

Smith searched the Serb. He found no weapons. They didn't need to be bogged down by prisoners.

"Get the hell out of here!" Smith pushed the man toward the woods. Jovanov hesitated, as if he were afraid he would get shot as he ran away. "Go!"

Jovanov cautiously stepped backward toward the woods, never taking his eyes off Smith.

"Go!" Smith shooed him away. Finally, the terrified man turned and ran into the woods.

They had to signal the choppers before they flew away.

• • •

The F-16 only took about twenty-five minutes to fly from the Stealth's crash site to the latest GPS coordinates reported for the anti-radar device. The GPS coordinates were received from the transmitter in the device by satellite and retransmitted to register on a receiver held by Marshall in Italy. Marshall would read the coordinates over the phone to the Combat Air Controllers who would then relay them to the F-16 pilot. From the constantly changing coordinates, it was obvious the anti-radar device was on the move.

The pilot still pondered why the Stealth blew up seconds before his bomb struck. He was glad the F-16's systems recorded the video because he was sure no one would believe him. He wouldn't believe it if he hadn't seen it with his own eyes. But now he had to complete the second half of his top-secret mission. He was told that Special Forces had attached a transmitter to a briefcase carried by a high-value target. It was his job to strike the high-value target.

As he approached the latest coordinates transmitted by Aviano, he scanned the mountainous terrain. Because of the unavoidable delay in the relay to him of the latest coordinates and the movement of the transmitter, the target was no longer there. He was in effect looking where the target had been moments ago. But the information was nonetheless useful. The data points were tracking a mountain road. So the pilot figured the target was in a moving vehicle. All he had to do was follow the road and see what vehicle was ahead.

While the road wound its way around the mountains, he flew in a straight line. So it took him little time to locate the prime suspect. Or, more accurately, suspects: two vehicles, one following the other. He used his targeting optics to gain a better view. The lead vehicle appeared to be a panel truck. The second vehicle appeared to be a cargo van. The pilot keyed his mike. "Any idea what sort of vehicle our target is traveling in?"

"Negative," was the reply from the combat controller.

"I've got two potentials and only one bomb." The vehicles were too far apart to both be destroyed at the same time.

"What do they look like?"

The pilot described both vehicles. Because of the delay inherent in reporting the GPS coordinates, it was impossible to tell which vehicle carried the target. While the GPS would provide pinpoint accuracy, the system for reporting to the pilot wasn't precise enough.

"Can you hit them both with one bomb?" the controller asked.

The pilot studied the scene below him. "Negative. They are

close together, but not close enough. I'm likely to miss both."

The controller paused. Then he chuckled. "Pick one. They're all bad guys. Do your job. Let God sort 'em out."

"Do I have clearance to engage the target?"

"Engage away. Drop your bomb and get your ass back home."

The pilot studied the two vehicles weaving their way along the narrow road. Who would live and who would die today? It was all in his hands. He made his choice and feathered the crosshairs for the laser on the direct center of the vehicle that lost his mental coin flip. He made his final system checks, armed the bomb and triggered its release.

The second 500-pound GBU-12 Paveway II dropped away from the F-16 and began its glide path toward the laser reflecting off the roof of the vehicle far below.

• • •

Smith's men drove one of the trucks at the site alongside the SA-10 launcher. Next they took some of the grenades from one of the dead Serbs. When they were ready, they pulled the pins, tossed the grenades into the truck, and ran for cover.

• • •

The overnight package had arrived. Delevic and Labus sat on their respective beds in the hotel room pushing ammunition into magazines. Food wrappers and cups were scattered about. Soon they would be ready for action.

• • •

Captain Olsen, pilot of the lead Pave Hawk, executed an evasive maneuver when he saw the fireball. The remnants of a SA-10 missile jetted up, corkscrewing like an errant bottle rocket. Black smoke rose above the level of the helicopters.

When it became clear that the explosion on the ground was not an attack upon his copter, Olsen edged over to investigate. On the ground, white-hot flames sprayed out in all directions as the solid rocket propellants were consumed all at once. Several trucks and tents were visible in the same clearing as the burning hulk that used to be the Grumble launcher.

Several men dressed in camouflage waved their arms. One of the men repeatedly flashed a mirror.

"Let's see how good my Morse code skills are," Olsen said to his co-pilot.

Olsen studied the pattern.

"P….J…..P….J. Hot damn, we found 'em!"

• • •

Paxton stared at McMurphy's green backpack. A brilliant flash in the rear windows of the panel truck surprised the hell out of him.

The GBU-12 struck the cargo van following Hashim. The F-16 pilot had chosen the vehicle that looked as if it carried the most people. An instant later the shockwave struck the truck, kicking its rear wheels high off the ground like a bucking bronco. Everything in the rear of the truck rained down upon the metal wall separating the cargo hold from the driver's cabin. Paxton was pitched onto his back, his feet in the air. All of his body weight squeezed his handcuffed hands between himself and the wall.

The two other men in the back tumbled down and impacted heavily with the metal wall on either side of Paxton. Mc-Murphy's pack fell and struck Paxton squarely in the chest, its arm straps landing on his face. He could taste the old canvas.

The rear of the truck landed heavily, right side up, snapping the rear axle. The rear wheels rolled off to the left and right as the truck scraped to a halt on its undercarriage. It was sitting at an angle in the middle of the road. Its occupants were momentarily stunned. A ball of fire rolled upward from the other van—it had been completely destroyed.

Paxton had only an instant to make a decision. The pitching up and sudden stop of the truck brought everything and everyone from the rear of the truck to him. He had nowhere to go, so he suffered the least impact and thus was the least disoriented. He looked to his right. The non-English-speaking soldier lay next to him moaning. He had a big bruise on his forehead; Paxton leaned back and head butted him in nearly the same spot with the bruise. The soldier's head hit the truck's left wall and he slumped down motionless.

Paxton quickly looked to his left. Moriz, the Chechnyan, had not been as stunned by the explosion as his comrade. He saw what Paxton had done and was scrambling around looking for his machine gun. Paxton spun around on his bottom until his head was toward the rear doors and his feet were toward Moriz, who was on the right side of the cargo hold.

Moriz grabbed the MP-40 trapped underneath him. He had to arch his back to get off the weapon. Paxton kicked out with this left foot and struck Moriz in the face. The Chechnyan was only temporarily fazed. He worked his weapon out from under himself. Paxton rolled onto his right side, his right leg bent, planning to turn on his hip like a turret. He stabilized himself with his bound hands on the floor of the truck. He kicked out with his left foot again, this time with more force, unleashing all his rage and frustration. He struck Moriz's mouth with his heel. Paxton felt teeth give way as he drove Moriz's head into the front wall. The back of the Chechnyan's head dented the thin sheet metal when it impacted. Moriz was injured, but undeterred. He continued to function like a killing machine. He lifted up the MP-40 and steadied it with his left hand, aiming it directly at Paxton.

Paxton performed a hook kick, snapping his left leg back, like a donkey, knocking the machine gun out of Moriz's hand and against the left wall. Moriz's eyes grew wide. Paxton kicked forward striking Moriz's right cheek. Then Paxton bent his knee all the way up to his chest, cocking his left leg like the launcher on a giant pinball machine. Moriz looked at him, terrified. Paxton stomped mightily and struck Moriz in the throat. His boot shattered the larynx and snapped the neck. The Chechnyan's body crumpled to the floor.

Paxton was certain Hashim, who had been driving, had heard the commotion and would be racing to the back of the truck to help his comrades.

Sweating, aching, and cursing, Paxton scooted to the machine gun. He backed up to it and stretched his fingers out to grab the cold metal. He leaned all the way back to pick up the weapon. He turned the weapon behind his back until he located the trigger. He bent backward, bracing the machine gun between his back and the floor, roughly aiming the barrel the best he could toward the front of the truck.

He squeezed the trigger.

The machine gun jumped in his hand. It was deafeningly loud as he stitched a pattern of bullet holes across the metal wall, hoping he hit the front-seat passenger and driver. For good measure, he fired rounds into the man he had head butted. The body jumped with the bloody wet impact.

Paxton dropped the machine gun, and it clattered on the bed of the truck behind him. His ears were ringing. He didn't have a moment to spare. He worked his way to his feet. He still had to crouch because of the low ceiling. He pushed one of the back doors open and stumbled onto the road.

The acrid smoke from the smoldering hole in the ground filled his lungs. He coughed and looked around. The rear of the truck was sitting on its chassis. The driver's side door was slightly open. Paxton stumbled toward the front of the truck. Hashim was slumped over the steering wheel. Paxton pushed the door open all the way with his knee. A pattern of bullet holes had pierced his chest. His machine gun, partially covered by a heavy coat on the passenger seat, was still gripped in his right hand. His left hand was on the door. He died as he had been climbing out to help his men. No one had been in the passenger seat.

Paxton turned his back to Hashim's body. He reached up with his bound hands and grabbed Hashim's left arm. He walked away from the truck, pulling Hashim's body out of the driver's side door. Paxton let go and Hashim's head made a sickening sound as it struck the road. Then Paxton sat down with his back to the body. He felt around with his hands until he located the keys in the dead man's pocket. He fished them out and sorted through them behind his back until he found the keys to his handcuffs. It was damned tricky, but he un-locked the cuffs and freed his hands. Paxton crawled across the asphalt to the edge of the road. Jesus Christ. He doubled over dry heaving, his body trying to throw up the contents of his empty stomach. Then he rolled over and lay there on his side, the world spinning around him. The asphalt was warm against his body.

Time passed. He wasn't sure how long he lay there before he came to his senses and realized he had to get help. He had to find a way to warn his family. At the very least, he had to get out of the immediate vicinity before he was captured again.

Paxton pushed to his feet. He lumbered to the back of the truck and opened one of the doors. He was numb from all the death and destruction. He reached in and grabbed one of the machine guns. Then he grabbed McMurphy's pack and tossed it onto the road. He opened the pack and looked inside. The electronic device was still in there. He wanted to take the thing and throw it into the fire raging behind him. He checked the urge. That device was the piece of evidence he was going to use against Reed. He was going to see to it that Reed never again saw the light of day. And if anything happened to his family, he would kill Reed himself. He didn't care anymore. He stood there, stooped over the backpack, shaking.

Paxton hoisted the bag onto his back. He then walked around to the driver's seat, stepping over Hashim's body. He grabbed Hashim's machine gun as well. Why not? He would have grabbed the third machine gun but that would have entailed moving another dead body. He'd had enough of dragging bodies for one day. He returned to the road.

The van was destroyed and Hashim's truck was a total loss. It looked like he was going to have to walk. But which way? He didn't have any idea of his location. West. He would head west. If he walked west, he would have to eventually hit either NATO-controlled Bosnia, or Macedonia and then the Adriatic Sea. If he continued west far enough, he would eventually reach home. So west it was. He checked the position of the sun, hitched the backpack higher and started walking.

CHAPTER 30

MARSHALL LOOKED AT THE SMALL RECEIVER IN HIS HAND and turned it to show Reed. "Sir, the F-16 dropped its bomb but the anti-radar unit is still transmitting." GPS coordinates kept appearing on the LCD screen every 60 seconds.

"Damn. He missed it," Reed said.

"There were two vehicles—the pilot picked the wrong one." Marshall plopped himself tiredly into the chair across the table from Reed.

"We have to hit it again," Reed said. "We can't let the transaction with the Iraqis occur. That would be disastrous."

"Yes, sir."

"Look on the map and determine how much time we have before it gets to Jashari."

Marshall laid the transmitter on the table and helped spread the map out flat. He then took a red pen and traced coordinates from each axis and marked an "X" on a roadway. "Here is where the bomb struck."

"And where is Jashari's headquarters from there?" Reed asked, leaning over the map.

Marshall circled a spot on the map. "His hideout is in this vicinity."

"Put some marks to show the anti-radar device's progress."

Marshall scrolled through the display on the receiver and then double-checked the readout. "Sir, look at this." Marshall marked red Xs on the map. "It's left the road."

Reed looked at the string of marks leading due west. "Obviously someone is carrying it on foot."

"Definitely. It is moving much more slowly than it was before. And look, sir, it's no longer headed for Jashari's headquarters."

Both men looked at the map and came to the same conclusion. "You know what that means, Marshall?"

"Yes I do. *Paxton*!"

"Unbelievable! We have to move very quickly before he gets much farther. Do we have any air assets in the area?"

"Yes, sir!"

"Send them now."

• • •

Paxton trudged through the mountainous terrain. In a couple of spots the climb became so steep that he nearly reconsidered his decision to head due west. Up ahead he saw a small mountain stream. *Water.* He was suffering from dehydration and needed a drink badly. He climbed up the hill and then down a steep slope toward the stream. He literally slid the last ten meters on his side, landing feet first in the ice-cold water. The stream was only ankle deep. He bent over and lifted handfuls of water to his lips. It tasted so good. He then splashed his face with the icy water. He felt better, but he was still exhausted. Maybe he could rest … for a moment. He found a flat spot of dry land near the edge of the stream and sat down. He took off the backpack and set it on the ground. Then he lay back, placing his head on the pack. The hard case of the electronic device inside made it of questionable value as a pillow, but it was better than nothing. He carefully arranged the two MP-40 machine guns across his chest, ready for action just in case. Then he drifted to sleep.

• • •

Marshall hung up the phone. "I gave them the latest GPS coordinates for the anti-radar device. I told them it was stopped in that location, but that they needed to hurry."

"How long until they are over the site?" Reed asked.

"Less than fifteen minutes."

• • •

Total exhaustion consumed Paxton. It was the most peaceful he'd felt since the start of the mission. A familiar sound startled him awake. That noise he'd heard tens of thousands of times before. But it was still so unexpected, so startling, that he thought it must be part of a dream. But it wasn't. It was real. And it was right over him. Hovering. The big black belly of a Pave Hawk helicopter. And it was loud as hell.

Paxton lay there on his back, blinking as he watched a figure climb out of the side door and get winched down toward him. Paxton didn't move. He didn't reach for his weapon. It was as if he were watching a training exercise. Soon, the figure's feet touched the ground mere yards from Paxton's boots. The man wore a helmet and protective glasses, but it was a face Paxton immediately recognized.

"Sorry to wake you, Pax," Smith shouted over the thumping of the rotor blades, "but it's time to go home."

Paxton sat up and put his hand on top of his head to protect it from the downdraft. "How the hell did you find me?"

"General Reed told us where to find you."

"How the hell did he know where I was?"

"I don't know. All I know is that he wants that device you're carrying back."

"I'll give it back to him. I'll shove it right up his—"

"Pax!" Smith laughed. "You might feel differently when you get home. Come on. Let's go."

"Home! My family! Smith, we have to get word—we have to contact Colonel Ward immediately!

"What's up?"

"No time to explain. I need a radio now!"

Paxton put on the backpack and Smith attached him to the winch. Then both men were pulled up together to the helicopter. Once they were safely inside, the side door was slid shut and the Pave Hawk headed for Brindisi Airbase, Italy.

• • •

"Detective Margolis, you won't believe what I've found out," Patrick Lambert, chief of forensics said.

"Good or bad?" Margolis plopped himself down across the desk from Lambert.

"Fuckin' incredible. We ran all the prints we found in the motel room. Amanda's were in there, of course. We were not getting any hits on any national databases, but I got a big-time hit for two different sets from INTERPOL. Names are Borislav Delevic and Milo Labus."

Margolis pulled out his notebook.

"And the photos from the bar appear to resemble the ones in their dossiers."

"No shit." Margolis scribbled notes.

"Real bad hombres. They're Serbs wanted for war crimes. Rape, murder, ethnic cleansing. They want to round these guys up and try them at The Hague along with Milosevic. If they ever catch 'em."

"I wonder what the hell they're doing over here?"

• • •

The rental car with the pizza delivery sign on its roof pulled in front of the nicely manicured lawn of 324 Casa Verde Way. In the driver's seat, Delevic looked at his watch. He was wearing a stolen pizza delivery uniform. Seated next to him was Labus wearing a similar uniform, although his did not fit as well. It was very tight across his large stomach. Delevic looked around. There did not appear to be any unusual activity in the neighborhood. Parked in the driveway in front of the house was the same Ford SUV that had been there the night before. The family was home.

The weapons had been delivered to their motel that morning by the overnight service. They spent the rest of the morning loading their magazines with the rounds they had purchased the night before. Now everything was ready.

Delevic grabbed the pizza insulation bag and opened the Velcro flap. Inside the bag was his MAC-10 submachine gun. With its silencer screwed on, it still fit nicely on its side and crosswise from corner to corner. The side ejector slot was on top since the gun was laying flat. If the bag were held in front of him, the barrel of the silencer was tucked into the front right corner of the bag. The 30-round magazine projected all the way to the right rear corner. To fire the weapon all he would have to do would be to hold the bag in front of him and open the flap like he was checking the address printed on the side of a nonexistent pizza box. He then could reach in, rotate the bag slightly to the left and pull the trigger. The bullets would pass easily through the fabric of the bag. He would aim by pointing the right front corner of the bag toward his target like a big red arrow. Delevic pulled back on the weapon's charging lever, cocking it and opening the bolt. The MAC-10 fired from the open bolt.

While Delevic checked his weapon, Labus inspected his Baretta. The .40-caliber automatic pistol had been fitted with a custom silencer. Both men could kill their prey without disturbing any of the neighbors. No one would think twice about the sight of a pizza delivery car parked in front of a house in a quiet suburban neighborhood. Labus tucked his weapon into a paper bag for concealment.

"All set?" Delevic asked.

"Yes," Labus replied. "I want the woman."

"You can have the woman. But we need to hurry, get the job done and get out of here."

Delevic checked his cell phone one last time. No missed calls. No messages from General Rugova. Nothing to call off the hit. It was time to go to work.

"Let's do it," Delevic said.

The two men opened their respective doors and climbed out.

"You cover the back," Delevic instructed.

"Okay."

The larger man lumbered up the driveway and around the side of the garage to the backyard.

Delevic carried his insulation bag like a hot pizza was inside it. He walked up the pathway to the front door and stepped up onto the front porch. He heard sounds from inside the house—probably a television. The mat on the porch read "Welcome." A wooden sign hanging over the doorbell heralded "The Paxtons." There was no doubt they had the right place.

Delevic positioned himself in front of the door and glanced over his shoulder one more time. No one was behind him. The coast was clear. He reached out and pushed the doorbell. He heard its ring through the door.

He raised the pizza bag in front of him and opened the Velcro flap. He reached into the bag and his fingers closed around the MAC-10's grip. With one practiced move he switched off the safety and his finger slipped into the trigger guard.

CHAPTER 31

Delevic stood outside the front door of the Paxton home. He was certain Labus had sufficient time to make his way to the backyard. The operation would be quick and ruthless. His plan was a simple one: Once the front door opened, he would burst in and kill everyone in the house. He didn't anticipate any resistance. The lone adult, Jill Paxton, would be the one most likely to answer the door. Maybe he and Labus would have a little fun with her first. Once she was dead, it would take only a matter of moments to clear the rest of the house, picking off targets as they appeared.

It was an operation he and Labus had performed many times at the houses of ethnic Albanians. They would be out of there and down the road before the bodies bled out. He would then dump the rooftop sign and blend into traffic.

He perceived movement on the other side of the door. He

raised the insulation bag containing his machine pistol higher. Then there was the sound of the dead bolt opening and then the sound of the door unlatching.

Show time.

The big white door swung partially open. He waited for the target to appear. He stood still and listened. The only sound was that of the television. Oh well. He pointed the corner of the pizza bag toward the slightly open door and squeezed the trigger.

The MAC-10 coughed through its silencer. Fabric from the insulation bag flew out and a series of 9 mm holes stitched their way through the door. With a cyclic rate of over a thousand rounds per minute, the thirty-round magazine could be emptied in no time—except for Delevic's disciplined use of exceedingly short bursts.

Delevic kicked the door. There was no resistance from the other side. He fired off another short burst from the machine pistol in a wider arc. He stood there for another moment to see if anyone moved inside the house. Everything was still. He looked over his shoulder to see if any of the neighbors had noticed what he was doing. No one was around.

He turned his attention to the task at hand. He stepped up close to the doorway and peered around the door jam on the side away from the hinges. Nothing. He adjusted the grip on the machine pistol and stepped over the threshold.

Delevic stood just inside the doorway. The floor of the foyer was covered with a nice Mexican tile. Delevic's right hand was burning. The MAC-10 ejected casings into the pizza bag.

Some landed on the backside of his right hand. He ignored the pain. In front of him was a stairway that led to the second floor. He could see a pattern of holes made by the bullets that passed easily through the front door. To his left the room opened up into a small formal living room. *Empty.* No sound of screams. No running footsteps.

Something's not right.

He turned quickly to his right and kicked the door the rest of the way open so hard that it swung back and smacked the front wall. Several meters away was a figure—not a slim, pretty woman, but a broad man wearing woodland BDUs. The man aimed at Delevic with a 12-gauge combat shotgun.

"Drop it!" he boomed.

Delevic swung the pizza bag around toward the man in one motion and pulled the trigger.

Click.

In the confined space of the insulation bag, one of the casings had fallen into the open bolt, jamming it from closing and firing. Immediately realizing what had happened Delevic yanked the machine pistol out of the bag and attempted to manually clear the jam.

BLAM!

The blast from the shotgun struck Delevic in the chest. Blood sprayed all over the living room furniture and carpet. The assassin's lifeless body thudded to the tile floor. The machine pistol clattered onto the tile next to his open hand.

Colonel Ward cycled the action on the shotgun and advanced toward Delevic's body to make sure he was dead.

• • •

Out back Labus heard the shotgun blast and immediately knew something was wrong. *This is supposed to be a silent kill.* He crouched down and moved to the French doors that opened into the backyard. He moved surprisingly well for such a large man. He pulled his pistol out of the paper bag and held it at the ready. He reached out and tried the door. It was unlocked. He carefully swung it open and dashed into the house, taking cover behind a kitchen counter.

Labus listened carefully for movement. He was breathing hard from his swift movements. He held the silenced pistol in his right hand. The tight pizza delivery shirt had crept up, exposing part of his round belly.

Labus heard a skittering sound. *Metal on tile.* What happened to Delevic?

The Serb reached the archway that divided the kitchen from the formal dining room. He peered around the corner. He could see the foyer. The front door was wide open. Delevic's body was splayed on the tile floor in a pool of blood. A man in camouflage with his back to Labus leaned over Delevic checking for vital signs. Labus raised his pistol and lined up the front sights with the back of the man's head.

The pistol shot sharply rang out and trilled throughout the first floor.

Colonel Ward spun around in time to see Labus's body slump forward onto the dining room carpeting, blood gushing from the large exit wound in his forehead.

"I got him, Colonel," Machette said proudly as he stepped out from his concealed position in the kitchen pantry.

"Thank you, Sergeant," Ward said as he walked over to inspect Labus's body. "Call the police and go get Jill and the kids from the neighbor's house. Let her know it's safe."

"No way, sir," Machette replied.

"Why not?"

"'Cause I don't want to be the one to tell her what a mess we made."

• • •

Onboard the Pave Hawk, Paxton and Smith had to use headsets to communicate because there was so much cacophony. Smith treated Paxton's injuries as they talked.

"I'm sure you got word to Colonel Ward in time. You're family is going to be okay."

Paxton stared out the window feeling helpless.

Olsen's voice crackled over the headset. "Sergeant Paxton?"

Paxton bolted upright. "Yes, Captain?"

"Great news! Just got a report that your family is safe."

"Thank God!" Paxton bolted up and pumped his fist in the air.

Congratulations were exchanged all around the interior of the helicopter.

"Apparently Colonel Ward got the bad guys," the helicopter pilot said.

"No shit?"

"That's what the word is."

The exhilaration was palpable as the helicopter continued over the water toward Italy.

When Paxton was able to think clearly again, his thoughts returned to his team. "So where is everybody?"

"There were two helicopters. The other one returned to Italy with the wounded and the rest of the PJs to help treat the wounded. I, on the other hand, stayed with these guys to look for you," Smith said, waving his hand to indicate the other PJs seated in the helicopter. "We got the call from Reed with your coordinates and picked you up pronto."

It was almost too much to comprehend. Paxton sat there in silence for a few moments while Smith knelt in front of him performing his physical examination.

Then it hit him. "What about Cue Ball?"

Smith shook his head.

"What?"

"I hate to say it."

"Shit. What happened?" Paxton asked sitting up, heart pounding again.

"I hate to admit it, but you were right. We were always the 'B' Team. Cue Ball is safe and sound back in Italy. If we'd looked for him, we would have risked our lives for nothing."

"Who got him? Who was the 'A' Team?"

"You're looking at them," Smith said, holding his palm out to the PJs seated across from Paxton. "They flew out of Brindisi and picked him up."

Paxton looked at the faces of the young PJs seated across

from him. The faces were familiar. They should be. Every one of them, to a man, was trained by Paxton.

"Son of a bitch!" Smith exclaimed.

"What's the matter?" Paxton asked, looking back down at him.

"What the hell did you do to my stitches?" Smith said pointing to Paxton's knee. "Half of 'em are pulled out. That thing's going to scar now."

Paxton smacked Smith's helmet with his open palm and the two men laughed until tears filled their eyes.

CHAPTER 32

THE PAVE HAWK HELICOPTER LANDED OUTSIDE THE PJs' hangar in Brindisi. The rotors slowed as one of the PJs slid open the door. Paxton pulled the pack containing the anti-radar device onto his back and stepped onto the tarmac. Colonel Hicks was waiting for their arrival. Paxton snapped off a smart salute to the PJ commander who promptly returned it.

"Welcome to Italy, Senior Master Sergeant Paxton," Hicks said, shaking his hand.

"Thank you, Colonel. I'd like to phone my family if I may."

"Yes. Please, use my office. There is someone waiting there to see you."

"Who?"

"General Reed."

"Son of a bitch! I can't wait to see him," Paxton said as he matched Hicks' long strides. They headed toward the hanger.

"Calm down, Sergeant Paxton. We don't need any trouble."

An Air Force Security Police vehicle pulled up next to Paxton and Hicks, cutting off their path to the hangar, its blue lights flashing. The door opened and a security policeman stepped out. He looked at the dirty and bloody man in the unusual uniform.

"Senior Master Sergeant Paxton?" the policeman asked.

"Yes, Airman?" Paxton stopped in his tracks.

"Sir, come with me. I have a warrant for your arrest."

"What the hell are you talking about? Arrest for what?"

"Attempted murder and destruction of Air Force property."

Paxton turned to the police officer. "I have no idea what you're talking about."

The officer looked at the piece of paper in his hand. "I have a sworn affidavit from a Major Thompson. It seems you attempted to murder a civilian by the name of McMurphy and you destroyed one C-17 Globemaster III owned by the United States Air Force."

"You have got to be kidding me," Paxton said, an extra space between each word.

"I'm not kidding, Sergeant. Please place your hands behind your back."

Paxton sighed and did as he was told. He could feel the outline of the electronic device in the backpack with his forearms. Once again handcuffs were placed on his wrists.

"Airman is this really necessary right now?" Colonel Hicks asked. "This man just returned from seeing action in Yugoslavia."

"I'm sorry, Colonel, but I have my orders," the policeman replied.

"Look," Hicks continued. "We have to debrief this man. Let us at least do that in my office and then you can take custody."

"Then I must attend the debriefing with you, sir. I can't let the prisoner out of my sight."

"I'm sorry, but you can't do that, Airman. His debriefing is classified." Hicks looked him over.

"But, Colonel," the officer said.

"Airman, what is your security clearance?" Hicks demanded.

"Top Secret," the police officer replied.

"That's not high enough. You can't attend. Uncuff him."

"Sir, I have my orders from the base commander."

Hicks turned toward the security policeman and glared at him. "Airman, I have a two-star general sitting in my office waiting to debrief Sergeant Paxton. If the base commander has a problem with that, he can take that up with General Reed."

"Yes, sir," the policeman said as he unlocked the handcuffs. "But I'll wait outside your office."

"Suit yourself," Hicks replied.

The freed Paxton walked with Hicks into the hangar. When they were out of the security policeman's earshot, Paxton said, "I really appreciate that, sir."

"There is only so much I can do. Ultimately, you are going to have to go with him."

"I understand, sir," Paxton replied.

Hicks opened the door to his office and ushered in Paxton.

Behind the desk stood General Reed. Next to him was a captain whose nametag read Marshall. Other than Hicks and himself, there was no one else in the room. Hicks pulled the door shut.

"You traitorous son-of-a-bitch!" Paxton shouted as he advanced to the edge of the desk and leaned over to jab his finger in Reed's face.

Hicks grabbed Paxton's shoulders and pulled the larger man back as best he could. "Stand down, Sergeant."

"You'll wish I was killed in Yugoslavia, General Reed." Paxton twisted his shoulders free of Hicks's grip. Paxton lunged and was almost over the desk when both Hicks and Marshall grabbed him.

"Sergeant Paxton! Do you want me to call the security police officer in here and have you cuffed again?" Hicks demanded. "Let's not add to the list of charges against you."

Paxton regained some of his composure, putting both feet on the ground and adjusting his shirt. "He and his stooge Mc-Murphy committed treason, damn it. I saw it with my own eyes and I have the proof."

"Committing treason? *That's* what you think we were doing?" Reed asked in a surprisingly calm voice.

"Damn right. I bet you are sorry to see this device back here with me."

"As a matter of fact, I am," Reed agreed, "but not for the reasons you think. Sit down for a moment and I'll tell you what's going on."

Paxton hesitated, and then he and everyone took a chair and looked at Reed.

"What I'm about to tell you never leaves this room," Reed said.

"I'm not making any promises," Paxton replied.

"That was an order, not a request," Reed said.

"Just get to the point."

"The Chinese are in the final stages of testing a new type of radar system—one designed to track and kill Stealth aircraft. As you know, neither the Stealth fighter nor bomber is invisible to radar; they just don't bounce very much of the radar signal back to the radar antenna, so it is much more difficult to detect."

"Spare me the science lesson," Paxton said.

Reed ignored Paxton's sarcasm. "The Chinese system works on a different principle. Instead of shooting a stream of microwave radiation at the sky and waiting to see what bounces back, it passively analyzes the background radiation.

"Background radiation is natural and manmade radiation is all around us, generated by television and radio transmitters, the sun and even the stars. This system maps the radiation patterns for a given area and keeps a database. Then when any aircraft flies, it disturbs the background radiation by its mere presence. By monitoring such disturbances, the Chinese system could track the path of the Stealth, and, of course, shoot it down. If it becomes operational, an adversary could ring militarily sensitive sites, or an entire country, with such sensors and render our Stealth aircraft obsolete.

"We've been aware of the principles behind the Chinese system for some time. Our physicists at a high-tech lab have found a way to exploit a weakness in the Chinese detection system. The result is a black box that has been added to each Stealth aircraft that renders the Chinese system blind."

"This box? The one that McMurphy took off the Stealth?" Paxton asked indicating the device he brought back. "He sold it to the Serbs. Still sounds like treason to me."

"You're a hard-headed man, Sergeant." Reed smiled. "The Chinese learned of the existence of the anti-radar device through some unfortunate leaks. They've been trying to get their hands on either the plans or the device. If they learn how we render them blind, it will be a simple matter for them to fix the weakness."

Paxton leaned forward in his chair. "I still don't follow. Why sell it to the Serbs?"

"You see, that was my idea," Reed said. "I'm the head of the Air Force Advanced Technology Department at the Pentagon. I felt the best way to protect our anti-radar system would be to let the Chinese get hold of a fake system. Then they spend the next ten years reverse engineering it and still wouldn't figure out how we beat their system. I had a bogus box produced and we tried a couple of times to feed it to the Chinese—agents pretending to be engineers selling secrets, that sort of thing. But it didn't work. Later we found out there is a leak somewhere in the Pentagon. But it was too late. Two CIA officers lost their lives trying to pass the thing off."

"You figured the only way the Chinese would bite was if they got a device directly from a downed plane," Paxton said. He not only saw the deviousness of Reed's plan, he also felt like a complete ass for not figuring it out sooner. "Where does McMurphy come in?"

"There were two devices. The real device already outfitted on the Stealth fighter. And the bogus one we cooked up. McMurphy carried the fake one in his tool box—underneath the tray. It was protected by Styrofoam peanuts." Reed leaned back in the chair, his gaze on Paxton. "His mission was to climb into the wreckage and remove the real one from the plane. Then he was to take the fake one out of his tool box, hide the real one in the tool box, sell the fake one to the Serbs, who would turn around and sell it for a profit to either the Chinese or maybe even the Russians, while he walks away with the real one."

"So you were hoping a Stealth would get shot down?"

"No! Of course not," Reed said indignantly. "Nonetheless, we always knew it was a real possibility, so we had to have a contingency plan in place just in case."

"That is crazy."

"Not really. If we didn't have such a plan, and a Stealth was shot down, the Serbs would have taken the box and sold it anyway. Only it would have been a real one."

"If it had the real one, how did it get shot down?"

Reed shrugged his shoulders. "Lucky shot, I guess."

"Lucky shot! You've got to be kidding me."

"The fact is, we have no idea how the Serbs were able to shoot it down."

Paxton was silent. He didn't know whether to believe one word of what he was hearing. Not knowing what to say, he asked the first question that popped into his head. "Who the hell is McMurphy anyway?"

"Ah, McMurphy works for an agency that shall remain nameless. He has been the government's man in Belgrade for almost five years. We had contacted him to lay the ground-work. He was to make the appropriate contacts there and plant the seeds of the idea with the Serbs. And, of course, to paint himself as just the man to make it happen."

"If he was your 'man in Belgrade,' what the hell was he do-ing in Texas with you?"

"We had recalled him to Washington for special training. He had to know how to locate and extract the device from the Stealth so he could live up to his cover as an expert. The plan was to train him, give him the device, and reinsert him back to his post in Yugoslavia through normal channels. But, un-fortunately, the Stealth fighter was shot down before we were ready. So we had to reinsert him back into the country in a hurry. That is where you and your team came in."

"So we were a diversion. You wanted to sneak him in under the guise of a rescue mission."

"McMurphy already laid all the groundwork. General Ru-gova couldn't wait to get his hands on the device. With a Stealth fighter down and McMurphy in Washington, there was a real risk the Serbs would just take the real one and sell it. Then we'd really be screwed. We had to move fast. And that was the reason for all the secrecy—we already knew there was a leak at the Pentagon. We had to operate completely off the books so word would not get back to the Chinese. It was the only way."

"It still makes no sense."

"As I told you, we weren't ready for a Stealth to be shot down. McMurphy never got his training. As a substitute, we had an engineer record in great detaila description of the procedure for removing the device from the plane. We burned it to a CD and had McMurphy listen to it over and over until he had it memorized."

"The headphones," Paxton said almost to himself.

"Yes, the headphones," Reed agreed. "As a result, McMurphy had never actually performed the task before. Had he had the opportunity to practice, he would have been able to remove the device, make the switch and pop out of the cockpit in no time. One of our engineers performed a demonstration in under thirty seconds. We considered sending him, but he would have been like a fish out of water in a combat zone. So we were left with McMurphy and you. McMurphy knew it was going to take a long time for him to do it, and if anyone saw what he was doing, it would be disastrous. You were the only one who fit the profile to serve in the role of watching his back. I'm aware of your background, Sergeant. I read about what you did in Iraq during the Gulf War. I felt you were the type of man we were looking for." General Reed looked him over. "Perhaps you were the wrong man for the job."

"Screw you, General. At least I got the device out of the Serb's hands and back here where it is safe," Paxton said holding McMurphy's backpack out at arms' length.

Reed shook his head slowly. "Sergeant Paxton, I think combat fatigue is getting to you."

"What the hell do you mean by that?"

"You brought back the wrong device. That bag contains the fake one."

"Bullshit!" Paxton said, tearing the bag open and spilling the device out onto Hicks' desk. "This is the one that was with McMurphy's stuff. I saw his toolbox there. And the Styrofoam peanuts. I'm sure of it."

"It's the wrong one," Reed said flatly.

"What? How can you tell just by looking at it?"

"Because we had planted a GPS tracking device in the fake one. How do you think we found you?"

It took a moment for that to sink in.

"The Serbs have the real one?"

"Our best guess is that after you and McMurphy were captured, the backpack was searched and the Serbs found the real device. They figured out that they were being scammed and made the switch. It's possible they've passed it off to the Chinese or the Russians."

"Where is McMurphy?" Paxton asked.

"No one knows. Somehow he was able to make a short phone call to us, but the phone cut out before he was able to tell us anything."

Exact GPS coordinates.

Paxton suddenly bolted upright. "So you were able to track the device the whole time? "

"Well, the whole time after McMurphy activated it when he was making the switch in the cockpit."

"But you knew where it was at all times after that?"

"Yes."

"Then why the hell did you bomb the convoy I was riding in with the device?"

"Sorry about that. We, um, didn't know you were with the device," Reed explained.

Paxton shook his head this time. "Even if I were to believe that you didn't know I was with the convoy, and I'm not sure I do, I still don't understand why you would bomb the device with the GPS transmitter. If it's the fake one, why bother to bomb it? I thought you wanted them to get the fake one."

Reed and Marshall glanced at each other. Even Hicks seemed interested in the answer.

General Reed cleared his throat. "It seems our allies, the KLA, are heavily infiltrated with some of our worst enemies."

"Yes," Paxton agreed. "They're al Qaeda. I killed three of them."

Reed looked at Paxton, stunned. "The al Qaeda elements intended to trade the device to some Iraqi agents in exchange for a hundred liters of Tabun."

"GA?"

"Yes."

"Shit."

"That's why we decided to interfere with their contract, if you will."

"You almost killed me you bastard!"

"I already apologized."

Paxton stared at Reed. "So let me make sure I understand. The Serbs have the real device and are about to deliver it to the

Chinese or maybe to the Russians, who will use it to render our entire Stealth aircraft program obsolete. Iraqi agents are ready to deliver nerve gas to *al Qaeda* in exchange for the fake device, 'cause they don't know it's fake, and no one knows where McMurphy is."

Reed nodded. "That sums it up."

Paxton sighed and put his head onto Hicks' desk. "Cluster-fuck," he said under his breath.

"Are you okay, Sergeant Paxton?" Hicks asked.

Paxton sat back up and looked at Reed. "I have to make this right."

"What do you mean?" Reed asked.

Paxton took a deep breath and let it out. "I have to go back."

• • •

The phone jangled on the desk. "Detective Margolis."

"This is Detective Barrister of the Bexar County Sheriff's Office," the voice on the phone said.

"San Antonio?"

"Basically."

"What can I do for you?"

"I think I have something for you on your Amanda Cole case."

Margolis bolted upright in his chair. "Whatcha got?"

"Two dead males that match the descriptions and photos in your APB."

"Dead? What happened to them?"

"A couple of Air Force personnel blew them away after they entered the home of another service member."

"No shit?"

"Yeah, pretty incredible shit. Your suspects came in heavy. Silenced machine gun and all."

"Holy shit."

"Yeah, good thing the zoomies were there. They were apparently tipped off."

"Really? By whom?" Margolis scribbled notes.

"They won't say. There's a whole 'National Security' cloak that's come down around this thing. The Fibbies have come in and taken over. Pushed us right out. But I thought you should know that your boys are dead."

"Definitely good to know. I may be able to close this case after all."

• • •

After all the shouting died down in Hicks' office, Paxton raised his hand, asking for silence.

"Look," Paxton said, "we can't leave things as they are. It's a big disastrous mess. And I'm the only one who can fix it."

"Hardly," Reed said.

"With all due respect, General, prematurely stopping the transaction between the KLA and the Iraqis was the wrong move."

"Says who?" Reed demanded.

"Says me," Paxton replied.

"What do you know about it?"

"What I know is there are Iraqi agents likely on their way to Yugoslavia at this moment carrying nerve gas. They are going to unload it somehow, somewhere. No way are they going to try to bring that back to Iraq. It would be too easily detected with the sanctions in place. So they are going to off load it somewhere. Wouldn't it be better to know the exact GPS coordinates of that transaction when it occurs? You could get two birds with one stone. You catch the Iraqis and al Qaeda and you can capture or destroy the nerve gas. As things stand right now, we're flying blind."

"What do you propose?" Marshall asked.

"We give the KLA the fake device and let them meet with the Iraqis. We track them and then we knock them all out. "

Reed looked interested in his proposal. "Why you?"

"Because as of right now, they are probably looking for me and the device."

"We send someone else to play you," General Reed said. "Jashari doesn't know what you look like. You killed his men—so no witnesses."

"Wrong. Hashim took pictures of me at the site of the wreckage with his digital camera. I guarantee you he knows exactly what I look like." Paxton wanted to sleep and to eat. God, he was tired. He wanted, more than anything, to hear his wife's voice.

"So what are you saying?" Hicks asked.

"Take me back. Reinsert me with the fake device. I let them capture me, and they think they are getting somewhere."

"Now who's crazy?" Reed asked.

"Have you got a better idea?" Paxton asked.

"No," Reed replied.

"But we have to hurry. If we wait too long, the KLA will stop looking for me and our chance of getting the GA will be gone."

"What happens after that?"

"Then I get away from the KLA somehow—we will work out the details on the way."

"You're crazy," Reed said. "I'm not ordering you on this mission. You're completely on your own. You can either go or not. It's up to you. I'm washing my hands."

"I thought you had the balls to see this through," Paxton said. "I still need one thing from you." He jabbed a thumb at the door. "There is a security policeman waiting outside the door ready to take me into custody. Buy me some time."

Reed nodded.

"Thank you, sir."

"Are you really sure you want to do this?" Hicks asked.

"No," Paxton said. "But I'm going to."

● ● ●

Hicks and the others cleared the office so Paxton could have a few moments of privacy to talk to his wife on Hicks' office phone. Paxton had tears in his eyes as he spoke with his wife and children.

"Oh, and honey," Jill said over the phone. "I have some very good news for you. I opened your mail. You were accepted."

"Hon, it's been a hectic few days," Paxton said gently. "Can you be more specific?"

"Your application was accepted! To med school, baby! You made it. Pending your graduation from night school in May, you start in the fall."

Paxton slapped his forehead. "Oh my God. I forgot all about that. I never thought they would take me. I thought I was too old."

"You're in, baby. You're going to be Dr. John Paxton one day."

If I don't get myself killed first, Paxton thought.

"We need to start making plans for your separation from the Air Force and where we're going to live and all that," Jill said. "The kids and I can't wait to see you. So when do you get home? Tomorrow?"

Paxton thought about Reed's words: *You can either go or not. It's up to you.* Then he sighed, "I'll be home soon, Jill. But first I have to take care of one little matter."

If you enjoyed Robert Capko's SAY GOODBYE, you won't want to miss any of the John Paxton novels. Read on for a sneak peek at the next novel in the John Paxton series

THE LONG ROAD HOME

Coming soon

from

ROBERT CAPKO

and

CLASS VI PUBLISHING

THE LONG ROAD HOME

Coming soon from
Robert Capko

CHAPTER 1

HEADQUARTERS 255th RESCUE SQUADRON
BRINDISI AIRBASE, ITALY

SENIOR MASTER SERGEANT JOHN PAXTON WAS CLIMBING OUT the window of Colonel Hicks's office because he had destroyed a U.S. Air Force C-17 Globemaster III.

The fact that the demise of the massive cargo jet wasn't entirely his fault meant nothing to the security police officer standing outside the door waiting to haul him away. Then again there was that little problem with McMurphy.

McMurphy!

Paxton wished he had never met the man.

If he hadn't, the police officer wouldn't be charging him with attempting to murder McMurphy. The plane was gone. McMurphy was missing. There wasn't anything he could do about either situation. But there was something he could do to clean up another mess. But he had to first avoid arrest, thus his unusual choice of an exit.

Colonel Hicks had left him alone in his office to give Paxton the privacy to make just one phone call—to his wife, Jill. He'd finally got to call her after being denied for so long. He finally got to say goodbye. And now it was time to leave.

Before Paxton had opened the window, he grabbed the electronic device belonging to Major General Reed. It had been left on Hicks's desk. He'd shoved it back into the ratty green backpack and put the pack on his back.

Halfway out of the window, Paxton looked to his left and right and seeing no one, jumped down to the concrete tarmac outside the hanger that housed the 255th Rescue Squadron. He turned around and pulled the window shut. Then he made his way around the backside of the metal hanger keeping his left shoulder close to the building. Time was short, so he had to move quickly.

Paxton approached a corner and stopped to peer around. Nobody there. He went around the corner and ran the length of the hanger. Then he stopped and peered around the next corner. He saw a green Pave Hawk helicopter sitting on the tarmac. It was facing him and he could clearly see through the cockpit windows the two Air Force pilots sitting at the controls. No obstacles were visible between Paxton and the helicopter.

He broke for it. He ran as fast as he could straight for the Pave Hawk. As he ran, sharp pain radiated from his wounded left knee. Sergeant Smith had done a fine job of field stitching the wound closed, but he'd managed to rip all but a few of the stitches out.

As soon as the Pave Hawk pilots saw the man running toward them, they did exactly what Colonel Hicks had told them to do.

They started the engine.

Paxton wore a bloody and torn Battle Dress Uniform (BDUs) with a cut and pattern unlike anything in the United States military. His uniform was bereft of any name, rank or unit identification. There was nothing on it to indicate that he was a decorated Air Force pararescueman. Indeed there was nothing on it indicating he was with any nation's armed forces, let alone the United States.

The helicopter's rotor blades began to move. They rotated slowly at first, but continued to gain speed as Paxton closed the remaining distance.

As Paxton passed the last metal wall of the hanger and emerged into the open he could see the rest of the tarmac. Over to his left was the security police officer's sedan, its blue strobes flashing. Farther to his left, near the large hanger doors stood the police officer with his back to the helicopter. He was occupied with what appeared to be an animated conversation with both Colonel Hicks and Major General Reed. Hicks and Reed were facing Paxton, but showed no indication that they saw him running like hell toward the helicopter.

Pacing back and forth in the space between Paxton's path and the police officer's back was Captain Marshall, General Reed's aide. He was engaged in an animated conversation on his cell phone, a feat made that much more difficult by the sharp increase in noise emanating from the helicopter's engine and rotor blades. He didn't seem to notice Paxton.

Paxton picked up the pace. He was almost to the helicopter. The pilots split their attention between watching him approach, watching the group around the policeman and watching the instruments in the cockpit. If they felt any tension, they didn't show it.

Paxton ran alongside the helicopter's port side, using its fuselage as cover. He hopped into the open sliding door and landed heavily on his bottom. He then slapped the bulkhead twice and shouted, "Let's go!"

The pilot twisted the throttle to full and the engine whine increased exponentially. Paxton got up, turned around and plopped into on one of the seats facing forward. As he pulled on his lap belt he looked out the open starboard door. The policeman was still talking to the officers. Paxton scanned the scene before him.

Movement in the backseat of the police sedan caught his attention. Someone was looking through the back window right at him. He immediately recognized the face.

Smith!

Paxton didn't at first comprehend what he was seeing. *What the hell was Sergeant Smith doing in the back of the security police car?*

The Pave Hawk helicopter lurched forward slightly. It was taking off.

But Smith needed his help.

Paxton unbuckled his lap belt as the rear of the helicopter lifted off the ground. Paxton pitched forward and almost fell out of the open door.

"No! Wait!" he shouted even though there was no way

the pilots could hear him. He reached up and pounded on the bulkhead again and then turned and leaped out of the open right door.

His boots smacked onto the concrete and he bent his knees to absorb the impact. Pain vibrated in his shins. He regained his balance and ran toward the police car.

The absurd sight of Paxton leaping out of the helicopter as it took off must have caught General Reed's attention because he stopped speaking in mid-sentence and looked over. The security policeman turned to see what had gotten the general's attention. He saw Paxton running toward the sedan and recognition was instantaneous.

Paxton reached the back door of the car and yanked it open. "Smith! What the hell are you doing in here?"

The young black pararescueman looked at Paxton, his hands zip tied behind his back. "I'm charged with insubordination in the field and assault and battery on an officer."

"What?"

"You know, when I kicked the pistol out of Major Thompson's hand."

"This is bullshit. Look I think I can get you out of this, but I've got to explain to you what's going on."

"You know what's going on?"

The helicopter pilot in the right seat had evidently seen Paxton hop out and run to the car because he eased the copter back down. Its rotor blades were still a blur.

Paxton glanced back at the copter. The pilot had his hands open and out waving them in a gesture that politely translated to *what are you doing, idiot?*

Paxton then looked up in front of him, across the roof of

the police car and saw the security police officer walking toward him with long strides, his hand on his pistol. Reed and Hicks were trying to catch up with him.

"There's no time to explain. Come with me," Paxton said as he pulled on Smith's arm.

He shook his head. "Pax I'm in enough trouble already."

Paxton gauged the distance between the car and the approaching policeman. "Now dammit!"

Smith looked up at Paxton. "I hope the hell you know what you're doing." He scooted to the open door and Paxton helped his former student out.

"Let's go!" Paxton ran toward the helicopter with Smith right behind him. They were slowed by the fact that Smith's hands were tied behind his back.

Seeing the men running, the security policeman pulled his pistol out of its holster. He leveled it on the men and shouted, "Halt!"

Paxton and Smith couldn't hear him over the noise of the Pave Hawk. They continued toward the open door.

Captain Marshall stepped up and blocked the police officer's view. "Don't do that, Airman."

"Get out of my way!"

"Lower the gun, Airman," Colonel Hicks demanded as he stepped beside the policeman.

The young policeman looked at Marshall and then at Hicks. His arms were still outstretched, pistol level.

"Listen to the colonel, son," General Reed said as he walked to the other side of the policeman.

The officer looked at Reed, saw the two stars on his uniform, and slowly lowered his gun.

"This never happened," Reed continued. "You will go back to your station and report to your sergeant that you were unable to locate either Sergeant Smith or Sergeant Paxton."

The policeman stood there slack-jawed, pistol at his side.

Across the tarmac, Paxton helped Smith onto the helicopter and then climbed aboard himself. The Pave Hawk took off once again as Paxton fastened Smith's lap belt and then looked around for a medical kit. He located one and used a pair of scissors from it to cut off the tie-wraps that secured Smith's wrists. He then sat down, buckled in and both men donned headphones to make communication possible.

"You're one crazy sonofabitch, Pax."

"Don't worry. This time the stars are on my side."

"I sure hope so. I don't like breaking rocks." Smith looked out at the ground falling away. "Where the hell are we going, anyway?"

"Yugoslavia."

"*What*? We're going back?"

"Afraid so."

"Shit."

"What?"

"I should have stayed in the police car."

• • •

Author photo by Maggie Benko

ABOUT THE AUTHOR

Award-winning author **ROBERT CAPKO** is a veteran of
the United States Air Force and lives in Central Florida
where he is enjoying the weather and working on his
next thriller, **THE LONG ROAD HOME** that
will soon be available from Class VI Publishing.

For more information check out:
RobertCapko.com

Or join the Robert Capko Fanpage on
FaceBook by clicking Like:
facebook.com/robertjcapkofanpage

Or follow on Twitter:
twitter.com/robertcapko

This book is also available in the
eBook format of your choice.

Cover design by KC Cali
kccali.com